Passion Project

PENGUIN BOOKS

PASSION PROJECT

London Sperry is a New York–based author of romantic comedies full of heart, humor, and hope. A lover of storytelling, she received her bachelor of fine arts in musical theatre from The Pennsylvania State University before finding her true passion for writing. *Passion Project* is her first novel.

Passion Project

A Novel

LONDON SPERRY

PENGUIN BOOKS

PENGUIN BOOKS
An imprint of Penguin Random House LLC
1745 Broadway, New York, NY 10019

Book design by Alexis Farabaugh

ISBN 979-8-89242-458-5

Printed in the United States of America

Set in Baskerville MT Pro

Mom—the pigs are flying.

Passion Project

Chapter One

I've been betrayed by pasta carbonara.

I sit back on my heels, trying not to tip over and smack my head on the bathroom wall or, worse, the rim of the green ceramic toilet in front of me. Dean Martin's voice wafts through the speakers, an embarrassing reminder of where I am—the bathroom of a fast-casual Italian restaurant on the Lower East Side. And I just puked my guts out in their toilet like a frat boy. I wipe my chin and press the flush tab, wincing at the seasick feeling of the room rocking back and forth.

I lied before. It's not really the pasta's fault. It was the wine. It was the two and a half bottles of Chianti I slurped back like one of the Real Housewives. Who on earth told me I could afford that? One single glance at my bank account would make me vomit again, I'm sure.

I squeeze my eyes closed and cradle my head in my hands. It's like my stomach knew to expel any evidence of tonight's disaster from my body.

I'm assuming my date left hours ago. I don't really know. I've already blocked his number. We were supposed to meet at a cocktail bar across the street called Rosencrantz & Guildenstern, where customers learn how to make personalized signature cocktails and sample them all night. Their Instagram advertises maple Manhattans with bourbon-soaked cherries, mezcal palomas with charred grapefruit wedges, and matcha martinis with mango honey. In other words, if you're like me and you have the anxiety of an entire therapy waiting room, it's the perfect spot for a first date. You can dodge eye contact and focus on the bartender-slash-instructor, and then get drunk and forget about it in the morning.

This was supposed to be a night one hundred percent curated by my roommate and oldest friend, Sonya, and honestly, she has to get at least some of the blame for this shit show. Sonya planned everything—the guy, the location, the day, the time down to the minute, and even *me.* She gathered pictures from my social media accounts and slapped together something resembling a dating profile. I have to admit, when I looked at her finished product, I was impressed. On the screen I look like a shiny twenty-five-year-old ready to take on life.

Oh, how misleading.

Henry had liked my fourth photo, which was a picture of me across the table from Sonya, taken on one of the nights I wasn't too depressed to let her drag me out to dinner. I'm grinning. A full toothy smile. A comically large bowl of guacamole sits in front of me. I look happy.

Liar.

Sonya insisted that *this* was what I needed to get out of my slump. *This* was the guy. I didn't have the heart to tell her that there was no guy alive who would tempt me to fall in love. Not even if he was the Swedish boyfriend from *Mamma Mia! 2*, or the British boyfriend from *Mamma Mia! 2*, or the other British boyfriend from *Mamma Mia! 2*. Not even then.

Henry's not really my type anyway. His profile was generic enough, one snap of him at a wedding with some friends, another rock climbing, a candid photo at the top of a mountain with a camera slung around his neck.

I rolled my eyes when I saw that one. Outdoorsy I am not.

I could see from his pictures that he had messy walnut-brown hair and a smile that was friendly, if a bit cheeky—cheeky in the "smirky" sense of the word. Not anything to do with his literal cheeks. His cheeks were normal. His eyes were forest-green behind a pair of wire-rimmed glasses. I know this because Sonya zoomed in on his eyeballs and said, *Do you have any idea how rare real green eyes are, Bennet?*

I agreed to go out with Henry because he seemed like a safe choice. It didn't appear we had much in common beyond being in the same city at the same time, but the wordy answers to the question prompts on his profile told me he would be able to carry a conversation even if I couldn't. The opportunity to smile and nod without the pressure to talk about myself goes a long way with me. Basically, he seemed nice. Nothing more, nothing less. I could tell by his profile that I was unlikely to be murdered by him, and even less likely to fall in love with him.

Sonya hyped me up as much as she could. She dressed me, swiped makeup on my eyes, and sprayed a fancy-looking perfume on my neck as she blasted ABBA on her phone. When the time came, she pushed me out the door like she was pushing me out of an airplane without a parachute.

She means well, I know she does, but is it too much to ask to be left alone? I'm not her project. I'm her roommate.

And it turned out, my gut was right. I couldn't do it. When I dragged my sorry ass to the bar for the date, I froze. I stood there in front of the door, panicking as the street closed in on me. *What if I'm not interesting? What if he's not interesting? What if I can't think of anything to say? What if he hates me? Or, worse . . . what if he doesn't?* I pressed my nose to the window, trying to catch a glimpse of him. If I could just see him, if I could just observe his mannerisms, maybe I wouldn't be so goddamn petrified. But all I saw were couples. Couples *everywhere*. Kissing cheeks, holding hands across tables, sipping their cocktails out of the same glass. I tried to picture myself as part of one of those couples . . . tried to pretend it wouldn't be so wrong.

I should've known then and there that my night would end with my head draped over the toilet, because the bile was already beginning to rise.

My body collapsed to the sidewalk, on top of chewed gum and cigarette butts. I couldn't muster up a deep breath or a coherent thought as the world shook and knocked itself off-kilter. All I could do was tuck my knees to my chest and wait it out until my fingers stopped tingling and I could stand up without tipping over. New York didn't even stop, didn't even bother to look at the girl with her head between her knees on the sidewalk. It must've been the least interesting thing any of the people who passed by me had seen today. I could almost hear their internal monologues as they walked by. *Oh wow! Someone's having a mental breakdown on the sidewalk? Business as usual, carry on.*

There was no way I was going to meet Henry. I couldn't. So I slinked across the street to L'italiano and sat at the bar to drink off the panic attack.

He probably thinks I'm an asshole. He's probably right.

Why is it always like this? Why can't I be normal?

Normal people's dates end with a good-night kiss, not a vomit carnival in the back of a nice restaurant.

I should get myself together before they send a medic in here. My head thumps as I pull myself up off the tiled floor to stand in front of the marble sink. I'm surprised that instead of my reflection, I see a white brick wall with the word BELLISSIMA! written across it in black paint—the subtext of this message being *Don't worry about what you look like! Go out! Enjoy life! Don't be vain!* It's like those terrible coffee shops that don't have Wi-Fi because they want you to talk to other people instead of looking at your devices. Torture. With no mirror in sight, I roll my eyes and open the camera app on my phone. *Bellissima, my ass.*

My eyeliner has magically stayed in place, but there's only a thin line of sweaty eye shadow left, tucked in the creases of my sockets. The layer of foundation I used to try to cover my freckles has all but disappeared, and my dark brown hair looks like it's been styled by a leaf blower. I keep it in a chin-length bob so I don't have to think about it. Most of the time it works out fine, but today I wish I could throw it up into a bun to air out the back of my damp neck. There's a small blob of something beige on the lapel of my shirt; whether it's carbonara or puke, I may never know.

I turn on the faucet and start to wash the grime from the bathroom floor off my hands. There's no soap in the dispenser. Of course.

A loud knock on the door spikes my blood pressure.

"Someone's in here," I croak.

It feels like a medieval torture device is clamped onto my skull. I splash water on my face so I don't look so much like a drunk psychopath. Almost immediately I regret it, because there are no paper towels, just an electric hand dryer. A fat drop of water clings to my eyelashes. I dab it with the back of my sleeve, smearing what's left of my mascara.

Another knock booms through the tiny bathroom. Does this person think I magically disappeared in here?

"One minute!" I grunt.

I pop a piece of gum into my mouth, wipe my eyes, and sling my bag over my shoulder.

Three deep breaths. *Act normal. You can do this.*

Another knock. Louder and more aggressive.

Who does this asshole think they are?

"I said one minute," I snap as I crank the door handle. "What don't you understand about that?"

I whip the door open to see a tall man standing in the way. He looks at me like I have three heads.

Brown hair, wire-rimmed glasses—just like his dating profile. An expression of pure shock and horror painted across his green eyes—decidedly *not* like his dating profile.

"Shit." I drop my gaze down to the floor. Maybe by some miracle he won't recognize me. "Excuse me."

"So this is where you've been." Henry leans on the doorframe, blocking my exit. His expression changes from shock to something else completely. Something almost smug. A tattoo on his bicep peeks out from under his pink short-sleeved shirt.

"I don't know what you're talking about." I let my hair fall in my face, obscuring his view.

He smirks. *Smirks.* "Bennet, right?"

My name sounds so stupid coming out of his mouth. I've always hated it. It makes me feel like an adolescent boy or trust-fund-douchebag-finance bro, which I know was not my mother's intention when she gave it to me.

"Nope." My voice sounds like my larynx has been run through a blender. "My name is Andy. Goodbye." I try to map out an escape route, but the way he's casually leaning on the doorframe and the unfortunate largeness of his body block my path. Why is he here, all these hours after our planned date? Why did he cross the street and turn into the same restaurant I had?

"Look, *Andy*," he mocks, doing air quotes around my fake name. "If you didn't want to go out with me you could've just said so."

"I'm late for a . . . uh . . ." *Come on, Bennet. Think of something. Anything.* "I'm late for a baptism." A *baptism*? What the fuck?

"Really? On a Wednesda—"

"I have to go."

I squeeze myself through the archway between his arm and the door and spill out into the dining room.

The space is almost pitch-black compared with the fluorescent light of the bathroom, and it takes a moment for my eyes to adjust. There are old-fashioned lantern-type light fixtures peppered through the dining area that glow red and orange like tiny matches. The tables are so close together that navigating the floor would be difficult for a sober person, let alone a drunk idiot like me.

I make my way through the darkness, barreling straight into the blond bartender who overserved me. She's handing a glass of red wine to an unsuspecting gentleman at a bar table as we collide. I don't have time to stop and say sorry, but I look back long enough to catch the gruesome sight of wine splattered across the man's chest like blood. The bartender curses at me as she grabs a rag from her belt and dabs his chest, soaking up my wreckage. Of course he was wearing a crisp white button-up. Why wouldn't he be?

I finally reach the door and frantically try to pull it open, but it won't budge. It won't move. *Dear god, why me? Why must I be punished? What did I do to deserve this?* My heart is pounding, sweat is dripping from my forehead. I feel a body behind me, his heat warming my back. An arm stretches over my right shoulder, a tattoo peeking out from under a pink shirt. He pushes gently against the door. It opens without a fight.

I turn around, once again pinned between a dude named Henry and a door.

"It's a push."

Chapter Two

I've never considered myself a particularly agile person, but I'm almost proud of how quickly I managed to haul ass out of L'italiano and book it to the subway. The only saving grace of this entire night is that I didn't have to wait too long for an uptown train. I now sit on the B across from a woman with a sleeping child slung across her lap. I massage my temples as the train pulls away from the station, knees bouncing in my seat as I try to shake the humiliation out of my body. I glance up to the woman across from me, who quickly looks away. She pulls the sleeping toddler on her lap closer to her chest, kissing the child on the forehead. I make a mental note not to be too offended when she inevitably moves seats at the next stop—I'm sure I smell like sewage and look a bit unhinged.

I never want to be myself, but today I'd especially like to melt into this subway seat and wake up in a new body with a whole new life. But, alas. Like always, I wake up as Bennet

Marie Taylor, and I wake up to the subway announcer's garbled voice calling a stop that is definitely not mine.

I must've dozed off somewhere between Columbus Circle and 125th Street. My eyes are heavy and saturated, and I blink away the tears. They say you're not a true New Yorker until you cry on the subway, but I never cared much about being considered a true New Yorker.

I stagger through the sliding doors and into the dark station, trying to get my bearings. It smells like any other station in the Bronx: stale, sweaty, and sour. I make eye contact with the butt crack of a man peeing on the tracks. My stomach churns. There are no boundaries in this city.

I scan the station to figure out where exactly I am, until I see a sign—YANKEE STADIUM. I'm at Yankee Stadium. It's a relief to realize I'm not actually too far from my apartment in Harlem, and that all I have to do is catch the D going in the opposite direction and I'll be home in a couple stops.

I pry my eyes away from the roach skittering across the station sign to check my MTA app. The next downtown train isn't arriving for twenty-nine minutes.

Well. It seems as good a time as any to finally see what all the fuss is about over a baseball stadium. Sam's favorite baseball stadium.

I climb up the subway steps, careful not to stagger and twist an ankle, and emerge into the cool night air. The stadium is across the street from the subway exit I chose, so I wait until I get the little walk signal, and then I cross the street. I hold my breath and stare at my feet on the pavement as I approach the sleeping giant, almost afraid that looking at it before I'm right underneath it will somehow ruin the experience. When I feel its stoic presence upon me, I stop, take a breath, and look up.

And up.

And up.

It's dark out, but the sign is lit up so bright I have to squint. It's huge. Bigger than I pictured it. Like a twentieth-century Colosseum where men come to fight. Although when Sam played, the game seemed more like a dance: delicate, elegant, and refined.

The Yankees were his favorite team. He used to take the train from Jersey with his dad once a summer to see them play. I imagine him, age seven, standing here, staring up at the huge monument. He's holding his father's hand while eating Dippin' Dots out of an upside-down batting helmet. His rosy cheeks are smeared with sugar and dirt and his sandy blond hair is mussed by the wind. I've seen pictures of him at that age, all joy, growing into himself. I stand, still as a statue, looking up at the towering stadium, feeling everything and nothing at the same time. Minutes pass, though it feels like hours.

It's colder than I'd anticipated at the end of May. I shiver as a breeze blows my hair across my face. I tuck it behind my ear as the chill delivers me back to reality. I have no idea how long I've been here, and I might have missed my train by now. I rush back into the underground tunnels of the city, making my train by a couple of seconds, and emerge in Harlem.

I live in a fifth-floor walk-up, and by the time I reach the top, I'm out of breath. I pray to god that Sonya is asleep so I can spare her the sound of my labored breathing and the scent of my L'italiano bathroom visit. Truthfully, Sonya has seen me far worse than this—we've known each other since our awkward middle school days—but living in New York has peeled me open in ways I hadn't expected. It takes everything in me not to let my mushy, tangled insides pour out into our tiny apartment and slowly drown her. So I try my best to keep our relationship in check. Safely distant. Sonya loves it here. She found her home. She found her people. And I'm a specter of the friend she once knew, haunting her apartment and shrieking like a harpy at anyone who gets too close . . . even my oldest friend.

I reach down into the dark pit of my purse, rifling through gum wrappers, Sour Patch Kids dust, Band-Aids, loose change, and two pairs of sunglasses, until I loop my fingers through my key ring.

I unlock the door and say a silent prayer. *Please, if there's a god above, Sonya will be asleep.*

When I push into the living room, she springs up from the couch like a bird in a cuckoo clock.

"How was it?" she asks, shuffling toward the door. I flinch. *Kill me.*

"I didn't go." I kick my shoes off and slip past her. "I wasn't ready."

She tilts her head, her brows wrinkling above her deeply concerned eyes. "Oh no," she says. "I'm sorry."

"It's okay." I rub my forehead and cross into the kitchen to fill up a glass of water.

She follows close behind. "Want to talk about it?"

Talk about it? No. I want to forget about it forever. I shake my head. "I just need some sleep. That's all."

I turn to face her, her big brown eyes fixated on me. She looks at me the way one might look at an abandoned kitten left in a box on a random stoop. She's worried about me. She's always worried about me.

We used to be so similar back when we were sixteen, skipping science class to go to Starbucks every Wednesday afternoon until her parents caught us and dragged us back to school. She'd knit me a hat every winter, and I'd return the favor by giving her a mixtape of old songs I knew she'd like, even as CDs became increasingly obsolete. We were silly back then. I don't know how to be silly anymore.

"I didn't mean to trigger you or anything," she says, shrinking.

"It's okay," I assure her, even though it's not. "I'm okay," I assure her, even though I'm not.

"Did you give any thought to what we talked about?" she asks, dodging eye contact. "I mean about—"

"Yeah," I say, crossing my arms. I've been toying with the idea of moving back to Pennsylvania for the past couple of months. I moved to New York for one very specific reason—one that I'm failing at miserably. If I can't do that one thing, what's the point of still being here? I'm sure Sonya's concern is well meant. But if I moved out, her girlfriend could easily move in and split her rent. She'd be fine without me. "I don't know yet," I tell her. "I'm still thinking."

"Okay," she says, shifting her weight. After a moment, she turns to walk toward her bedroom. Just when she's finally there, she pauses, taking a moment to look me up and down. "I'm right here if you need me, Bennet. You know that, right?"

"Yeah. I know." I nod and gulp down some water. "Good

night, Sonya." I turn my body toward the sink to refill my cup and also so that I don't have to see her looking at me with a mix of pity, exasperation, and concern.

I let the water from the faucet flow out of the cup and over my fingers. Someone somewhere once told me that the water in the city has microscopic shrimp in it, but I don't think I mind. Imagining little shrimp in my water glass actually makes me smile.

By the time I look up, Sonya has disappeared.

I wish I could still be the girl she remembers, the one who loved baking brownies with her and her mom. The girl who loved cheesy movies and playing laser tag and going on adventures. But that was before every atom in my body rearranged into who I am now.

I gulp down the rest of my glass of water, hoping it keeps tomorrow's hangover at bay.

Why hadn't I just gone to Rosencrantz & Guildenstern, made complicated cocktails, and had meaningless conversation with a guy named Henry? Why had I instead spent an entire evening punishing myself and placating my emotions with wine and pasta that I can't afford? I don't understand it, and if I could, I think I'd unlock the secret of life. I'd be the most powerful self-help guru on earth, and I'd make millions on a book titled *You Don't Have Anxiety, It's Just a Made-Up Thing in Your Head That Causes You to Do Crazy Things!* and I'd spend my days in a villa in Greece never worrying about anything. I'd live my life and not ask questions.

Most of my days are spent asking questions.

Why do I hide when Sonya comes into the kitchen to make coffee?

Why can't I be nicer to her?

Why do I spend days mulling over a single text?

Why did that guy catcall me?

Why didn't *that guy catcall me?*

Why can't I go on a casual date?

Why can't I leave my bed?

When I'm safe behind my bedroom door, I take off my shirt and shudder at the reflection in the mirror. I let Sonya rope me into wearing a stick-on bra to avoid bra strap lines, and it migrated south a couple of inches below my nipples. I peel it off and feel along the sticky part. Beads of sweat lick my thumbs. Gross.

I change into sweats as I scan my dark, messy room. Clothes cover the hardwood floor. Books that I'll never open clutter every surface. My bed is unmade and littered with Chap-Sticks, makeup remover, underwear, and socks. This place is my sanctuary, my haven, and I've turned it into a landfill.

Before I let myself get into bed, I make a mental note of all the people I disappointed today.

Sonya.

Blond bartender.

Man with wine-stained shirt.

Sam.

Me.

Henry.

As I crawl under my comforter, I'm no longer at risk of human interaction for at least eight hours, and that thought alone is enough to put me into a deep, peaceful sleep.

Chapter Three

It would be an understatement to say that single, friendless, and directionless was not how I imagined my life would look when I moved to New York. Sam had this vision for us when we were in college. We'd rent a small apartment on the Upper West Side and grow old shopping at Zabar's, taking walks in Central Park, and going to Yankee games on Saturdays. He always said he saw our future here, where there are museums and theaters, where culture is baked into every brick. He said I was too big for a small town, that together we would take on the world. I loved imagining our future together, what we would name our kids, if they would have his nose or my eyes. But I never imagined us living in New York. This dream was singularly his.

Despite everything, I decided I had to give it a try. But now that I'm here, my life looks nothing like what he had imagined. I don't go to museums. I don't go to theaters. It's sad, pathetic, and lonely, and I don't think I'm cut out for it. And if I'm not cut out for it, what am I even doing here?

The apartment I share with Sonya is tiny. There aren't that many nooks and crannies, but every one of them is stuffed to the brim with cookware. My French press lives above the fridge next to our toaster and hand mixer. I have to stand on my tippy-toes to reach it.

There are only a few items stuck to the front of our fridge. A picture of Shakespeare, a set of magnetic poetry, an invitation to Sonya's cousin's graduation party, and a save-the-date for a wedding. *The* wedding.

The parents of the bride and groom cordially
invite you and a guest to witness the union of
Alexandra Chase and Theodore Brightwood.
Please save the date of our celebration: September 15th.

I trace the edges of the embossed postcard. Alexandra looks like Sam here. Just a little bit in her smile.

It dawns on me that I used her nickname as my fake name last night with Henry. This save-the-date says Alexandra, but to me, she's Andy. Sam's younger sister and my best friend.

The couple in the picture stand in a field of tulips. Andy's hair is nectarine-red, Theo's dark as licorice. I know that Andy will be a beautiful bride, and I've known since the first time I met Theo that he loved her. I guess if there ever was an appropriate time to use the phrase *power couple*, it would be in reference to Andy and Theo.

I turn the card over so the picture is facing the fridge. This way I don't have to look at it and acknowledge the fact that my old friend is almost a stranger now. That our lives splintered away from each other and now we barely talk.

I can't think of what happened the last time I saw Andy. The last ugly thing I said to her.

I fill our rusty kettle with water, place it on the burner, and fill my French press with coffee grounds from Sonya's girlfriend's coffee shop. The nutty scent breathes life into my lungs.

Sonya has a nine-to-five at a jewelry store in SoHo, so I know I'm alone. I don't bother changing out of my stretched-out senior-skip-day tee, putting on a bra, or even putting on pants. My short hair sticks up in all kinds of odd directions and I have a tiny white drool stain on the corner of my lip. How could Sam possibly have found me attractive in the morning? He'd take me home looking like Cinderella and wake up next to the evil stepsister. Nonetheless, he would roll over, kiss me, and tell me I was beautiful.

I haven't felt beautiful in years.

Sam used to get me coffee from a Quik Mart on baseball practice mornings. I'd wake up to the smell of watered-down black coffee and chewy bagels and I knew before I even opened my eyes that I was loved. When I think of Sam, I think of those mornings. He smelled like any college boy might, a little musty and faintly sweaty, but mixed with something sweeter, vanilla maybe, and always Quik Mart coffee.

My mom said I was lucky I got someone to deal with me, someone as patient as Sam. I've always been prone to anxiety, and sometimes even depression, though the brunt of that came much later. After Sam. Back in college, I was able to manage that kind of thing on my own. Not that it was ever easy, but it was nothing like it is now. Sam was like a balm. With him, I was more focused, more level. He was such a peaceful person, while I had a hurricane stirring inside me at all times. We were incredibly different, but it surprisingly worked. For a time, it worked.

The whistle from the teakettle drills a hole through my skull, and I tip it over the press. I can't believe I'm going to have to wait ten more minutes before the coffee is ready to drink, but when I moved to New York I insisted that I'd be the kind of person who uses a French press. I love coffee, but if I were honest with myself, I'd acknowledge that I much prefer coffee from Quik Mart.

My head feels like it's full of cement. I can't wait any longer. I press the grounds to the bottom of the glass beaker and pour myself a cup. It's definitely too weak, but I can't bring myself to care.

I take my mug into the living room, which is as cluttered as the kitchen. Our gray futon sags under my weight as I sit. A crappy coffee table covered in chipped black paint—which we found on the corner of 149th—sits in front of me, and the walls are mostly bare except for a few abstract canvas prints we bought at HomeGoods and one piece of beige macramé Sonya got at a thrift store. We have a small TV stand (also found on the street), a blue rug, and a couple of mismatched trays we use for meals. Nothing in here is very heavy—heavy furniture is too permanent, too serious, so everything in here is cheap and light and will leave almost no proof that we were ever here when we inevitably move out.

I check my phone. One text from Andy Chase.

> Hi Bennet. Thank you so much for the KitchenAid! So sorry you couldn't make it to the shower, but we're all hoping you'll make it to the wedding. Let me know ASAP.

I close the message. Buying that KitchenAid practically bled my bank account dry, but I had to get it for her, especially considering that the thought of going to her wedding makes me physically ill, and the guilt is eating me alive. Andy and Theo's wedding will be perfect, as was their unseasonably early spring-themed wedding shower I assume. Theo is a successful entertainment lawyer in L.A. and his paycheck combined with the Chase family money will definitely cover the cost of the extravagant wedding Andy is surely planning. Every detail will be prepared with exquisite and modern taste, from cakes baked by celebrity chefs, to flowers arranged by famous boutiques, to the bridesmaids' ballet slipper fingernail polish. It will be a citrus-scented Los Angeles dream with orange and purple sunsets across the horizon and people so gorgeous they should all be featured in magazines. Andy will leave nothing to chance, and the results will be worth her painstaking efforts. The weekend will be beautiful. And I will be miserable.

I'll answer her later.

I crack open my laptop to check my schedule. I have a shift at two. I can probably squeeze in a grocery run before then.

Out of curiosity, I type *Yankee Stadium* into Google. Turns out the stadium I was standing under last night didn't even exist when Sam was seven. I was picturing that moment all wrong.

Fantastic.

If you think you know the worst place to be in New York City, think again. It is without a doubt the Trader Joe's on Seventy-Second Street. It seems like the entire upper half of Manhattan is holding court in the two-story grocery store at any given time, and today is no different. Open-toed shoes aren't safe in New York in general, but especially not in cramped NYC markets. Last summer, a woman ran over my foot with a shopping cart and my toenail split in half. When I had the nerve to shriek in pain, she only rolled her eyes and kept it moving toward the gnocchi, leaving me and my poor toe to bleed out next to the Two-Buck Chuck.

I grab a basket and descend down the escalator into the store.

I stock my cart with mostly junk food and frozen meals, considering that's all I ever have the capacity to prepare. When I'm at the checkout line, I grab a bag of gummies and dark chocolate peanut butter cups that are placed at an end cap.

My cashier looks no more than nineteen, with straw-blond hair and adolescent acne. He's got the longest eyelashes I've ever seen. Boys have it easy in life, born with all the beauty and none of the beauty standards.

"Hey," he chirps. "Find everything okay?"

I lug the heavy basket onto the counter and nod. This is the part I hate, when there's clearly supposed to be social interaction, but conversation falls between us like a brick. I pray he lets the brick fall and smash to the ground and doesn't attempt to pick it up with a comment, or god forbid a question. I hold my breath as one by one my basket empties and gets repacked into brown paper bags.

"Your total will be $189.45. You can insert your card whenever you're ready."

I cringe. I cannot afford this. I spent most of my food money last night. But it would be far too embarrassing to ditch and run now, so I dig into my bag in search of my wallet. I pause when it's not in the normal pocket. Odd. I rifle through all the random crap at the bottom of my purse, but I can't find it. *Shit.*

"Sorry, one second," I mumble.

I remember that there's a huge tear in the purse lining. Sometimes stuff gets lost in there. That has to be where my wallet is.

The cashier cocks his head, smiling. "Do you have Apple Pay?"

Of course I don't have Apple Pay. Sonya begged me to let her set it up a few months back but I couldn't be bothered.

"I know it's in here somewhere," I huff.

His smile starts to fade as I stick my hand in the hole between the lining and exterior of my purse and feel around. I find two mismatched earrings and a dinner mint, but no wallet.

"I'm sorry, I—I must've left my wallet at home."

He clutches the bags like I'm going to run off with them.

"Then I can't give you these. I'm sorry."

Oh god, oh god, oh god. He's looking at me with a condescending smile that makes me feel as small as a grain of Trader Joe's frozen jasmine rice.

"It's fine. I, um . . . I'll leave." Mortified, I book it out of there. As I tumble out onto the street, I realize that I know exactly where my wallet is.

It's on the bathroom floor of L'italiano in the East Village.

Chapter Four

God, can I please catch a break? It's like all the events that happened in the past twelve hours are ripples in the water after the catastrophic belly flop that was last night, and together they are trying to drown me. I can't believe I have to go back to that awful restaurant. I even called them a couple times to see if the stupid wallet was still there, but of course the line was busy and they don't have an answering machine. What kind of restaurant doesn't have an answering machine?

L'italiano is open till midnight, so hopefully I'll be able to pick up my wallet after my catering shift. With any luck, some alien life-form will have wiped the memory from all the employees there and no one will remember me.

As a woman with no skills and no direction in a big city, naturally I temp. Sometimes I cater, sometimes I hand out postcards to people on the street, sometimes I dress up like a hot dog and pass out little cups of relish to yuppies in Whole Foods. All these jobs have the same requirements: strip yourself of your personhood and do what you're told.

I make my way into the New York Athletic Club loading dock since serving staff aren't allowed to use the front entrance, and hang my jacket on a rack beside the kitchen door. NYAC is for people with old money. Everything has history, from antique trophy cases to busts of famous athletes. This place even smells rich. Lots of heavy furniture.

I've worked here a handful of times. It can be grueling, but the pay is well above minimum wage and most of the staff here don't suck. Once, a cook saved me a full plate of filet mignon with pureed potatoes, roasted carrots, and gravy to take home after my shift, and it fed me for the following two nights. As long as management doesn't see, I can usually eat for free, which is good, since my life is a huge embarrassing joke and I couldn't get groceries today.

I've opted for my super-sexy black Dansko clogs this afternoon. I used to try to look semi-presentable when I came to work, but cute shoes aren't good for your joints when you have to spend eight hours on your feet. Besides, there is a strict uniform at NYAC and that includes black shoes, a white collared shirt, black slacks under a maroon coat provided by the venue, and a gold bow tie. Today the coat given to me fits pretty well. The name tag says ANYA. Sure, I can be Anya.

"You're late," a voice nips my ear. It's headwaiter and asshole extraordinaire, Mr. Kirk. Yes, we are asked only to refer to him by his last name.

His scrawny body and narrow face tower over me, hands on his hips, lips tight. If a knitting needle came to life and started ordering people around, it would be Mr. Kirk.

"It's two o'clock. I got here five minutes ago," I retort.

His black eyes bear down on me. "That means you should be working by two. Not standing by the door looking lost."

"I haven't even been given an assignment yet. I don't know what room the event is in."

His thin, cracked lips form a straight line. "How many events have you catered here?" he asks firmly.

"I don't know, ten or so?" I pull at the scratchy bow tie around my neck.

Kirk crosses his arms. "After ten events you need to be told what to do at every step of the way? Do I need to hold your hand? Is that it?"

"No, sir." Kirk's eyes narrow in on me. "I'll start polishing the silverware," I mutter.

Yeah. *Most* of the staff here don't suck.

"Good. Don't be late again," he says, his voice nasal and grating.

I nod. "Yes, sir."

Douchebag.

He whooshes away like a comic-book villain.

The kitchen is like a labyrinth. It's probably big if you measured its size by square footage, but it feels as small as a bathtub with all the people, dishes, jugs of condiments, boxes of produce, and industrial appliances cluttering the space. When I enter, the smell of garlic and onions makes my mouth water.

I grab a bin of silverware, a clean kitchen rag, and a glass of club soda. I find my way to an empty corner and start to polish. Dip, wipe, dry, set aside. Dip, wipe, dry, set aside. I continue polishing until every fork and knife is sparkling and the sounds of my brain quiet into nothingness.

There's a fine mist in the air when I finish my shift. It's the kind of night that's hot and cold at the same time. I can't tell if my shirt is sticking to my back because of the rain or because of my sweat. I wipe my brow with the sleeve of my jacket as I cross the street to catch the train downtown. My stomach grumbles. Mr. Kirk caught me taking a plate of chicken cordon bleu and I was forced to give it back. I watched him toss it in the trash as I threw my maroon jacket and bow tie in the hamper by the door, trying hard not to say something that would get me fired.

It'll be ten by the time I get to L'italiano, which is well after the dinner rush, but there may be some straggler tables. I hope there will be enough action going on that I will be able to sneak in and out with little fanfare, but not so much that I'll have to wait for hours to get someone's attention.

I ride the F train down six stops until I hear the conductor call "Delancey Street" over the rumble and screech of the tracks. I pass Rosencrantz & Guildenstern, a monument of my fear. The doors taunt me. Mock me. *Screw you, doors,* I think as I cross the street toward the warm glow of L'italiano. *Screw you and all you represent.*

It would be a hell of a lot easier for me to just cancel all the cards in my wallet and head home, but I know that I can't let my fear hold that kind of power over me. I run my hand along the iron door handle until, finally, I pull it open.

The scent of buttered bread and lemon zest wafts through the air as I survey the restaurant. There are two tables with people in the dining room and one couple sitting at the bar—other than that, the place is empty. The couple are glued to each other in a very . . . *intimate* embrace. He's practically got his fingers in her mouth.

I go to the bar, but I don't sit on a stool. I don't want to look like I'm staying for a drink. Instead, I lean on the bar and try to look busy by burying my face in my phone. It's pathetic, really. No one has texted me in hours and I exhausted all the updates on my Instagram feed on the way down here, so I'm stuck studying a picture of Andy and Theo from their joint wedding shower. In college, Andy always insisted that it was silly and sexist to separate bride and groom for the shower because they'd mostly be getting kitchen appliances and houseware items, and it would be *absolutely ridiculous that those gifts should be just for the bride in the twenty-first century. Do we not expect the groom to do housework?*

She's wanted to get married for as long as I've known her, and has had strong opinions on the wedding industry since she started watching *Four Weddings* on Sunday mornings when nothing else was on cable and Sam was at baseball practice. *When I get married, I won't separate the bridesmaids and the groomsmen, because I want Sam on* my *side. And when you two get married, I better be in both of your parties. I'll be maid of honor* and *best man.*

I bite my bottom lip, using the pain to cast aside that memory. The lost potential of that statement. Sam won't be at either of our weddings.

Come on, Bennet. Keep it together.

Finally the soft-core porn next to me stops and the couple head out into the dark street, his arm pulling her flush against his body. It feels like hours are passing as I stand here awkwardly, refreshing my Instagram feed. How can they expect to make money with service like this? I could be a paying customer.

Just as I'm about to give up and leave my number at the host stand with a note to call me if they find it, my wallet slides onto the bar in front of me. My eyes follow the path of the person's fingers up to their wrist, forearm dusted with light brown hair, up to a bicep and a tattoo peeking out from under a short-sleeved shirt.

Henry.

"Well," he says with a raised eyebrow, "didn't think I'd ever see *you* again."

Chapter Five

F*uck. Fucking fucking fuck.*

"Hi," I sputter.

"Hi, Bennet." He leans on the bar between us. "Or did you say your name was *Andy*?"

"I . . ." *Shit.* "I might have said that."

"Good thing there's an ID in here so I have proof it's you." His hand stays tightly gripped around the wallet as he looks at me over the rim of his glasses. "How was the baptism, by the way?"

He's baiting me to take the wallet right out of his hand, but I don't want to touch him, let alone play tug-of-war with him.

"You work here?" is all I can manage to squeak out. My mouth has gone completely dry and I feel as if I might once again vomit in the bathroom of L'italiano.

"Why'd you think I picked a spot across the street for our date?" The sound of the word *date* coming from his lips makes my face get unbearably hot. I'm suddenly aware of the fact that I'm wearing my cater waiter pants and button-up, which are probably the least sexy things a human being could be caught in. I've got brown mustard stains smeared across my thighs and I'm sure I smell like gorgonzola.

"You're a bartender and you picked a bartending class. That's not fair."

"Maybe I wanted to impress you." He leans in, fingers tightening around my wallet.

"Give me that," I snap, finally snatching it out of his hand.

He cocks his head, frowning. "You know, you might want to be nicer to the guy who spent all night waiting to hear from you."

"I had a bad night," I say, shoving the wallet in my bag.

"Yeah." He gestures out the window at Rosencrantz & Guildenstern with his thumb. "I had a bad night too." He sort of shakes his head and frowns in a half-scolding, half-dejected manner. I couldn't have actually hurt this guy, right? We don't know each other.

"Sorry. I didn't think you'd care. It was just a first date," I say.

"I took the cocktail class by myself, and when I was done, hours later, I came to the conclusion that I had indeed been ghosted. All of this, only to cross the street, have my coworkers ask me how my date was, and find you drunk in the men's bathroom. Gotta admit it was pretty surprising. From your profile, you didn't seem like the type to be that—"

"Sloppy?" I say, cutting him off.

He shakes his head. "I was going to say *callous*."

"You clearly don't know me at all," I say under my breath.

"Nope." He smirks, leaning a hip on the ice trough under the bar. "And now I never will."

For some reason this makes my stomach clench, the blood in my veins run cold. As if I could control what happened last night. As if I *wanted* to insult him and humiliate myself at the same time. "Guess not," I mumble as I back away from the bar. My throat starts to sting as I reach the exit. Fuck this restaurant. I push the door open, feeling the cool spring air whip against my face.

"At least you won me twenty bucks."

His voice stops me in my tracks. I turn on my heels toward him, one hand still holding the door open. "What?"

"Sarah, the bartender last night, she bet me twenty bucks we'd never see you again. I had a feeling you'd be back, so I took it."

"That's kind of fucked up."

"Not really." He rests his elbows on the bar. "I bet on you, remember?"

"That's not fair." My chest hitches with a short breath. Why should this guy make money off my panic attack? "And I feel like I deserve half of that twenty dollars."

He dips below the bar, grabbing his wallet from wherever he stashed it for his shift. He rifles through, pulling out a ten-dollar bill and holding it between two fingers. He smiles. "All yours."

I walk back to the bar, closing the door behind me. He barely moves as I approach him. When I go for the ten-dollar bill, I half expect him to pull it out of my reach, but he doesn't. He lets me slide it out of his hand. Cautiously, I retreat back a few feet.

"Thanks," I mutter.

"It's only fair," he says.

"Okay . . ." I scratch my chin. "Goodbye, then."

"Why didn't you show up to our date?" he asks, ignoring my goodbye.

"I, um . . ." I bite the inside of my lip and glance to the floor, crinkling the bill in my fingers. "I had a panic attack."

"Because of me?"

"Um . . ." My hands tremble. "I haven't been on a date in a really long time, and . . ." I shake my head. "My roommate made the profile. I wasn't ready."

"It's okay." When I look up, he's studying me. I think for a second that he might be looking behind me, so I glance over my shoulder. He laughs. I don't get it.

"I've never had a panic attack," he finally says, shrugging.

Of course he hasn't. "Lucky you," I say. "They're not fun."

"I didn't mean to stress you out," he says. "It was just a date."

His eyes are softer now, but I remember the way he looked at me earlier. Somewhere in the cross section between angry, hurt, and amused.

I clear my throat. "Look. Until you knocked on the bathroom door, I didn't consider that there was a real person attached to your profile. You were just this hypothetical guy on my phone screen. And then there you were, very, very real. And I felt even worse, and I ran."

His face drops and he dodges my eye. "I kind of felt like crap for the rest of the night after you booked it out of here. Like maybe I said something wrong or did something wrong, or . . . I don't know. You got to the bar, took one look at me, and wanted to throw up."

"I *did* throw up . . ." I whisper under my breath. The scope of the absolute fuckery of last night comes into full view in my head. Me spilling wine, puking in the bathroom, I don't even remember paying for dinner. "Ugh." I cradle my forehead in my hands. "I humiliated myself and I made you feel horrible and I'm sorry." My chin twitches and I feel the edges of my eyelids grow heavy and my nose starts to sting. I will not cry in front of this random dude. "Shit," I mumble. I turn my face away from him so he won't see my eyes get watery.

"Crap," he says. "Are you okay? Do you need a napkin?"

He grabs a cocktail napkin from the bar and offers it to me. I try my hardest to recall the tears back into my brain.

"No." I clear my throat. "I'm fine."

"Wine?" he suggests.

I groan, shaking my head. "I'm really okay."

"Pizza?"

I freeze for half a second at the suggestion, feeling my stomach growl in response. One simple fact is shackling me to this spot, and that fact is: I'm starving.

"Pizza," Henry says, grinning wide. "Winner, winner, chicken dinner."

"Winner, winner, pizza dinner," I say, immediately cringing at myself. "I mean . . ." My stomach growls again—louder this time.

Henry smiles, but quickly covers his mouth. He definitely heard it this time.

Drat. I've been betrayed by my own stomach. But I realize

that I might not have another opportunity to eat something besides Lean Cuisine until my next NYAC shift, so I reluctantly turn toward him. "Do you have pepperoni?" I ask.

"Of course we have pepperoni. We're a respectable establishment."

I glance toward the door, freedom in reach. Then I glance back to Henry, pizza in reach. It's genuinely a tough decision.

"Come on," he says, checking his watch. "We have five minutes until the kitchen closes. It's now or never."

My stomach gurgles again and I wince. Clearly this is out of my control.

"Fine," I say. "I'll use my bet money." I fish the ten-dollar bill from my pocket.

He shakes his head, punching the order into a tablet. "I get a staff meal for free," he says. "We can split it."

Then he grabs a bottle of wine from the well. "Wine?" He places a wineglass on the bar in front of my stool.

"You're being awfully nice to someone who stood you up," I say. "What's that about?"

"Are you always this skeptical of people?"

"Are you always this nice to people who ghost you?"

"No." He grins. "I usually don't meet them."

I feel my face get hot. "Right. Because of the ghosting."

"Right," he says as he pulls the cork from the bottle. "Kinda the point."

Now that I'm here, now that he's in front of me, I realize it's not so scary to have a drink with a stranger. Maybe this is my chance to vindicate myself for last night.

I take a breath, swallow, and climb up on the barstool.

"Hey, you're staying! Look at that." He smiles as he pours a glass of red.

I hold up one finger. "One glass of wine. That's it." He slides the glass toward me. I groan and shake my head. "Please . . . anything but the Chianti."

"Fair enough." He smirks and takes a sip out of the glass. "This will be mine, then. How about white?"

I nod.

His hair falls onto his face as he bends down to the wine cooler. He twists the cap off a bottle of white and pours some into a fresh glass. It's dark in the restaurant, but the vintage light fixtures on the walls make everything glow like marshmallows over a fire.

He finishes pouring my wine and returns the bottle to the cooler. "I'll be right back. Don't disappear," he says before he vanishes into the dining room, I'm assuming to make his rounds with the remaining tables.

The wine tastes like grapefruit. I sip it cautiously. What the hell am I doing? Why am I even here? Why is he being nice to me? This isn't a date, right?

Henry closes out one of the tables and starts cleaning plates off the other. He moves like there's nothing weighing him down, like the only thing surrounding him is air. It's a skill I never had. I don't make good first impressions. I get tongue-tied and awkward, and usually I can't think of a single thing to say no matter how far back into my brain I dig. It's like all the words in my vocabulary fall out of my ears and my personality gets flattened into a pancake.

Henry hands the last diners their check and disappears into

the kitchen. If I want to bolt, now is my chance. But I don't move.

He appears behind the bar with a tray of pizza and two plates, and I've never been so proud of myself for not letting my urge to flee win, because, *god*, does that pizza smell divine.

"So," he says, placing the food on the bar. "Tell me." He grabs a slice of pizza and pulls it toward him, creating the most perfect cheese bridge I've ever seen. It stretches between the slice and the rest of the pie until it finally snaps.

Oh god, I'm more turned on by that pizza than I have been by a man in years.

"Tell you . . . what?" I ask, trying not to seem more focused on the pizza than the man eating it.

"Anything."

I shrug. "Not much to tell."

Henry covers his mouth with a napkin while he chews. "Listen, if we're going to be friends you're going to have to tell me something about yourself."

I gaze at the pizza on the bar between us. I could swim in the grease in one of those curled-up pepperoni cups and be happy forever, but taking a slice of pizza feels like a commitment. Like I'm cosigning on whatever weird thing this guy wants from me. So I hesitate. "We're going to be friends?"

He folds his slice in half. "Sure."

"Why?"

"Why not?" He takes another big bite.

I take a sip of my wine. "Don't you already have friends?"

He shrugs. "I moved back to the city after a couple years at home in Denver, and my network shrank. I joined the dating apps to make friends just as much as to date or whatever." He wipes his hands on a cloth.

"Why me?"

"Because you're here."

I scowl. Henry continues. "And because you won me twenty dollars."

"Ten dollars."

"Yes, of course. Ten dollars."

I grit my teeth. What is there to tell? I feel so dumb. I used to be good at this. "I don't know what to talk about," I say.

"We'll start easy," he says. "You're from Pennsylvania, right?"

My stomach drops. "How did you know that?"

He shifts away from me, his neck flushing red. "Um . . . because . . ." He glances at his phone, which is face down on the bar. "Because it's on your profile," he says.

I squint at him. Did I put that information on my profile? I deleted it when I got home last night, so there's no way of checking. But if Henry knows I'm from Pennsylvania, he had to have gotten it from somewhere. After all, Sonya is the one who made me the profile, so I suppose she could've put my hometown on there without me noticing. Though I did ask her to keep it vague.

He clears his throat, tearing me from the thought. "Where in Pennsylvania?"

Hesitantly, I answer. "Lancaster County."

He nods. "Amish country."

"Yup," I say, picking at a splinter in the bar. "Where I'm from, and probably where I'll go next."

"You don't like New York?"

I shake my head. "It doesn't like me."

"Why are you in the city, then?" he asks as he notices me picking at the wood.

"My dead ex-boyfriend."

He chokes, turning away from me, pounding a piece of pizza free from his windpipe. After coughing for a minute he turns to look at me, his eyes watery from the ordeal. "Oh my god, I'm so sorry."

"You want to be friends? Well, that's my baggage. Figured I'd get it out of the way up front."

If I went to therapy, they'd probably tell me that I say shocking things about Sam to disarm people and deflect from my true emotions, but I don't go to therapy. Sam is gone and sugarcoating it won't bring him back. If Henry has any sense at all, this'll be enough to scare him off from trying to be my friend.

Henry looks at me with soft eyes, the muscles in his jaw working as he studies my face. He takes a breath as if to say something before thinking better of it. He drums his fingers on the bar between us to punctuate a subject change. "Hold that thought."

He crosses into the dining room and grabs the credit card from the last of the remaining customers. The man at the table stands up to shake Henry's hand.

I look down the front of my shirt to see a splotchy red rash on my chest from nerves. I close the top button of my blouse and then I check my phone. A message from Sonya:

> You okay if Jamie spends the night? We're going to watch both Mamma Mias back to back. Join us!

I type a response.

> Of course Jamie can stay. I'm not feeling well though. Next time maybe.

I click my phone shut, knowing there probably won't be a next time. Any day now, Sonya will get sick of begging me to spend time together, and I won't blame her.

Suddenly Henry's back in front of me.

He takes off his glasses and rubs his temples before looking up at me. "I think my dad is dying."

I stare blankly back at him, at the labored expression on his face. Where did *that* come from? "What?" I frown as I take a sip of wine.

"That's my baggage," he says. "He's pretty old."

I swallow, feeling the wine warm my belly. "Is that why you were in Denver?" is all I can think of to say. I'm not used to being on this side of the depressing conversation.

He replaces the glasses back on his face. "Yep."

"How old?"

He scrunches his nose and squints at me. "Does it matter?"

"Yes."

He frowns. "Dementia-old," he says. "He forgets a lot. It makes me nervous. But my mom is there with him and I was able to hire a nurse to come by every week." He adjusts his glasses on his nose. "It's not as big a suitcase as yours, but it's baggage nonetheless."

"Is this your way of getting me to trust you? By sharing that?"

He shrugs. "Depends. Did it work?"

No, I think. "No," I say.

"You're . . ." He crosses his arms and tilts his head. "You're funny."

I frown. "I don't think anything about this conversation has been funny."

"That's not what I meant," he says, scratching his elbow.

"What *did* you mean?" I cross my arms, mimicking him.

He shakes his head slightly, smiling. "I mean I think it's going to be really easy to be friends with you."

"You're nuts," I say. "And I haven't agreed to any friendship here, no matter how many times you say it."

"You don't think the cosmos is bringing us together?" he asks, grabbing his wineglass. "What if Sonya never made you that profile? What if you didn't forget your wallet here?"

"Then I'd have had a peaceful night alone," I say. "And how do you know my roommate's name?"

He rolls his eyes. "You told me over the app," he says. "Why are you so untrusting?"

"Why are you so persistent?" I challenge.

"Why are you still here?" He smirks.

"I—" I swirl the golden wine in my glass, making a little whirlpool. Why *am* I still here? "I don't know. The pizza."

He rolls his eyes. "Not the company?"

"Nope. The pizza and the wine." I raise my glass; the

restaurant lights burn amber through the liquid. "Cheers," I say. "To your really old dad."

Henry smiles, raising his glass to mine. "To your dead ex-boyfriend."

We clink them together.

Having Sam out in the open feels good. I don't talk about him earnestly with anyone. When he inevitably crosses my mind, I do everything in my power to change the mental channel to anything else. There's safety in sharing him with this stranger. There's no threat that I'll *actually* have to be vulnerable with Henry. I'm never going to see him after tonight. Turns out, even a pretend friend sort of feels real when you're lonely enough.

Henry changes the music from Ella Fitzgerald to Alabama Shakes as soon as the last customers leave the building. It feels a little naughty to be in a restaurant after hours with the lights on. It's like I'm seeing a person naked for the first time and I'm not supposed to. Henry throws a rag over his shoulder to pick up some dirty dishes. I finally slide a piece of pizza onto my plate. My mouth waters as I unroll a silverware set and cut off a bite.

"You've got to be kidding me," Henry says, peering over my shoulder. "Cutting your pizza?"

"I don't want to get my hands dirty."

"I'm starting to second-guess this whole being-friends thing." He gets a spray bottle from a waiter station by the bathroom and starts cleaning tables. His hair is always falling over his eyes.

"Not friends," I say as I take a delicious bite and try not to shiver with pleasure.

"Not yet." He stacks a couple plates and brings them to a busing station.

"You lied on your profile. How am I supposed to trust you?"

"I didn't lie," he says, cocking his head.

"Your profile said you were a photographer, not a bartender," I say, taking another bite of the most delicious pizza I've ever tasted.

"I am," he says, wiping a nearby table.

"Why are you at this restaurant?"

"Because I'm no Annie Leibovitz." He continues to clean. "I work here to pay the rent until I can get my business off the ground."

"What do you take photos of?"

"People." He stops wiping the table and stretches one arm across his chest before picking the rag up again. "Mostly engagement shoots and family portraits, but I also do weddings and concerts and other stuff like that."

"Cool," I say as I take another bite.

"And you? What do you do?"

I hold up a napkin to cover my full mouth and mumble, "Next question, please."

"That's a softball."

I sip my wine to wash down a clump of cheese. "Not for me."

"Well, that's obviously a catering uniform," he says with a smile, gesturing to my clothes.

"This is actually how I dress every day, and I'm offended you would think otherwise."

"All right. Don't tell me." He raises his eyebrows, baiting me. "But that's really boring of you."

I groan. Fine, I'll play. It's not like I'm going to see him again anyway. "Tonight I was a cater waiter. Tomorrow I'll be a desk receptionist. The next day, who knows? President, maybe."

He laughs and scratches his chin. "You temp?"

"Real winner, aren't I?"

He pulls a chair out from the table he was cleaning and sits. "Nothing wrong with temping."

"Oh yeah, my passion is serving mimosas and cocktail wieners to the one percent. I'm building my future brick by brick every day." I give a sarcastic smile, batting my lashes.

"What *is* your passion, then?"

I shake my head, tossing my napkin on the bar. "I don't have a passion."

"Come on." He drapes one elbow over the back of his chair. "Everyone has something they're passionate about."

"Not me. I think it's what they call apathy."

If you asked me in middle school, I would've said my passion was journalism. If you asked me in high school, I would've said my passion was acting. If you asked me in college, I would've said my passion was poetry, or, more accurately, the embarrassing poetry I wrote about Sam. Now the only thing I'm passionate about is making it from one moment to the next.

"I don't buy it," Henry says, wringing the bar towel between his fingers.

"It's the truth whether you buy it or not. I'm a directionless loser in her twenties who doesn't have a passion." I gulp down the rest of my grapefruit wine. "If you want to retract your offer for friendship, now's the time."

"I don't pick my friends based on their jobs," he says.

"No, you seem to pick your friends based on nothing at all."

"Everyone needs a passion," he says, ignoring my comment. "It's like the only reason I get up in the morning."

I discard my wineglass on the bar. "Is this you telling me you're actually a life coach? Are you going to pitch me a three-step plan to change my life? Are you going to try to sell me supplements next?"

"No . . ." He looks out the window. "But you're giving me an idea."

"I was joking," I say. "Please don't try to sell me supplements."

Henry turns back to me, suddenly with bright eyes. I might actually be seeing a light bulb go on in his brain.

"What if I help you find it?"

"What?"

"Your passion," he says, beaming. "What if I help you find it?"

Henry looks at me as if he just said something *normal* and not *very weird and strange.*

"Hello?" He snaps his fingers in front of my eyes. "Are you alive in there?"

"Sorry." I blink. "What?"

"Do you want me to help you find your passion?"

I violently stab a piece of pizza with my fork. He flinches. "That's such a weird thing to say to a stranger, Henry," I say.

He shrugs. "What about this interaction gave you the impression that I'm not weird?"

"I didn't think you were *this* weird," I say.

"Well, we barely know each other. Plenty of room for surprises." He smiles.

I roll my eyes. "You're a little drunk, and I'm a little drunk, and we're going to part ways after tonight and never talk to each other again. Even if I said yes to whatever you have in mind, that's what would happen. And we're both going to feel really dumb tomorrow."

"That is not going to happen," he says. "I'm weirdly committed to this."

"Why?" I feel my heartbeat in my neck and I smooth my palm over it to quiet the thrum of the sudden and strange bodily reaction. "What reason could you possibly have for offering to help me, a complete stranger, and someone who ghosted you, find a totally vague and existential thing?"

"Because . . ." He dodges my eye contact, looking over my head.

"Because, why?"

"Because . . ." he says again. Have I stumped him? It looks like he's about to say something, but then decides against it. "Is it so hard to believe that I just think it would be fun?"

The only word I can think of when I look at him now is . . . *sincere*. He's being sincere. What if he's right? What if the only reason for doing this is that it would be fun? When was the last time I had fun?

I clear my throat. "Say I agree to this. . . ."

"Yeah?"

"Which I'm not," I say, causing him to playfully roll his

eyes. "But say, hypothetically, that I do. . . . What would that even look like?"

He shrugs. "Don't know. We could just try some new things. Take classes, go to new places . . . once a week we could get together and try a new passion. I'm a lot of fun once you get to know me, you know," he says, smiling. "Some might call me an expert in fun."

"Who calls you that?"

"Doesn't matter. Come on," he says. "I can tell you want to say yes."

"No, you can't."

"Yes. I can."

"No, you can't," I say in a huff. "And you're honestly pretty full of yourself if you think you can help me do this."

"Nope." He clasps his hands under his chin. "Just passionate about passion."

"Ugh." I cross my arms.

I think about the girl I was before everything went down with Sam. I was so excited for life to start. So excited for what my future would hold. I felt like life was a series of endless possibilities, surprises around every corner. But in chasing those opportunities, I lost the person I loved most. Now I have no spark left. Only guilt and grief.

Would it be so bad to try?

I lift my eyes to Henry, who's looking at me expectantly. "What do you get out of it?" I ask.

He rests his elbows on his knees, holding the rag between them. "Why do I have to get something out of it?"

"Because otherwise this makes literally no sense."

"I get a new friend. The presence of Bennet in my life."

"Don't be patronizing."

"I'm not." His mouth blooms into a smile. The single dimple on his cheek draws my eye for just a flicker of a second. "I'm being *spontaneous*."

"You're being *crazy*."

"Come on," he says. "I have a bunch of fun shit I want to do and no one to do it with. You'd be doing me a favor, really."

I squeeze my eyes shut, trying to imagine what this would look like between us. On one hand, I don't have anything else to do in the foreseeable future besides several depression naps and a Netflix marathon. On the other hand, depression naps and Netflix marathons are my safe space. It would be so easy to keep myself hidden from the world, sheltered in my cocoon knowing that I can't fail if I don't really try. On the third hand, if there are allowed to be three hands in decision making . . . I'm a little tipsy and it actually seems possible right now. Things I would normally never consider are suddenly worth considering.

"I don't even know you," I respond, opening one eye.

"There's this really wonderful thing I'd love to introduce to you. It's called *getting to know someone over the course of more than one hour-long conversation*." He flashes that bright smile at me, the restaurant's light reflecting in his glasses. "Care to give it a go?"

"This won't be a boy-saves-girl-and-teaches-her-how-to-live-life type of situation," I say. "I'm not a damsel in distress."

He raises three fingers in the air in Scout's honor. "Never."

"Because feminism."

"Because feminism." He nods.

"And I'm only going to agree to this if you promise we'll just be friends."

"You've made that very clear. You did stand me up, remember?"

"I mean it. I'm not . . . It's not the right time for me."

"Heard," he says, his face suddenly serious. "I'm not in the business of crossing boundaries, Bennet."

I swallow, my throat dry as ash. "Agh." I wince. "This is ridiculous. I feel stupid."

He tosses his head back and laughs. "Oh my god, it's not that serious, Bennet. Do you wanna hang out with me and do fun shit, or do you want to keep ghosting guys on dating apps?"

"Both, kinda."

"Good." He smirks. "Every Saturday. We'll do something new. The ghosting you can do on your own time."

He holds out his hand to shake. It hangs between us in dead air, waiting for me to grab on.

Despite the fact that part of me thinks this is stupid, part of me thinks that Henry isn't telling me everything, and most of me thinks I'm not made for a life of passion, I grab his hand and we shake on it. Even if I'm just playing along, I need to prove that I can. To prove that I'm not scared of everything.

Chapter Six

Sunshine pours from my window and casts a streaky shadow across my floor, revealing the true disaster state of my living quarters. Seeing it in the light is a sobering experience. I've always been a messy person, unable to keep a clean house, but when I moved in with Sonya I knew I'd have to confine my mess to my room and not let it spill out into the kitchen. Maintaining order in the shared living spaces has worsened the chaos behind my closed doors.

I stretch in bed, waking my body up. I've been grinding my teeth all night, so I give my jaw a quick massage before rolling over to check my phone. No messages. I half expected a text from Henry. He has my number from our initial date, and I assumed he'd use it by now. So far, though, he's proving me right. He was never serious about being friends, and I was never serious about finding my passion. And I *do* feel stupid. There's not a chance in hell that I'll text him. That's for damn sure.

My feet ache from NYAC last night, and my knees crack when I get out of bed.

The hinges squeak as I open the door and head to the bathroom. I stop when I see someone sitting on the couch. She's in head-to-toe black, with a messy pixie cut as if someone just ran their hands through it.

Jamie.

"Morning." She stands to greet me. I'd forgotten that Sonya had her over last night. "I made coffee," she says. "Want some?"

She lifts my favorite clay mug to her lips and I try to keep from scowling. She made coffee in *my* French press. She's drinking out of *my* mug.

I remind myself that I do like Jamie, even though she's always catching me at the worst moments. She's got a calming aura about her, and her rocker chick vibe balances out Sonya's type-A senior class president personality.

"No, thanks," I say, even though it smells delicious and the dull pain behind my eyes would be cured with one single sip.

"Sonya told me you had a date the other night," she says. She is far too *awake* for this hour.

"Yeah." I yawn, padding across the room. "I'm sorry, Jamie. I'm not really up yet."

"Oh." She shrinks back. "Sorry."

I shut the bathroom door behind me, brush my teeth, and splash water on my face.

When I make my way back to my room, Jamie has vacated the couch. I feel bad for scaring her off, but I'm nursing a two-day hangover and I cannot be social right now.

—

I sit down on my unmade bed and open my laptop to my calendar.

> Friday, May 29th: 11:00am–5pm
>
> Desk Attendant at The New York Public Library, Celeste Bartos Forum. Dress code: Business casual.

I check my phone. 10:27.

Shit.

I forgot I was working today. I had to walk out the door ten minutes ago if I was going to make it to Bryant Park in time.

What the hell does business casual look like? I dig through the piles of dirty clothes on my floor looking for anything that might work. I check the train times as I pull on a pair of black high-waisted jeans. Is denim business casual? I don't have time to second-guess.

I'm a mess, yes, but I'm never late. The perfect time to arrive at an event or job is four minutes before the start time. That way you're not disrespectful by being late, and you don't have to commit to more than five minutes of awkward small talk with the neurotic early comers. It's always my plan to be exactly four minutes early, no more, no less.

I dart to the station and hop on the first train that approaches, barely checking to make sure it's the right one. This is what happens when you let people catch you off guard. I let Henry distract me and now I'm late to a shift. I stayed out too late, talked too much, and let that weird night get the better of me. Also, why hasn't he texted? And why am I thinking about that when there are clearly more pressing issues at hand? I have very few things keeping me going in New York, and even though it's soul-sucking and there's no upward mobility, this job is one of those things. Losing it would be the final sign that I'm truly not meant to be here.

When I finally make it to Bryant Park, I hike the subway steps and cross the street to the closest building New York City's got to a Parthenon: the New York Public Library. I take one millisecond to pause and look at it—to admire the odd sense of time travel I feel in its presence—the grandiose arches above the doors, slate-gray pillars holding them up, the intricate statues carved into the building's face. This city is so fast, so industrial, that I sometimes forget that there's also history here. This building feels out of place, a relic, but I feel a sudden rush as I start to ascend the marble stairs toward its gaping maw. The library isn't out of place—no, it will outstay everyone and everything here. It's everything new and shiny that are merely tourists camping out in New York's stoic, unchanging facade.

Me, I think. *I'm the out-of-place one.*

I catch my breath and dash up the marble steps, feeling like the carved lion statues on either side of me are judging me as my thighs and lungs burn. Now . . . where the heck is the Bartos Forum?

I spot a map on the far side of the gigantic stone atrium and shuffle over, footsteps echoing in the massive room. I've worked a few jobs here, but there are so many tiny nooks and crannies of the library that I could never memorize every single one. I pull out my phone, praying that no one from my temp agency has called to scold me for being late, and I open my email assignment for details.

Enter the library at 42nd Street.

I used the wrong entrance. *How about next time you actually read the email, Bennet?*

I rush out the door and clomp down the stairs onto the busy sidewalk, rounding the corner to Forty-Second Street, where I finally spot the correct entrance. I suck in a breath of air and shove my way inside, hoping one of my supervisors isn't on site today to notice my tardiness.

I spot Sal, another temp I work with often, behind a small table. There's an empty chair next to him for me.

"I'm so sorry. I slept in," I bluster at him.

"It's okay, sweetheart, they didn't even notice." Sal's complexion is similar to an eggplant. It makes me worry about his cholesterol. He's wearing an ill-fitted white button-up that's yellowing a bit around the seams. His hairline is damp and balding, but his features bear the faint whisper of someone who used to be handsome. Sal's the kind of guy who could never lie to you. He's also the kind of guy who gives you his full life story in a single six-hour shift—and I've had many six-hour shifts with him. He wears his emotions on his big expressive face, always close to the surface. He's the only person who can call me *sweetheart* without making me want to rip his throat out. It's a paternal *sweetheart*, not a creepy one.

I've seen him around the other temping venues, but the library is turning into his home base. He knows all the ins and outs, and where to get free coffee. Valuable information for an employee who never stays at one place long enough to get comfortable.

"What's the event?" I ask as I slide into the chair. The air in here is musty, but in a good way. It smells of old pages and dust and real marble.

"Some corporate thing. They got a stage set up in there and a brunch buffet. You should peek inside before they get started. It's real nice."

"Oh," I say, craning my neck to see inside the forum. "Okay. I'll be quick."

I sneak through the entrance to a flurry of caterers and event planners making final touches on an absolutely breathtaking room.

The domed ceiling stretches over my head like the top of a wire birdcage. It's dark inside, but not in a sullen way—in the same way that a planetarium is dark. Maybe it reminds me of a planetarium because the ceiling is lit up in cerulean blue and electric violet, deep and vibrant as a faraway galaxy. There's a stage toward the front of the room, with two large screens on either side. Seats are set up auditorium-style, with a few grazing tables in the back for those who are eating breakfast or drinking brunch cocktails.

I can't help the bewildered look that must be plastered on my face when I return to our rinky-dink desk in the lobby. It's not even a desk. It's a folding table.

"Told ya," Sal says, scratching his chin. "Fancy."

I shake my head, feeling the immeasurable distance between me, sitting *here*, and those people in *there*. "Wow," I say. "A whole different galaxy."

"We'll have more fun out here," he says, smiling.

Probably not, but I smile back at him anyway. "What do we do?" I ask.

"When they come to the desk, we hand them a name tag and a folder and tell them to head inside." His voice is low and robust, colored by years of barking drills at high school football players.

"That's it?"

"We gotta check their name off on this clipboard too, but that's easy."

"What time does it start?"

"Any minute."

"Great." I tuck my hair behind my ears, but it pops back out immediately. I take a deep breath and try to enjoy the calm before people start checking in.

I glance over at Sal, who's staring at his phone with laser focus.

I suddenly remember that he's expecting his first grandchild—a fact he told me the last time we worked together. I swivel toward him. "Texting your daughter?"

"Oh." His face brightens. "Yeah."

"How's she doing?"

"They got her on bed rest until the little guy comes. Something about her blood pressure. But Mary and me are so excited."

"It's a boy?" If the kid looks anything like Sal, he'll be a little chubby eggplant baby.

"A boy," he says, beaming. "I can't believe I'm gonna be a grandpa. You wait and see, sweetheart, it goes fast. Soon you'll be doing what I'm doing."

I am doing what you're doing, I think to myself.

The first businessman approaches our desk, bringing me back to the task at hand. Sal greets him, gives him a lanyard, and sends him to the room. Person after person comes to our desk, each dressed sharply, each outshining the last with confidence and poise. These people are my age, yet they seem to be in on something that I don't understand. How did they get that way? What am I missing?

It's like my grief has tethered me to myself, the walls of sadness like shrink-wrap surrounding all sides of me until I can barely breathe. Any movement I make, any step forward or back, is too painful. The smaller and smaller my world becomes, the more daunting it is to try to move out of the hurt. I feel close to Sam in my grief. It's the only thing I have left of him.

If Andy were here, she'd be inside that room—hell, she'd probably end up as a keynote speaker. She's always been that way—audacious, fiery, spirited—partially because of her privileged upbringing, and partially because it's just her nature to be like that. I've never seen her waver—not even since Sam died. She's still Andy, still finding ways to be happy.

I blink as I hand a girl in a perfectly tailored suit a name tag and check her off the list. She disappears into the beautiful conference room, red hair flowing down her back. Reminds me of Andy.

I'm an outside-of-the-room person, and I always will be—no matter if a boy with green eyes and glasses made me feel differently for one fraction of a moment over white wine and pizza. No matter if Sonya tries to convince me I'm not.

Sal and I continue the shift, and I go to the place I always go to when life starts to feel too overwhelming: autopilot.

Chapter Seven

Okay, what the hell? This stupid guy practically begged me to be his stupid friend and now I'm stupid waiting for a stupid text. I crawl into my unmade bed and pull the covers over my face. What on earth was I thinking last night? And why do I feel so . . . disappointed?

Something familiar is happening in my body—a tightening of my muscles, slither of darkness up my spine, a desire to curl up, close my eyes, and bear down until it passes. It's small now, but it's happened enough times that I know it will grow from my stomach to the tips of my fingers—it'll grow until it envelops me whole, and the best I can do is endure.

The first time it happened was when everything went down with Sam. The darkness surrounding me, pulling me deeper and deeper into a pit that I couldn't crawl out of if I tried. I dropped out of college, I stopped talking, I gave up.

I screw my palms into my eyes, trying to physically squeeze some dopamine into my brain. I can't hold off the bad feelings forever, but I can try to distract myself.

I open my laptop and put on an episode of *Criminal Minds*. Garcia is trying to track the unsub by using his cell phone, but all the numbers he called were blocked. I know this show is wildly unrealistic and that technology hasn't advanced enough to do half the fancy stuff Garcia does to find the bad guy, but I don't care. I like a story that has a neat ending, one in which they always catch the killer.

Wait.

The cell phone numbers were *blocked.*

I blocked Henry.

What an idiot. Heart beating fast, I scroll through my contacts until I find *Green Eyes Henry*—Sonya named his contact in my phone. I select "unblock." Just like that, messages start pouring in.

> Hey, Bennet! I'm at the bar wearing a red rose on my lapel, so you know who I am. Also I'm wearing a top hat.
>
> I'm joking about the rose btw.
>
> And the top hat.
>
> Unless you're into it?

Oh my god. He's insane. There are even more texts from later that night.

> I'm not stalking you, I promise. I work at L'italiano. I was picking up my paycheck.

You left your wallet here. You're lucky I'm not a thief or I'd steal all your money.

Jk there's only like 47 cents in here.

I'm working tomorrow night if you want to pick it up.

At the bottom of the string of texts is the one I was looking for. Or *not* looking for. I don't know.

Good morning, new friend. I know you're supposed to become the President this week, but if you have a free day for an adventure, let me know.

I start to type. What do you even say in a situation like this? Do I even want to reply?

Sorry, I blocked your phone number before I knew we were going to be friends.

Delete.

Sorry, I had work all day and didn't look at my phone.

Delete delete delete.

Sorry, I'm not sure if being friends with you is altogether a good idea considering I have a track record of disappointing people and myself along the way so it might be better to call the whole thing off.

Delete. I try one more time.

Apparently my stint as President has been postponed. Turns out there's a pretty rigorous job interview for the position including a countrywide election? Did you know about this?? Seems unfair.

Send. *Don't think about it. He's just a person.*

I tiptoe into the bathroom and turn the shower on as hot as it will go. I slide the curtain open, drop my clothes in a pile, and sit down in the tub, clutching my knees to my chest, and I let the scalding water run down my back until it stings. I sit there long enough that the water's heat tapers off and my fingers go pruney. Long enough that when I stand up, I'm lightheaded and dizzy.

When I get out of the tub, I wipe the steam from my phone screen.

One message.

Any idea where to start? Passion wise? Since you can't be President :(

I wipe my hands on my towel so they're dry enough to type the first thought I have, because if I think about it too long I'll never respond.

I used to like to draw.

Sonya is the artist, not me, but there was a time when I'd doodle in the corners of every piece of notebook paper I had. I was never particularly good at it.

Hmmmmm okay. Noted.
Indoorsy or outdoorsy?

I shudder.

Indoors.

He types for a second and then his message pops up.

Great. I have an idea for tomorrow.

My heart drops.

Tomorrow? So soon . . .

He types for another moment.

Your enthusiasm is palpable!

I roll my eyes. Before I can respond, he's texted again.

Meet me at 2. Washington Square Park.

I tighten the towel around my body, the air cooling in the bathroom around me. I take a deep breath and respond.

No need to bring a rose.

Chapter Eight

Saturday morning started out perfectly average. I woke up, threw on some clothes, went grocery shopping (take two), scanned my email for shifts this week at Carlyle Staffing Solutions, and signed up for six of them. Two events at NYAC, one at a corporate event space, and three at the library.

What *wasn't* normal about this morning was the feeling that I was going to keel over and pass out at any moment. I have plans today. Actual plans.

Who *am* I?

I have one hour before I see Henry. I pace around my tiny apartment.

Calm down. I fan my armpit with a paper plate. *You can always bail.*

I don't know what he could have planned for midday in Washington Square Park. I usually avoid that area of the city due to all the college students and music and general chaos.

I rifle through my clothes. Everything I try on looks stupid. My favorite jeans make me feel lumpy, my favorite top looks babyish, and my favorite jacket makes me look like I'm trying way too hard. I *am* trying way too hard. After several failed outfits, I give up and collapse on the floor in my underwear. I could make snow angels in the piles of clothes.

I consider texting Henry to reschedule. And then the next time we have plans, I'll reschedule again. It'll be a never-ending chain of rescheduling until one or both of us die. I'm fine with that.

I slide open my phone screen to a text from him.

> I know you're thinking about ghosting me, but I'm not above threatening you with a pizza embargo if you do. I can have every pizza joint in the city blacklist you, you know. I have that power.

And then:

> Meet you at the fountain.

I think of how weird he got when I ghosted him. How surprising it was that it bothered him even a little bit. How I didn't even consider his feelings when I blocked his number. I can't do that to him again today. I have to get through this, just once, and then maybe he'll let me off the hook and we can go back to being strangers and I can go back to being the recluse of 155th Street.

Just once.

I close my eyes and repeat my mantra. The mantra that gets me back down to earth when my heart feels like it's beating so fast it might fly away.

My cheeks are real. My chin is real. My lips are real. I am real.

When I was a kid and I started to get this way, my mom would crouch in front of me and ask me to point out things in the room. *Show me something pink, Bennet,* she'd say. I'd point to something pink. *Show me something blue.* I'd point to something blue. She'd always end on whatever color I was wearing, to ground myself back to my body. Slowly, over the years, it morphed into my mantra. Remembering that all I am is a body, a pile of organs and flesh, eases my anxiety. It balances me. Brings my breathing down.

When I was with Sam, it became *Tell me something good, Bennet.* He'd smile, his palm laid across my stomach. *Sunflowers,* I'd say. *Andy's denim jacket. Spaghetti. Summertime.* He'd pull me close and bury his face in my neck. *You,* I'd whisper. *You.*

I dig into the back of my closet and find Andy's jacket. It got mixed up in my things when we both left school after Sam died. Neither of us really paid attention to what we were packing, and I kept it all these years like a little treasure. I pull it on over a plain T-shirt and hope that her strength gets me through this.

I grab my bag and I'm out the door.

No backing out. I'm doing this.

I walk up the steps from the subway at West Fourth and emerge onto the bustling sidewalk. I don't see Henry, so I nudge my way across the street and into the park. I cup my hands over my forehead, blocking the sunlight from my eyes as I head toward the massive carved white arch at the far end of the park, dodging caricature artists and skateboarders zooming past. I make my way to a footpath, greenery on either side, and feel a bead of sweat roll down the back of my neck. It's hot with all these bodies around. I can never get used to being near so many people. I like to keep at least three feet of space between me and everyone else if I can help it. And in this city, I usually can't.

College students whiz past on scooters, buskers play clashing music on each corner, a woman conducts a flock of birds on the wind like they're her own private orchestra. I walk past a bench that smells distinctly like piss as I approach the big round clearing at the center of the park and the beacon in the middle—the fountain. It spews water from its core, casting a thin mist over the general area. The fountain is a large bowl—people sit inside its rim, sketching, chatting, sunbathing in the mist. A couple of children splash around in the spray, and a rainbow shimmers out of the corner of my eye. Couples kiss, old men play checkers, women breastfeed their babies. There's a couple being entertained by a magician. I weave through the mass of people until I see him.

He's chatting with another guy who's sitting on the fountain's lip. They're both laughing. The guy is holding a paperback with his finger wedged between the pages as a makeshift bookmark.

Henry's wearing a blue T-shirt and jeans, throwing his head back in appreciation of some joke I can't hear.

Three deep breaths.

"Hey." My voice cracks as I approach them. Great start.

"Bennet!" Henry looks up and smiles big and bright, revealing his single dimple. "This is Martin. Martin, this is Bennet."

"Nice to meet you," I say, trying not to let my nerves come through in my speech.

"You too." Martin's husky voice doesn't match his appearance. He's got on a brightly colored plaid button-up and khakis, and he sits properly with his legs crossed.

"Well." Henry checks his watch. "We better get going. Let me know if you want to grab a beer sometime."

Damn. This new guy isn't coming with us. I was hoping for a buffer. Henry shakes Martin's hand and turns to me.

"Ready?" His tousled hair waves in the breeze. An air of anticipation sparks in his eyes, like there's something on the tip of his tongue.

"No."

Henry rolls his eyes and smiles. "Come on."

I can barely keep up as I follow him through the crowd. His pace is somewhere between a walk and a jog, as if at any second he could take off.

"Hey!" I call, hoping to slow him down.

It works. Henry pauses briefly in his tracks, looking back at me.

"Was that your friend back there?"

"A new friend, maybe." He continues walking, but I'm able to keep pace with him now.

"What does that mean?"

"I saw he was reading one of my dad's favorite books, so I asked him about it, and, I don't know. We got to talking. Turns out his girlfriend dumped him and moved into a one-bedroom with his best friend last week. He teaches at Brooklyn College."

"You just . . . started talking to him?"

He shrugs. "Yeah."

"And he didn't think you were crazy?"

He dodges a woman whizzing by with a stroller. "Why would he think that?"

My breath shortens as we speed-walk through the park. "Is that like a hobby of yours? Talking to random people like Martin . . . and *me*?"

"Sure," he says with a smirk.

"Why?"

"You know what I'm going to say to that." He stretches his arms over his head like a cat, and I hear a tiny crack of vertebrae. "Why not?"

"I think it's a little suspicious, that's all."

"I like people. Is that a crime?" He looks both ways before crossing the street. "Always have. I like talking to them, I like listening to them, and I like taking pictures of them."

"Sounds like *Humans of New York* but murdery. Which, by the way, actually *is* a crime."

"I like following them home at night. I like hiding them in my basement. I like the taste of human flesh. You know, normal guy stuff."

"Serial killers are overwhelmingly charming men, so you're not really helping your case here."

"Ah." He raises an eyebrow. "You think I'm charming."

"Ugh." I groan involuntarily. "I think you're clinging to the wrong part of what I said. I believe *serial killer* was the operative term in that sentence."

"Right, right. I'll hold off on showing you my torture room, then. You're not ready."

Even though I desperately try to hold it in, a chuckle bubbles from my chest. I clip it fast.

"Where are we going?" I say flatly, pinching the end of the lit fuse of the conversation and snuffing out any potential banter.

Henry stops in front of a weathered storefront. "Here."

The crumbly brick exterior is painted black. Vines crawl around the building like garter snakes. There are two birds spray-painted on either side of a sign that says THE RAVEN TATTOO PARLOR.

"Oh my god, no." My heart skids to a halt. "No, no, no, no, no." The word *no* echoes through my brain and spills out my mouth like an involuntary compulsion. "Are you insane? There's no way I'm getting a tattoo. Not a chance in hell."

Henry starts to laugh. I'm so glad this is funny to him, because I actually hoped this project wouldn't be a mistake, that maybe he'd suggest something normal and I'd have two hours today in which I didn't feel like a massive disappointment to the human race. But no, Henry wants to see me squirm. His laugh burns my skin.

"This was a bad idea," I say, taking a few hurried steps away from the door. I tuck myself into a shady corner beside the tattoo shop's vestibule, and fan myself with my hand—a tableau of a scandalized lady in one of the historical romance books my mom loves to read.

"Whoa, whoa, whoa!" Henry enters my hiding spot, folds his arms, and leans against the vestibule. "What's wrong?"

"So many things. First of all, getting a tattoo is not a passion. I can't make a career out of that. Second of all, you're crazy if you think I'm going to get one with *you*. And third of all, I can't just do something like this on a whim. It needs planning and thoughtful consideration. So thank you for your attempt to embarrass me, but it won't work."

Henry laughs, a bit awkward, and steps back a few feet. "First of all, you don't even know what we're doing yet, so don't freak out before there's a reason to freak out." He raises his eyebrows. "Second of all, of course I don't expect you to get a tattoo today. Do you think I'm nuts?"

"A little bit, yeah."

"Third of all, I offered to help you find your passion. Not your career. Those are two different things. Not that I need a fourth of all, but you did tell me yesterday that you liked to draw. This shop holds a tattoo class every Saturday. They teach you to use the needles and you practice tattooing on a honeydew."

"Oh." I cross my arms and frown.

He looks at me like I'm on the ledge of a building, and he's talking me off. "It's just a class," he says, smiling. "It's low stakes. If you don't want to do it, we don't have to."

I believe him when he says it. He won't try to force me.

"Henry," I say, embarrassed. "I really don't understand why you're doing this for me."

"This isn't going to be any fun if you keep asking me that. Just go with it." He tilts his head. "Okay?"

I deflate. *Just go with it.* "I'm not good at this whole making-friends thing. I haven't done it in a while."

"You're doing fine."

"I'm not." I uncross my arms. "This isn't going to be as easy as I thought it was."

"Nah." He shakes his head. "I think you're making it way harder than it has to be. Relax."

"Didn't anyone ever tell you that you never tell a woman to relax?"

"Yeah, but I kinda want to take this class and I'd kinda like you to join me, so . . ." He pulls a puppy-dog face. "Can you relax for me?"

Sigh. How can I say no to that? "Fine."

"All right, then." He cracks that stupid smirk and gestures toward the shop. "Shall we?"

The tattoo shop is small, dark, and dingy. The sounds of rock music and the high-pitched buzzing of tattoo guns echo through the air. Portraits of naked women, anchors, skulls, and flowers cover the walls. I picture Henry here, pointing to one of the designs and sitting in one of these chairs. I still haven't been able to get a good look at the tattoo on his bicep, and I hate that I'm so curious about it.

Henry waves at a woman tattooing a dragon on a large gentleman in a white tank top.

"Henry," she says through a big smile. "I'm almost done here, you can head downstairs to the rest of the group."

"Thanks, Kira." He forges ahead. "This is Bennet, by the way."

"Welcome."

The stairwell opens into a small room that's set up like a high school science lab, with six double-wide tables and a chalkboard at the front. Each lab table has two melons, and two sets of what look like surgical tools wrapped in plastic, and a couple people sitting and chatting.

Henry and I are seated in the last row on the left, behind a group of girls in matching pink sashes (bachelorette party, I assume), which is a good spot for me. There's safety and comfort in the back row.

"So . . ." I clear my throat. "You've been tattooed here before?"

"Yeah," Henry says, annoyingly not showing me his tattoo. I don't know why I'm so curious, but it's driving me sort of nuts not to see it. I'm not sure it's good etiquette to ask about tattoos, and he's not offering it up, so I keep my mouth shut. "Kira's great. My friend Sarah recommended her when I got back from Denver."

Sarah. He's mentioned Sarah before. "Sarah, your bartender friend?"

"Oh yeah, I forgot you met her," he says with a slinky smile. "She got grilled by our manager about overserving after your visit."

"Oh my god." I cover my face with my hands. I can feel it going red. "I'm probably famous at your restaurant for being an absolute disaster."

"I was kidding," he says playfully. "You're very easy to tease."

I take my palms from my face and rub my temples. "I don't usually drink like that."

He drums his energetic fingers on the desk. "It's okay, no one thought it was weird. We've all had nights like that. Most of the time it's in a club or at a party and not in an Italian restaurant, but hey, to each their own."

"Shut up."

"See?" He smiles. "Easy to tease."

Kira bursts through the door at the back of the classroom. She's wearing a racerback tank top with black jeans and thick heavy boots. Almost every visible inch of her skin is covered with tattoos. On her clavicle there's a woman's face with tears flowing down her cheeks. There's a portrait of Edgar Allan Poe on her shoulder. That's probably where the name for the shop came from. The Raven. She wears a literal representation of who she is on her skin. It tells me that she knows who she is, that she's bold and unafraid to make a statement, that she's proud of being Kira.

What do my plain T-shirt and denim jacket say about me? Little to nothing.

She shows us diagrams of the tattoo guns and goes into detail about how they work. Then she holds up her own tattoo gun and demonstrates how to turn it on. We follow along with the guns at our stations. At once, a choir of buzzing machines erupts, vibrating my eardrums.

"Before we go any further," Kira says, setting her gun down, "we have to learn to draw the tattoo."

On the chalkboard, she shows us step-by-step how to draw the shop's logo, a raven. The class breaks into a low roar of conversation and laughter as everyone clumsily tries to copy the little black bird in paper and pen.

"How are you doing?" Henry leans over my station to see my work.

"No cheating," I say, covering my paper with my arm.

"It's literally impossible to cheat," he says, tugging at the corner of my paper. "We're doing the same thing."

I snatch my paper away from his grasp and hug it to my chest. "Paws off, wise guy."

"*Wise guy?* What are you, a 1920s mobster?"

"Keep trying to see my drawing and you'll find out," I say, squinting menacingly.

"Well, if you won't show me yours, I won't show you mine. And I know you want to see it. It's probably a masterpiece."

"Fine," I huff. I *am* curious. "On three. One, two, three."

We hold our drawings up to our chests.

"Oh my god," I say before I can stop myself. Henry's is terrible. Truly awful. A scribbled mess. I can't control my laughter. "That's one of the worst things I've ever seen in my life," I wheeze.

"What?" He studies his work. "It's . . . it's abstract."

I'm laughing so hard a tear comes to my eye. "It looks like an evil toddler drew it with a blindfold on." I gasp for breath. "No, it looks like someone stomped on a bird and then tried to put it back together by memory."

"You're so mean," he says, but he starts to laugh at my laughter.

"Henry, it's possessed."

He turns the paper toward him and examines it closely

for the first time. He bursts out laughing at the sight of the monster.

Kira makes her way to us. We choke down our laughter in front of the teacher. "What's so funny over here?" she asks with a displeased smile.

"Nothing, I just drew a portal to the underworld," Henry says.

Kira leans over his shoulder to get a better look at his paper. She places her hand on his upper back.

"It's not so bad." She pats him gently between his shoulder blades. "Keep trying, you'll get better." She gives him a charged look, one any girl can recognize as flirty. She doesn't even look at me as she moves on to the next table.

"Teacher's pet," I mutter under my breath.

"It's not my fault she can recognize true genius."

"Yeah, right." I roll my eyes. "She's real interested in your *art*."

"I can't help it if you're jealous of my skills. I think someone should get this tattooed on them forever. I'm happy to do it for you, all you have to do is say the word."

"I'm just saying, no one would ever describe that drawing as *not so bad* unless they want to sleep with you."

"Ah, so I shouldn't be encouraged by the fact that you described it as, and I quote: the worst thing you've ever seen."

I swallow back any response. This is too close to flirting. "Yeah," I say, slumping over my paper. Henry returns to his as well, and we draw in silence for a few minutes.

Finally, it's time to tattoo on the melon. Kira instructs us to start with straight lines, and then curls, and then try to tattoo the bird.

My first attempt is honeydew slaughter. If it were human

skin I was tattooing on, the poor person would have to go to the hospital. The sticky juice leaks out over my hands and I have to wipe them on my jeans after I set the gun down to watch Henry work. He's not that bad. Despite his laughable art skills, his hand is steady and gentle.

By the end of the class, we each have a little melon that looks like Vin Diesel's head if it were covered in raven tattoos. I'm impressed with myself, if I'm honest. Most people toss their melons on their way out, but I choose to keep mine. I know it will rot quickly, but I'm not done looking at its beautiful imperfections, all created by my hand. I might stare at its ugly skin for days.

Henry and I take a lazy walk to the train station along the outskirts of the park. Trees and vines entwined in a wrought-iron fence along the sidewalk blot out the sun, giving us pleasant speckled shade as we walk. I inhale the smoky scent of Sabrett hot dogs from a nearby pushcart and listen to the muffled sound of a Caribbean steel drum being played in the park. Moments like these, when you're able to get away from the chaos of certain areas of New York but are still close enough to hear and smell it, are the moments when I like this city the most. It's like listening to the ocean through a conch shell, like closing your eyes and inhaling the scent of fresh-baked cookies. A moment between real life and a dream state. Almost hypnotic.

Henry tosses his melon back and forth between his hands.

"So?" he says, like a kid awaiting approval. "Did you have fun?"

I scrunch my face, trying not to give him the satisfaction of a smile. "What do you think?"

He tucks his melon under his arm. "You did. You loved it and you're going to have a full sleeve by Christmas."

"Something like that," I say. "Minus the sleeve."

"I know you probably won't end up a tattoo artist, but at least it was an adventure."

"It was." I turn the melon in my hands, studying the lines and shapes. "Thanks for, uh . . . talking me off the ledge."

"Eh." He gestures with his hand. "You would've done it without me, I know it."

He's wrong, but I let him think he's right.

"Till next time?"

He moves in for a hug, but I dodge him by stretching out my sticky hand to shake. He cocks his head, smiling.

"Yeah," I say. "Next time."

Chapter Nine

Almost a week has passed since I last spoke to Henry. Sunday, I had a shift handing out magazines in front of the Flatiron Building in the pouring rain. Monday was a plated dinner at NYAC honoring its retired members. Tuesday, Wednesday, and Thursday were at the library with Sal, which brings us to today. One more catering shift at NYAC and I'm free for a weekend of *Criminal Minds.* I have two whole days ahead of me with nothing planned.

My phone buzzes in my back pocket and doesn't stop—which is weird, since hardly anyone calls me nowadays. I open the screen, inhale sharply when I see Mom is calling. I swallow and clear my throat, willing my voice to sound chipper and bright. To my parents, I'm living my dreams in the big city, happy as a clam.

"Hi," I say, my voice slightly too high to sound natural.

"Hi, angel!" There's soft music playing in the background—she's probably cooking.

"Hey, Mom, I can't talk. I have a shift."

"You're always working," she says, the whir of a blender blasting through the phone speaker. So not cooking—making a smoothie for Dad. "I wish you'd call more."

"I know," I say, pacing back and forth in front of the NYAC loading dock. "I'm just really busy," I lie. "Can we talk later? I really gotta go."

"Of course," she says, a hint of worry in her voice. "Be well. I love you."

"Love you too," I squeak in before hanging up. I take a deep breath through my nose and out my mouth.

I think back to that horrible year at home between dropping out of college and moving to New York. My mom was so worried about me. I wasn't eating. Food lost its taste, and my stomach couldn't hold anything down anyway. I wasn't watching TV or reading books or scrolling through Instagram. I was existing. Catatonic. Sonya came over once or twice, I think because my mom assumed that having her there would bring me out of my room, but it just made me burrow deeper.

One night, Mom sat on the edge of my bed sobbing, begging me to let her help me. But there was nothing left to help. I wasn't human. I wasn't interested in getting better.

I can't admit to my mom that I still feel like the girl in bed, lying still as life passes by. If I did, I'm not sure she could bear it.

I miss my parents, but it's better this way, with a couple of fake phone calls and the occasional snapshot of Sonya and me looking normal and happy and *fine*. Better they don't know the truth.

Standing at the NYAC loading dock, I dread the coming shift. Maybe it's the anticipation of Mr. Kirk being a total dick, or the idea that a bunch of ancient men will send me running around the building like a madwoman to get them a side of mayo, or maybe it's because I'm tired of being invisible. Sometimes I come home from these shifts with the eerie feeling that I don't actually exist at all, that I'm a figment of my own imagination, made to smile and serve.

Unfortunately, I'm stuck here because the paycheck is fat, and I'm desperate. I pull on my maroon jacket and bow tie. My name tag today is BRAD. At least Kirk is nowhere to be found. Maybe it's his night off.

I grab a tray of shrimp cocktail and head into the party. The guests all adhered to the black-tie dress code, men in tuxedos, women in fine silks and satins. Everyone smells like lemon perfume and lavender soap and looks like they brush their teeth with mineral water. I only get to see this side of New York through a looking glass, but never to touch. They're all the same wolf in different clothing, these places I temp at. Or, I should say, the same wolf in different sequined pashminas.

After I spend a few hours passing out shrimp, the guests take their seats at their assigned tables. I carry a white cloth with a big bottle of sparkling water from table to table, refilling glasses until a woman in an electric-blue pantsuit pulls me gently by the elbow out of the dining room.

"Darling," she says in a hushed southern accent, "I have a favor to ask you."

The glass bottle of water sweats in my hands.

"I'm embarrassed to ask you this, but do you happen to

have a . . . a tampon on you?" She nervously eyes her table. She must be no less than forty years old and is too flustered to ask any of her posh friends.

"I'm not supposed to leave the dining room," I say, biting my lip.

"Please . . ." She shifts her weight in her kitten heels. "It's an emergency."

A drop of cold water rolls down my sleeve as I remember the scolding I got from Kirk. "I could get in trouble."

She crinkles her eyebrows and frowns, glancing back to her table. "I'm supposed to make a toast."

Maybe I'm tempted to help her because she's the first fancy guest to speak to me, or maybe it's because I'm tired of pouring water and wine. "I think I have one in my bag, but I have to run downstairs. Can you wait here?"

"You're amazing," she says, relaxing from her tense posture into a more relieved stance. "I won't move a muscle."

"Five minutes," I call back to her as the service elevator doors close behind me. It takes a lot longer than five minutes just to get down to the basement and sift through the contents of my bag, but I find what I'm looking for and head back upstairs. I press the elevator button, but it doesn't budge. The light at the top of the door indicates that it's on the fifth floor.

It's already been ten minutes.

I don't have time to wait.

The stairs in this building are like a game of Chutes and Ladders. It is so easy to get lost, but if I keep climbing up, I hope I'll eventually reach the rooftop lounge where the event is happening. I hike up and up and up until I come to a door that leads me to a carpeted staircase. I keep going up until I hear the music from the party again. My heart is pounding, my thighs are burning, and I'm out of breath. *God, Bennet, would it kill you to work out once in a while?* I get my bearings when I spot the familiar doorway that leads to the event. The handle is barely out of my reach when a hand grabs my shoulder, spinning me around.

Mr. Kirk.

He looks at me with his evil little snake eyes. "Why aren't you on the floor right now?" His voice is nasally and sharp.

"I was heading there," I say as I try to scoot away from him.

He steps in front of me, cutting off my path. "Fredo said you stopped water service fifteen minutes ago. That is unacceptable." He acts as if a rich person not getting their sparkling water fast enough is as bad as if I personally punched one of them in the face.

"A guest asked me to do something for her," I explain, slipping the tampon up my sleeve.

"What was so important that you had to leave the floor?"

"It's a feminine issue."

"Why didn't you come find me?" He puts his hands on his hips. He reminds me of a cartoon paper clip, with big bulging eyes.

Because I didn't want to embarrass the nice lady in the cool pantsuit, and also you and everyone else on staff here are cis men.

"Forgive me for not assuming that you had an extra tampon, Mr. Kirk," I say coolly.

He purses his lips and glares at me. *Wrong thing to say, Bennet.*

"I'm going to have to file a complaint with Carlyle."

My heart skips a beat and I immediately pivot into grovel mode. "It'll never happen again. Please, I promise." I hate myself for pleading with him and not fighting back, but I need this job, no matter how much of a twerp Mr. Kirk is. "Please, sir."

"This is strike two, Bennet. Strike three, and you won't be asked to return."

"Strike two? What was strike one?"

"You were late last week," he growls. "Don't you remember?"

"I wasn't late! I was here—"

"Do you want me to add another strike right now? Because I don't like this attitude."

"No, I—I'm sorry. Please." I take a deep breath. "I need this job." I can't fail at yet another thing.

Kirk grinds his teeth and squints down at me. He takes his sweet time thinking over what to do with me, putting on a three-act play. Finally, he speaks. "Don't let it happen again."

I nod. "Of course."

He turns on his heels like a spinning top and heads down the stairs to the kitchen.

Fucking bastard.

I tear off my bow tie and ugly maroon jacket and stomp out the door into the cool night air. What did he expect me to do, let the poor woman bleed onstage?

If I ever got this mad at school, Sam, Andy, and I would go to the batting cage. I wasn't good at hitting baseballs, but holding a bat and smashing things always made me feel better. Andy said it was healthy for us to let out our anger instead of bottling it up. Sam was always there to pitch for us. He never got mad or upset. He was always kind, always levelheaded, always looking for rational solutions to problems. He was a fixer.

Andy sucked at baseball. It was one of my favorite things about her—that someone who seemed so good at everything could not figure out how to make contact between a bat and a ball, no matter how easy Sam pitched it to her. I loved having something to tease her about, though it drove her absolutely insane. Our only true fight before everything went down with Sam was on one of those nights—Andy couldn't hit the baseball no matter how many times she tried, and she insisted we stay until she got it. Sam and I were exhausted, and tried to usher her toward leaving, when she snapped—yelling that we weren't on her side anymore, that Sam and I were leaving her out. It was shocking. Andy always seemed supportive of our relationship, but I was friends with Andy before I fell in love with Sam. She introduced us. We screamed at each other until Andy stormed off, and Sam drove me back to his apartment in silence.

The next morning, when I opened Sam's apartment door to head to class, there was a baseball sitting on the mat. I picked it up, turned it over, and saw *I'm sorry. I love you*, written in red Sharpie. It became sort of a white flag between me and Andy—anytime we got in a fight or wanted to apologize, we'd sneak the baseball someplace where the other would find it, and it was instantly better. Instant forgiveness. *I'm sorry. I love you.*

Our apology ball worked until I screwed up so bad that I don't even know where the stupid baseball ended up.

I don't have a batting cage at my disposal in Columbus Circle, so I decide I'll walk off my anger. I pass heaps of garbage, a man collecting empty soda bottles in big plastic bags, a woman pushing a granny cart of flowers. I smell the sweet cinnamon aroma of a sugared-nut cart. I pass a man packing up a display of graffitied shirts, and a child playing with glow sticks. I pass Lincoln Center.

God, it's like everything is compounding, the pressure cooker inside my skull zipping from my dead-end job to Andy to Sam to Sonya back to Mr. Kirk, and I just feel so damn *frustrated.* I'm frustrated with Andy for moving on. I'm frustrated with Sonya for trying to set me up before I was ready. I'm frustrated with Sam for dying. And I'm frustrated with myself for . . . for everything.

Come to think of it, I'm also frustrated with Henry for thinking it would be so easy to fix me. That it would be so simple to find a passion and turn my life around.

I pass a man asleep on a flattened cardboard box. I pass an empty bodega and a couple making out on a stoop.

My cheeks are real. My chin is real. My lips are real.

I pass a woman walking a cat on a leash. I pass a man covered head to toe in silver paint, clearly on a walk home from his shift as a human robot in Columbus Circle.

Breathe.

Kirk is just an insecure man who didn't have enough power as a child and is taking advantage of it now. He probably won't even report me. I'm a good caterer. I keep my mouth shut and I do my job. He's just talking a big game.

Henry is just being nice. Andy is just trying to survive. Sonya and Jamie are just existing. Sam is just . . . gone.

Come back to earth, Bennet.

My body aches from the eight-hour shift and the fifteen blocks of tantrum-walking, so I cave and take a train the rest of the way home. I calm myself, decrease my heart rate with every stop on the train.

Tomorrow is Saturday, which is supposed to be the day I spend with Henry, but it's now eleven on a Friday night and I haven't heard from him.

It occurs to me only as I reach the front door of my apartment building that *I'm* also capable of texting *him*. I shiver. The thought of asking someone to hang out gives me agita. I can't remember the last time I did that.

I weigh the pros and cons of texting him as I avoid going up the stairs to my apartment to Jamie and Sonya cuddling on the couch.

Pro: it will feel good to nurture a friendship.

Con: the friendship is with a weirdo who likes to talk to strangers.

Pro: I might be able to discover my passion.

Con: discovering my passion will mean I have no more excuses.

Pro: I will have plans tomorrow.

Con: I will have plans tomorrow.

I pace back and forth on the sidewalk. It's just one text. This shouldn't be such a big deal. I open my messages and draft one.

I think your demonic raven drawing
gave me powers? I found a couple of
feathers in the shower drain this
morning, and I crushed a water glass

with just the strength of my talon. Oops, I meant my *hand*. Is this normal?

Send. Don't think about it.

I walk to the corner bodega for a bag of salt-and-vinegar chips and a ginger ale, my favorite nighttime snack. I'm about to pay when my phone vibrates in my pocket.

I've consulted with the tattooed honeydew man living in my closet. He came to life shortly after our class. He said it's fine.

The cashier catches me chuckling. I quickly insert my card into the reader and pay for my food. When I'm out on the street I type:

Does this honeydew man have a medical degree? He's a little too young to be giving out advice so freely if he was only born a week ago . . .

Henry takes more than a minute to respond. I open the bag of chips and lean on a streetlamp. There aren't too many people out right now, but I make eye contact with the chunkiest bulldog I've ever seen. He's being walked by a fit twentysomething in head-to-toe Lululemon. I chortle at the juxtaposition. My phone vibrates.

He says that it's best not to question him.

The message comes alongside a selfie of Henry with the melon, except the melon now has an angry face scribbled across it in Sharpie. He holds a butter knife to his throat as if the melon is threatening him.

Please tell me you had to get up and go get that knife and you don't sleep with one by your bed. Major serial killer vibes.

He starts typing immediately.

The blue dots appear at the bottom of the screen, but they quickly vanish. I guess it's not very nice to accuse someone of being a serial killer all the time. Eventually the dots return and Henry responds.

What's one thing you wish you had as a kid?

I click my phone off, tucking it under my chin to think. The Lululemon girl and her bulldog pass me again. He grumpily trots alongside her, stomach almost grazing the pavement.

It gives me an answer to his question.

A pet.

He starts to type but stops. I wait for a few moments, but when he doesn't respond, I put my phone in my pocket and head upstairs.

I tiptoe to my bedroom and sidestep the piles of dirty laundry on my floor to collapse on my bed. I kick off my clogs and they land with a thud. I rest my computer on my boobs so the screen is inches from my face and I bury my hand in the bag of chips. I try my best to forget that it's Friday night in one of the most populous areas in the world and I'm alone.

I pop a couple of chips in my mouth and scroll through Instagram while *Criminal Minds* plays on my laptop. Andy posted another gorgeous picture from her engagement shoot. The crunching of chips echoes loudly in my ears as I zoom in on it.

Andy met Theo a year after Sam died. She had just started interning with an art buyer who worked for one of Theo's celebrity clients, and Andy apparently impressed. She has always had gorgeous taste, and her and Sam being raised with a silver spoon meant that she had *expensive* taste too. Mr. and Mrs. Chase made sure they wanted for nothing, and when I showed up, their generosity spread to me. Sam was always embarrassed by their wealth, but Andy wasn't. Not in a vain or selfish way, just in a way that felt natural to her. She thrived out in L.A. at her fancy internship. It seemed like she was always destined to rub elbows with the world's shiniest people, even a fancy, early thirties, entertainment lawyer named Theo.

I've seen them together in action only once, when Andy flew me out to L.A. They had just started seeing each other, and I was still in my near-catatonic state. Theo took us to fancy dinners, on tours of record studios I can't remember the names of, and even introduced us to a couple of his clients. I hated every second of it, seeing her happy. The sanitized haze of L.A. The palm trees. The fakeness of it all.

I hated that I hated it too, but I couldn't stop.

Andy begged me to come live with her at the end of that

trip. I remember that last conversation—the one that ended everything.

"Bennet, you can't live like this. It's not what Sam would want for you."

We were lying on the bed in her oceanside apartment, only a couple hours away from my scheduled flight home. The windows were cracked slightly, letting the smoggy L.A. air waft gently through her curtains.

"I know what Sam wanted, and that was for us to live in New York."

"He would want you to be happy. He would want you to move on." Andy's red hair spilled over her silk comforter.

"I can't." I pressed my eyes shut so I wouldn't have to look at her.

"What happened to the girl that wanted to travel Europe with me after graduation? Hmm? What happened to *that* Bennet? I haven't seen you smile the whole time you've been here."

A not-so-kind laugh bubbled from my throat. "*You* have no trouble smiling."

She shot up quickly, hair whipping around her shoulders. "Jeez, Bennet."

"You look completely unfazed."

"What's that supposed to mean?"

"Nothing." I rolled over in a ball, facing away from her. "Forget I said anything."

"No. Say it."

I lay there in silence, refusing to answer. Andy shook my shoulder. *"Say it."*

"Fine." I sat up in bed to face her. "How can you move on

like this? Do you even miss him at all? Because it seems like you don't, and it's only been, what? Two years? It seems like you're more than happy to live your glamorous life out here with this *stranger* and not be bothered at all that your brother is dead. It's disrespectful, Andy."

As soon as I said it, I wanted to take it back.

Her jaw tightened and her eyebrows lowered, crinkling together. I'd only seen this face once, at the batting cage, right before she lost it on me and Sam. This time, when she spoke, her voice was calm and level but dripping with anger. "Just because I continue to live my life doesn't mean I don't miss my brother. How dare you suggest otherwise."

"Andy—"

"No, you had your turn to talk. Now it's mine. Don't forget that I loved him a hell of a lot longer than you did. I think about him every second of every day. When I'm with Theo is the only time my heart isn't actively shattering into a million pieces. So go ahead and judge me, but I *know* my brother, and he would be happy for me."

My breathing was ragged and shallow. "Andy, I—"

"You know what? I don't care. Go to New York. Never finish your degree. Live in your world of misery. Do what you want, Bennet, but don't you dare question my grief or my love for my brother."

She stood up and started for the door, curling her fingers around the knob. At the last minute she turned to me and spoke with a wobbly voice. "I love you, Bennet. My family, we all love you so much, and I know you're too lost in your own pain to realize how much your words hurt me." A tear rolled down her cheek as she spoke. "Um . . ." She looked as if she might say something more, but she changed her mind and shook her head. "If you need a ride to the airport, Theo gets home from work in ten minutes."

She shut the door behind her, and I finished packing my bag.

Our relationship faded after that. I know I hurt her feelings by pulling away. I knew it when I said those awful things, but I couldn't stop. It was like this sickness was overcoming me, consuming my body, and there was nothing I could do but succumb to it. In the months following, she'd call and I wouldn't pick up. She would text me and I'd get back to her days later, if at all. And now she's sent me one final gesture: a save-the-date to her wedding.

I get to the bottom of the bag of chips and toss it in the trash can next to my bed. With greasy salty fingers, I open my phone to a message from Henry:

> Secured a location for tomorrow.
> Don't dress nice.

I text back a thumbs-up emoji and a melon emoji.

Chapter Ten

Everyone loves Henry, even the dogs. They paw at his leg, fall asleep in his lap, lick his nose. What am I, chopped liver? No, because dogs actually *like* chopped liver.

Spring is about to turn to summer any day now, as the trees are still flowering and blooming. Puddles of grime on the sidewalks are lined with milky yellow pollen and people walk around with tissues in their pockets. Spring might bring mud and dirt and allergies, but it sure does feel good to defrost after a long winter.

Henry and I sit behind a fold-up table in Morningside Park. We're wearing matching royal blue shirts that say PUPPY PALS across the chest and sitting next to a pen full of dogs playing and basking in the sun. Henry took my childhood wish for a pet literally, volunteering us at an adoption event.

The dogs vary in age from newborns to full-grown satos rescued from the streets of Puerto Rico. There's an elderly reddish-brown basset hound named Fred that was abandoned when his owner died. After a year in the shelter, he has yet to be adopted. I feel bad for Fred as he watches the tiny puppies get adopted one by one while no one pays attention to him. He's the one I hope gets adopted today, with his dark, droopy eyes and wet nose.

The cute dogs attract passersby, and then Henry and I take down the names and email addresses of interested adopters. Henry is, of course, a natural salesman, despite the demonic Chihuahua in his lap snipping at prospective adopters' fingers.

The organizer, Terrance, is a small guy with shoulder-length curly hair and a faint mustache. He introduces us to the dogs, sets us up with clipboards and pens, and gives us a stack of postcards with sad dogs on them to hand out.

"Did you have a dog when you were a kid?" I ask Henry as I scribble the raven logo on the corner of an adoption form.

"Nope," he says, grinning. "But I did have a pet."

"Cat?" Henry does not seem like a cat person. Not at all.

"Nope," he says. "I had a lizard named Falkor." He scoops up a chew toy from the table in front of us, giving it to the dog in his lap. The animal snaps it up immediately, growling as Henry starts to play tug-of-war with it.

"I don't know if I mean this as an insult or not, but I literally never know what's going to come out of your mouth next. *A lizard? Really?*" The Chihuahua snarls as Henry wins a round of tug-of-war. This thing is out for blood.

"I was a reptile guy. Total freak."

I sink back into my chair and set the pen down on the table, a shiver snaking up my spine thinking about a scaly reptile. "Falkor like from *The NeverEnding Story*?"

"What else would it be?"

"Wow, you were a nerd," I say. "Next you're gonna tell me you have a rock collection or something." The Chihuahua stares into my soul with its beady black eyes. It's growing very protective of Henry.

"I . . ." His cheeks turn pink and he looks down at his lap.

"*No*," I say.

"I might have a rock collection, yes."

"Oh my god."

He grins so wide the skin around his eyes crinkles. "They're all named after characters from *Star Wars*."

"Tell me you're joking. Right now. Please."

"Afraid not. Hey, maybe I'll adopt this little guy and name him Falkor Junior," he says, and then gives the Chihuahua a series of dog-treat bribes. Falkor Junior almost clips Henry's finger off.

The image of a little boy pressing his nose to a lizard tank, surrounded by action figures and pet rocks, makes me smile—I don't know what I expected Henry to be like as a kid, but it wasn't *that*. It makes him feel more real—less like a handsome stranger full of energy and mystery and crazy ideas.

"Please don't adopt that dog. That thing is a demon. Watch." I reach out to pet Falkor Junior and he immediately makes the most horrifying noise I've ever heard from such a small creature, his lip rising above his shark-like teeth. "See? Hates my guts."

"He can tell you don't like him. Isn't that right, Falkor Junior?" He scratches Falkor's neck and the dog melts like putty into his hands.

"Yeah, well, the feeling is mutual." I sneer. He yips.

Henry sets the dog in the fenced-in playpen to wander around and attract more adopters. He's vicious, but I suppose he's pretty cute too.

Henry sits as far back in the folding chair as he can, crossing his legs. "Marry, fuck, kill: Han Solo, Luke, or Finn?"

"No." I shake my head. "I'm not eleven."

"Humor me," he says, batting his eyelashes. "Please?"

I know how persistent this man is. He's not going to let it go, so I decide to indulge him. It's been a while since I've seen those movies, but I remember enough to play along. "Marry Han, kill Luke, fuck none of them because I'm not a nerd."

He laughs. "Kill Luke? Such a contrarian."

"My turn. Marry, fuck, kill: Chewbacca, Jabba the Hutt, Jar Jar Binks."

His face goes pale. "No way."

"You can dish it but you can't take it. I see how it is."

He looks at me, horrified. "You're sick."

"Yes, I am." I raise my eyebrow. "Go."

"Fine." He closes his eyes and concentrates. "Marry Chewie because he's loyal." He winces at the thought of his other two choices. "Uhhhh . . . kill Jabba the Hutt I guess. That leaves . . ."

Laughter bursts from my stomach like popcorn. "You sick fuck."

"You're evil." A bright red flush creeps up his neck and ears.

"I can't believe you'd sleep with—"

"Don't even say it." He laughs, his cheeks starting to turn red too. "Please."

"You'd make a beautiful couple, you and Chewie."

He slumps and puts his forehead down on the table in front of us, covering his face. "I'll be here for the rest of the shift. Please don't bother me."

"It's my payback for you dragging me out here."

"I think we're having fun, no?" he says, lifting his head and resting his chin in his hand.

I mimic his position, facing him. "Hate to admit it, but I guess I am."

"Why do you hate to admit it?"

I . . . don't know.

"Hello?" a voice interrupts. We shoot to attention at the sound of an angry woman on the other side of the table.

"Sorry." I clear my throat. I have no idea how long she's been standing there.

"I'd like to see that dog, please." She points to a gorgeous sato puppy named Gumby.

"Bennet, wanna take this one?"

I nod and smile at the lady. "Follow me."

I lead the woman into the dog pen and give her a handful of treats for Gumby. Gumby wags her tail, her caramel-colored fur glistening in the sun. It's almost like she smiles at us.

"I didn't know shelter dogs could be this cute."

I crinkle my nose at that comment. "All dogs deserve homes, especially shelter dogs."

"Of course." The woman picks Gumby off the ground. "She's perfect."

I glance at Henry, who's watching intently. "Would you mind if I showed you another dog we have up for adoption?"

He shakes his head no. *Don't do it.* I shoot him a dirty look.

I lug Fred's heavy body up off the ground and cradle him in my arms. "This is Fred. He's a little bit older than the other dogs, but he's loving and gentle and . . . just look at his floppy little face." I pat Fred on the top of his head.

She frowns. "I'm sure he's sweet, but I'm only interested in a puppy."

"Fred has been in the shelter for a year. Gumby has only been here for two weeks—"

"I want to be able to have my own people train the puppy. Who knows what kind of training this dog has had? And it's hard to make a commitment to a dog that might not be around for that long."

"Fred is the only dog available today. All the other ones have been adopted. It's Fred or nothing," I say, lying through my teeth.

She shakes her head, annoyance flooding her cheeks. "Maybe next time."

I hug Fred to my chest and return to my post in a huff, stroking him on the forehead. "She wouldn't even look at Fred. None of these people will even look at him. I hate that he's forgotten just because he's different."

Henry places a hand on my shoulder and squeezes. "We'll keep trying," he says.

"I would adopt you if I could," I say to the hound. "I'm sorry."

As Fred burrows his wet nose into my elbow, an old man in a newsboy cap approaches, wearing a tweed blazer far too heavy for this early summer heat. He looks at Fred, walking up hesitantly to our table.

"What a beautiful dog," the man says, eyebrows crinkling together.

Henry looks at me, wide-eyed, as if to say, *Him. Him. Him. Him.*

I stand up, holding Fred so his droopy face is in position to be adored by the man. He pauses, taking one meaningful look at the dog, and his eyes begin to water. He laughs, dabbing the corner of his eye. "Sorry," he says in a raspy voice. "I had a dog who looked like this one once. It's like staring at a time capsule. Uncanny."

"This is Fred," I say, bouncing him like a baby. "Say hi, Fred." The dog wiggles in response.

The man inhales, nearly choking down a cry. "My old girl's name was Ginger."

It's enough to make Henry and I both gasp, almost in unison.

I smile, squeezing Fred against my body one more time. "I think it's meant to be, then, sir. Would you like to adopt him?"

He nods, an expression of childlike glee spreading across his wrinkled face, eyes glossy and full of emotion.

I fill out his paperwork, heart thundering in my chest the whole time, and I tell him the shelter will have to do a home visit before handing Fred over, but assure him he is in the best hands until then. I can't stop staring at Fred for the next hour—picturing a soft-spoken old man with two lovely pups in one lifetime. Fred and Ginger. It couldn't feel more cosmic.

Henry looks at me out of the corner of his eye, smiling, as if he knows how much placing Fred meant to me. I feel lighter, brighter, slightly more buoyant, and I chance a smile back at him as the spring breeze blows some tiny white petals through the air in a shower of confetti.

And in this moment, as if on cue, Falkor Junior pisses on my foot.

Terrance comes running like a superhero, waving a pair of Tevas in the air. When I squealed, feeling Falkor's *gift* seep into my sneaker, Terrance dashed to the shelter's office a couple blocks away for a pair of spare shoes.

"They won't fit, but it's better than walking around in pee sneakers," he says as he hands the sandals to me.

I peel my sock off and rinse my foot with bottled water before strapping the sandals on. Henry holds my shoes and socks in a plastic bag.

"Thanks." I examine my feet in the sandals. They're at least three sizes too big. "I'll bring them back as soon as I can."

Henry and I turn to leave, and I stumble, tripping over my flippers. He catches me by the elbow and helps me get my balance. His fingers grip me tightly.

"You okay?" he asks.

"Yeah." I nod, standing up straight. "Thanks."

Henry lets me go, and I brush my fingers against the spot on my arm where he was just touching. "Thanks," I say.

"You said that already."

My face gets a little hot. "Let's go."

"Wait," Terrance calls. "You guys wanna hang out?"

Henry agrees right away, of course. Feeling like I have no choice, I tag along.

Terrance takes us to Tom's Restaurant, just a couple blocks from the adoption event. The front of the diner is familiar, at first I don't know why, but I notice a couple people snapping photos of the red-and-blue neon sign that says RESTAURANT over the door.

"*Seinfeld*," Henry whispers as we push the door open. "Where you recognize it from."

Of course, the image of that neon sign across my TV screen on nights I fell asleep with the TV on zooms through my memory. But this is such a normal diner—a cultural flagship under everyone's noses, casually sitting here on an upper Manhattan street as if it's not a celebrity.

We get seated in a small booth, Terrance across from Henry and me, a little bit crammed in side by side. The diner smells like sizzling bacon, maple syrup, and coffee. It's divine.

I order a milkshake and suck it down so fast I nearly bring myself to the brink of brain freeze.

Henry mixes his strawberry shake with a straw as Terrance sips a root beer float.

"I appreciate you guys helping us out." Terrance speaks in the back of his throat, his words all clipped and staccato, sort of like Jesse Eisenberg in that Facebook movie. "Milkshakes are on me."

I tilt my cup so the last remaining melted ice cream is in the corner and try to dig it out with my straw before I realize that Henry and Terrance are both watching me. "Thanks," I say as I place the cup on the table and push it away with two fingers. Henry snorts a laugh next to me.

"So, what made you guys volunteer today?" Terrance asks.

"Just trying something new," Henry says, shrugging.

"Cool, cool, cool. That's rad." Terrance nods his head like thirty times.

Henry's eyes flicker to me. "Bennet fell in love with Fred."

"I'm so glad you found him an owner today, otherwise my girlfriend probably would've adopted him." He takes a sip from the cup; the foam from the ice cream gets stuck in his mustache and I watch it bubble away into nothing.

"Why do you work at the shelter, Terrance?" Henry asks.

He clears his throat as if he's been waiting his whole life for someone to ask him that. "My mom groomed dogs in the basement of our house, so I always liked animals. Mostly I'm a bank teller, though. That's what pays the bills while I pursue my real passion."

"Which is?" Henry smirks at me. I stifle the desire to kick his ankle.

"I'm in a band," Terrance says. "We're called the Curtanas. We cover rock songs but we also write songs about American history. My girlfriend, Molly, is our lead singer and she's incredible." He pats his legs. "You guys should come see us play."

Henry and I are audience members for Terrance's babbling one-man show for the next hour. If it wasn't for Henry, I never would've said yes to hanging out with him out of fear of awkwardness or that he'd try to hit on me, but I'm surprisingly surviving this. It's honestly a bit shocking to find out that human interaction over the past couple weeks has yet to kill me.

Still, I find myself wishing Terrance would leave so I can debrief with Henry alone.

After we finish our round, Terrance heads to band practice. Henry promises that we will go see the Curtanas play one day, and they exchange numbers. When Terrance leaves, I half expect Henry to follow, but instead he picks up a menu and switches to the other side of the booth, sliding in across from me.

"Hungry?" he says, grabbing a menu from the table caddy to inspect.

Thank god. "Starving."

We order a plate of tater tots, a stack of pancakes, and a couple of Coca-Colas from our waitress.

He runs his hand through his hair and takes off his glasses, setting them on the table upside down. "Well. Now I officially know more about Terrance than I do about you."

"You know my full name. I don't even know your last name."

He smiles. "Adams."

"Oh no." I frown. "That's bad."

He cocks his head. "It's like the most normal last name on the planet."

"No, I mean, *Henry Adams*. You have two first names."

"Excuse me, *Bennet Taylor*, may I point out that you *also* have two first names?"

I shake my head. "Actually, I have a first and a last name, they're just switched around." I raise my eyebrows at him as I pop a tot in my mouth.

"Where did it come from? Your name?"

I wince as I swallow the crispy little tater tot. "I've always hated it."

He leans one elbow on the table. "At least your name doesn't sound like a Founding Father."

"Oh my god." I laugh. "Henry Adams does sound like a Founding Father. And you look like one too."

"I do not," he says, offended.

He does. He definitely does. He's got an American pie smile and a sharp jawline and wavy hair that falls into his face. The bridge of his nose has impressions where his glasses normally sit, and his body looks like it was made for building a nation with his bare hands—not that it's ripped or anything, but he looks strong. He's got this disarming energy about him that my guarded nature can combat. Terrance, Martin, Kira, even Falkor the dog have all been attracted to him like moths to a bright light.

I feel Sam's memory tap against the back of my brain, telling me that I should feel guilty for noticing these things about Henry. I try to quiet the noise, remind myself that all of these things are objective facts. I'm noticing things about Henry like one might notice strokes of paint on a mural, or . . . I don't know . . . warts on a toad.

"All you need is a powdered wig," I say, turning away.

"Fine." He raises his hands. "I accept. But I'm not too happy about it." He shifts in his seat and his knee accidentally brushes against mine under the table. "Sorry," he says as he pulls back.

I inch a bit to the left, giving us both more space. "It's fine," I say, trying not to touch the spot on my knee where we made contact.

"Now that I've conceded to Founding Fatherdom, you have to tell me. Why Bennet?"

I blow air out of my lips. "My mom was obsessed with Jane Austen, and she wanted to name me after Elizabeth Bennet, but Lizzy or Beth wasn't unique enough for her. So she took the last name and made it my first name."

Sam used to call me Lizzy sometimes, if he was feeling particularly affectionate. He'd lean over in bed and kiss me when he thought I was sleeping and whisper, *Good night, Lizzy.*

I smooth away the goose bumps that appear on my forearm.

"Okay . . ." Henry squints at me sideways. "Elizabeth Bennet, huh?"

"Don't tell me you don't know *Pride and Prejudice.*"

He scratches his chin. "I think I read it in school, but I don't remember."

"The Keira Knightley version is a masterpiece and the best movie ever made."

"Strong words."

"I mean them."

"I'm going to have to watch it, then, aren't I?" He smiles. I really wish I didn't notice that dimple every time.

I purse my lips. "Only if you don't mind love stories."

He thinks for a second, letting his eyes wander to a table next to us—a toddler in a high chair grabbing at a pancake in his bare fist, maple syrup dribbling all over the table.

Henry plucks a tater tot from the plate in front of us, pops it in his mouth, chews, and shrugs.

"All stories are love stories."

Chapter Eleven

It's getting bad again. Out of nowhere.

This morning I watched my phone ring three times—twice from Andy and once from my mom. Finally, Andy gave up and texted me:

> Are you still at the same address?
> Sending our invites soon.

I couldn't answer her.

Now Sonya and Jamie are on the couch and I'm stuck in my room. I've been here all day. Their presence in the apartment is like a moat keeping me locked in a tower.

I press my forehead to the door and rest my hand on the doorknob, willing myself to open it, but I'm frozen. My muscles won't budge. I slide down the wall and collapse into the pile of clothes on my floor. I need to eat, but if I go into the kitchen, Sonya and Jamie will want to talk, which of course isn't a bad thing, but I don't want to talk to them right now. I must've gotten in and out of bed and walked to the door four or five times by now trying to build the courage to open up. I feel powerless.

I was doing so well with Henry, talking to people, laughing, eating, smiling. How could I have found myself back here?

Nothing has to go wrong for me to feel this way. Everything can be fine, and I'll still find myself here. WebMD calls it a chemical imbalance. I call it the guilt of killing your boyfriend. Either way, this is just a part of being Bennet.

I bring my hands to my face and feel along my cheekbones down to my chin. I run my hands along my bottom lip. I trace my neck down to my collarbones and rest my hands on my chest.

Feel what's real. *My cheeks are real. My chin is real. My lips are real. I am real.*

It doesn't work.

I crawl to my bed, unable to stand with the weight of grief on my back.

I sleep for two days. I don't answer texts, I don't check my email or sign up for shifts, I just sleep. If I sleep, I don't have to feel. I hear Sonya come and go. She knocks gently on my door at one point, which makes me feel sick. I get out of bed and lock it.

When I sleep, I dream of Sam. Sweet Sam. Sand-blond hair, somber eyes. Always calm, always carefully analyzing the world around him. I walk toward him, to touch him, kiss him . . . but he gets farther and farther away. He smiles from across a black moat, then he's gone. I press my eyes closed, hoping that when I open them he'll be back. But when I do, I see someone different. *Henry.* He stops when he's just close enough that I can make out the color of his eyes, green as lily pads. He stretches his hand out to me. I don't move. He raises his eyebrows as if to say, *It's okay. Take it.* Panic surges through my chest and I whip my head around looking for Sam, but he's nowhere. My eyes sting as I turn back to Henry, but all I see is his back, walking away toward the never-ending horizon.

After three days, I defrost. The first precious drop of serotonin enters my bloodstream. The elephant gets off my chest. I'm lighter. I made it through.

I open my eyes to the dust in the air dancing in the golden light.

With weak fingers, I check my email for any potential Carlyle shifts that haven't been snatched up yet. I sign up for four, and then I carefully tiptoe into the living room. I smell like sweat. My mouth is as dry as cotton balls. I stop in my tracks when I see her.

Jamie.

I anticipate what she's going to say to me with dread. Probably something like, *Look who decided to leave her room*, or *Thank god, we thought you died in there.* But she looks up at me through her dark eyes and smiles.

"Want some coffee?"

As if nothing happened. I'm so grateful to her I could cry.

I nod, unable to use my voice.

"I made lavender syrup. Do you want some?" I nod again, blinking back a tear. The coffee is as delicious as it always is when Jamie makes it, bitter and floral, with a little touch of sweetness. She looks at me like she's about to say something, but decides against it. I watch her walk toward Sonya's room through the steam rising from my mug.

She stops, turning back toward me. "You know . . ." She gestures to my bedroom door, looking almost sheepish in her delivery. "That happens to me too."

I feel my throat tighten. "What does?"

"The, um . . ." She takes a deep, calculated breath and clears her throat. "The depression stuff. Sonya doesn't really get it all the time. But I do."

My fingers shake as I sink my gaze into my mug. "I don't understand it."

"Me neither."

"It's horrible," I say, wiping my eye with my knuckle and looking up at her again.

"The worst," she says with a shrug.

The tiniest twitch of Jamie's mouth, the mere hint of a smile, sends us both bursting out in laughter. I lean on the countertop to keep my balance as I laugh. My abs hurt from crying and now from giggling. A bit of coffee from my mug splashes onto the floor.

I shake my head, trying to get myself under control. "The fucking *worst*."

"It shouldn't be funny," she gets out, covering her mouth.

"It's really not," I say, choking back the last of my snickers.

Jamie's laughter subsides into a gentle stillness, a knowing smile. "Sonya and some of my friends and I are going to see a movie tonight. Want to come?"

"Oh . . . um . . ." I start making up excuses in my mind,

ways to get out of the invitation. Maybe I have an early shift tomorrow. Maybe my stomach hurts.

"It'll be chill, I promise," Jamie offers, pushing a bit.

I think to myself, no, no, I don't feel prepared to face the world and meet new people, but to my shock, I find my head nodding yes.

She smiles, as surprised as I am that I agreed. "I'll text you the details." And then she disappears behind the door.

I've always liked movie theaters. I like the smell of the popcorn, the sticky floor, the snacks . . . but most of all, I love sitting in a big room with a bunch of strangers and not feeling pressured to say a word.

I had to haul myself all the way to Prospect Park, since there is only one artsy little theater in New York playing the exact movie Sonya and Jamie wanted to see. They're at the ticket booth with a short guy and a tall blond girl when I walk into the theater.

"Yay!" Sonya sings. She grabs my hands and squeezes, jumping up and down. "I've missed you."

"Me too," I say, giving my best attempt at a smile.

She pulls me slightly away from the group to whisper in my ear. "I feel like you've been avoiding me," she says, frowning. "Ever since . . . you know. The Date."

"I've just been busy," I grumble, even though that's a total lie.

"We need to catch up," she says. "Plus I have semi-sort-of good news. Harper & Jane might sell my earrings!"

"Oh," I say. "Ones you picked out?"

She frowns and drops my hands like hot potatoes. "Ones I designed."

"Right." I cringe at myself. Designing jewelry is Sonya's new passion. She's always been an artist, but her medium constantly changes and sometimes it's hard for me to keep up. "That's great!"

"Thanks," she says, picking at the pendant on her necklace. "I've only been begging my bosses to sell something of mine all year and talking your ear off about it."

Ouch.

"I'm sorry, Sonya. I forgot." Last year it was ceramics. The year before that it was acrylic. Can I really be that bad of a friend for forgetting which one she's doing now?

To her credit, she shakes it off. "They're going to tell me if they'll sell them by next week. If they do, I want to throw a party. If you don't come, I'll absolutely kill you."

"Of course I'll come," I say. "Send me the details."

Jamie sidles up to us and puts her hand on Sonya's shoulder, ending this awkward moment. "She already has a Google calendar event."

My phone buzzes as I get the invite. "I'm manifesting," Sonya says, clicking her phone shut. "You're supposed to act like you already have the thing you want in order to get it."

"Makes sense," I say. "I'll be there."

"Bennet, this is Kevin and Sarah." Jamie gestures to the two people standing with us. "Some old work friends of mine." Now that I'm closer, I can tell one of them is definitely *not* a stranger. *Sarah.* Sarah the bartender from L'italiano who served me glasses of Chianti until I puked in the bathroom. It's not like I needed more evidence that my life is an absolute joke, but the universe keeps sending it to me nonetheless.

"We've met," Sarah says, chomping on a Raisinet. Yes, the last time I saw Sarah I barreled into her and made her spill an entire glass of red wine onto an unsuspecting gentleman.

"Sorry about that . . ." I say, barely able to hear my own words. "I wasn't in the right state of mind."

"You guys should've seen it. It was hilarious. I got her way too drunk, and she—"

"I puked in the bathroom," I blurt, trying to control the narrative. "And then I . . . I spilled wine everywhere. It was a mess."

"She was supposed to go on a date with our friend Henry but the poor guy found her in the bathroom instead. We teased him about it for like, the next week," Sarah chirps. My heart squeezes.

"Oh, you're *that* girl," Kevin says. "I've heard so much about you."

Great. Apparently everyone at that restaurant has heard of me.

My chest gets hot and my neck starts to itch. "It was supposed to be a date, but we're not . . . It's not like that. We're friends."

"This was the night of your date? Since when are you friends with him?" Sonya asks, cocking her head.

"I should call him, tell him to come," Sarah says, pulling her phone out of a yellow cross-body purse.

"No!" My voice is louder than I anticipated. "No, don't bother him." This weird friendship with Henry is not for anyone else to witness. Not yet, anyway. "I didn't expect to be friends with him, Sonya," I say. "It was . . . an accident. I didn't plan it."

She twists her mouth, glancing at Jamie before looking back at me. "I think that's great, B. But we definitely need to catch up, okay? Soon. I miss you."

"Okay," I say, relieved. "We will." I turn toward Jamie, Sarah, and Kevin. "Jamie, you said these guys were friends from work? I didn't know you worked at L'italiano."

She clears her throat, looking suddenly uncomfortable. "Oh yeah. Before I started at the Angry Bean. I couldn't handle the late-night hours, so I switched from red wine to coffee."

"So . . . you know Henry?" I ask.

She shrugs. "Not really. Met him a couple times, but that's it."

Sonya leans against Jamie's shoulder. "That's probably why he came up on your dating profile. Mutual friends."

Jamie shoots Sonya a stern look. Sonya sucks on her straw and shrugs. "What?"

"Why didn't you tell me you knew him?" I ask. Surely that would've been valuable information for me to have before going on a date with him. "Sonya, did you know Jamie knew Henry?"

Jamie nibbles on her lip and glances at Sonya, who seems to be communicating silently with her eyes.

"I didn't tell her I was setting you up until after," Sonya says. "Figured you'd want to keep it private. Then when I showed Jamie his picture she told me she knew him. I didn't think you were going to see him again, so why bother bringing it up, you know?"

That's . . . actually pretty considerate. "Oh," I say. "Thanks."

"No problem," Sonya says. I can't shake the feeling that she looks relieved.

"Henry can't come, anyway. He'll be working tonight since we're both here," Kevin says to Sarah. Poor Kevin, I'd completely forgotten he was standing there.

Jamie pulls five ticket stubs from her pocket, holding them up for us to see. "Should we go in?"

I exhale, praying we've moved on from this topic for the rest of the night.

We follow each other single file into the theater and take our seats for the showing of *Eternal Sunshine of the Spotless Mind.* Unfortunately, I get separated from Sonya and Jamie and end up next to Sarah, who takes the opportunity to chat over the previews.

"Henry's a good guy," she says, in a comedically loud whisper.

I turn my phone on silent and hum in semi-agreement.

"He'd be a good boyfriend," she says, shoving a huge handful of popcorn into her mouth.

I shudder. "No, no, no. I'm not looking for a boyfriend."

She shrugs. "Someone'll definitely snatch him up soon."

"He can do whatever he wants. We barely know each other."

She sizes me up, squinting. Then she takes a dramatic sip of Diet Coke.

I can't get a read on Sarah. I can't tell if she blabbed to everyone about my bathroom incident out of malice or just because she thought it was funny. I can't tell if she's grilling me about Henry because she's protective or because she's *jealous.*

How could she be jealous? There's nothing going on.

I don't like talking about Henry like this. Or at all, really. Making it into something it's not. It's like speaking his name too many times will ruin it. Gossiping about him will trivialize our new friendship, diminish it, like when you touch a shiny surface so many times it loses its polish. It's barely anything, anyway.

"I think the movie is about to start," I say, burrowing deeper in my seat.

"Fine," Sarah huffs and returns her attention to the screen.

We watch Jim Carrey and Kate Winslet fall in love and then forget each other. I close my eyes and imagine what a relief it would be to forget, to go back in time and stop myself from meeting Sam, to stop myself from falling for him, to stop myself from fighting with him, to stop him from driving to see me in the middle of the night. To just stop. Stop everything.

To my right, Sonya and Jamie hold hands. Kevin tries to be sneaky with a vape pen. Sarah texts, the blue light from her screen illuminating her face. I suck on a Sour Patch Kid and the acidic flavor stings the back of my jaw.

Chapter Twelve

Sal is wearing a green bow tie today. His meaty cheeks squish against his eyes when he smiles. He accosts me as soon as I get to the library.

"Sweetheart! You'll never believe it." He shoves his phone in my face. "Look!"

"Wow," I say, not entirely sure what I'm looking at. Sal is shaking with excitement, so I can't get a good look at his screen. "Sal, hold it still so I can see."

"Sorry, I'm too excited." He thrusts it in my face so close the screen goes blurry.

"Let me hold it." I grab the phone out of his hands, and finally focus on the picture. All I see is an orange blob.

"What exactly am I looking at here?" I say, tilting my head.

"Ultrasound of the kid! Isn't he beautiful?"

"Ohhhh." I squint. How this orange blob can be eggplant

baby, I do not know. "That's amazing," I say, handing the phone back to him.

"Did you see his hands? You can see his fingers." Sal pinches the screen, zooming in on a particularly blobby section. "We never could've seen something like this back when Marjorie was born."

I can't bear to tell him that I can't make out any human features on his screen, so I smile and nod. "It's beautiful, Sal."

"I can send it to you. Are you on Facebook?" He opens the Facebook app and looks at me expectantly.

"Oh, it's Bennet Taylor. I think I'm the only one." My phone buzzes when he sends the request.

"I'll post everything to my wall too so you won't miss a thing."

I've never seen someone so excited about anything; it would be a crime to shut him down. "I can't wait to see the updates," I say with a genuine smile.

"I got him this little sleep sack that's shaped like a football. You gotta see it." He starts scrolling through his photos, but his sausage fingers can't keep up with his brain and he keeps pressing the wrong pictures.

"Maybe we should get to our desk first, Sal."

"Shoot. You're right." He tucks his phone away and whispers, "I forgot we're on the clock."

Sal and I settle in at our desk outside the forum—I gather enough information from the people checking in to know it's some kind of psychology event. We get into such a rhythm, handing out lanyards and swag bags, that I barely notice someone call my name.

"There is no way the world is this small," he says, stepping up to my desk, a huge boyish grin spread across his face.

Of all people in this world, of all people on this godforsaken planet, Henry.

"What are the odds?" He leans on the table, cheeks pink from the heat outside.

"Are you secretly a psychologist?" I ask, looking him up and down.

He shakes his head and points to my clipboard. "Vendor. I'm here to take photos."

I scan the clipboard looking for confirmation, and sure enough, there's his name. "Really?"

He shrugs. "Yeah."

"Don't be mad," I say, "but when you said you were a photographer I assumed it was in a hipster thirty-five-millimeter way and not, like . . . a real way."

"Believe it or not, people actually pay me to do this sometimes." His eyes flick to Sal. "Sorry, hi. I'm Henry. Bennet's friend."

There's two people I never thought would meet each other.

"Nice to meet you." Sal stands to shake Henry's hand. He aggressively pats Henry on the back. The man coached high school football for decades, he knows how to pat a guy on the back. "Hey, do you want to see something?"

Henry nods. "Sure."

Sal shoves the phone in his face like he did to me. Henry's eyes light up right away. "Who's this?"

"My grandson!"

He takes the phone from Sal and zooms in. "Wow." His eyes scan the screen, his jaw hanging slack before he smiles in awe. He takes it in, takes it seriously. He gives a shit. I don't know why, but it makes my stomach somersault.

He holds the phone up to compare it with Sal's face. "He looks just like you."

It's like he knows what to say to slice through the hearts of everyone around him.

Big, emotional Sal starts tearing up. "That's crazy that you said that. I was thinking the same thing."

"You must be so proud." Henry shakes his hand. "Congratulations."

"Bennet, I like this guy," Sal says, half crying, half laughing.

"Everybody does," I say.

"Everybody?" Henry glances at me, smirking.

I roll my eyes. "Don't push it."

"Hey," Sal says, shoving his phone at Henry. "What's your Facebook? I'm going to put you two in a group chat."

Henry joins the group without a second thought.

Sal practically squeals as he sends us the ultrasound photo over Messenger. Both of our phones light up at the same time, and I find myself smiling in silent thanks at Henry.

"Here," I say, handing Henry a vendor pass. "The event is through the doors behind us. Have fun."

"Thanks." Henry slides the lanyard over his neck and adjusts the large camera bag on his shoulder. He disappears into the forum behind me, and I feel suddenly off balance.

A real photographer. Henry is a real photographer who gets paid real money to take real pictures. I imagined him failing at his goals like me, but he's not. He's doing it. It's equally admirable as it is depressing.

After an hour or so, the flow of check-ins slows down, and Sal and I are left to twiddle our thumbs. Of course, to Sal, that means sending Henry and me a constant stream of ultrasound photos in the group chat.

Despite being on the job, Henry responds to almost every one of Sal's messages with enthusiasm. I find myself wanting to watch him in action, see how he works.

"Hey," I say, leaning toward Sal. "Would you mind if I snuck inside to watch for a bit?"

Sal shakes his head. "Go ahead, sweetheart, I got it under control here."

"Thanks," I say, scooting out of my chair and through the door of the forum. When I enter the room, I'm still caught off guard by its beauty, despite seeing it once before. It feels like standing in an observatory, inches away from the stars.

Henry's on the far side of the room, watching the speaker intently, camera at the ready. I follow the line of his camera lens toward the stage, where a tall man with a salt-and-pepper beard is speaking.

I hold my breath when I see the name of his talk on the screen behind him:

Helping Patients Heal through Grief

Keynote Speaker,
Dr. Carlos Barrera, PsyD

Everyone is scribbling in their notepads vigorously, retaining everything he says. Henry's camera clicks in the distant background of my mind. I swallow hard. My heart thunders against my rib cage as I zero in on Dr. Barrera.

He's in the middle of telling a story about a patient he calls Ross, who lost his wife after fifty-two years of marriage. Ross felt physical pain in his chest after his wife's death that led to several trips to the hospital. Turns out, Ross was carrying a suitcase of guilt with him wherever he went. Guilt that he wasn't in the room when his wife passed, guilt because he felt like he deserved to die first, guilt because he didn't tell her he loved her one last time. The guilt distracted him from the pain, and the pain manifested itself physically in his chest.

I'm mesmerized by Dr. Barrera, by his words. I can't move.

Sam, Sam, Sam is all I hear.

My throat tightens and my teeth clench. I try to hold back the inevitable tears spilling out of my eyes, but I fail miserably. My lungs start to burn, and I let out a puff of air in a desperate sigh.

"You okay?"

Henry's voice shocks me back to reality. He's right next to me, and I have no idea how long he's been standing there, how much he saw.

I turn away, taking a deep breath to clear away the moment. "I'm fine." I dash toward the exit, hiding my face.

Sal is at the desk, scrolling on his phone, when I bluster through the door.

"Sweetheart," he says, concerned. "What's wrong?"

I shake my head and swallow the knot in my throat. "I just need a second. Can you watch the desk?"

"Of course," he says, the crinkles between his eyebrows deepening with concern. "Take your time."

I splash some water on my face in the bathroom and compose myself. Now is not the time to fall apart. Now is not the time to miss Sam. As if I have a choice. As if missing Sam isn't a part of my DNA. As if I weren't just reminded of how much I ache. How I feel like a weight thrown into the ocean, sinking slowly down, and no matter how hard I kick, no matter how many life preservers I'm thrown, I can't help but fall farther and farther into darkness. How badly I wish I could jump out of this life into another one. Another one where Sam is still here and maybe I'm not. I'd trade. I really would.

I step out of the bathroom, pausing before returning to my desk. I breathe in through my nose, trying to force my body to go back there, but, as if on instinct, I turn the other way.

I pick a stairwell and I climb. I hear the clacking of my shoes echo against the marble walls, the monotonous sound rattling around in my brain. I explore hallways, turning down different corners, not bothering to refer to a map as I lose myself in the labyrinth.

Eventually I get spit out in a room that feels like a Gothic cathedral. I let my eyes take in the beauty, the intricacy of the large wooden tables lined up, row by row, each with a lamp in the center, the stacks of books lining the walls, the massive arched windows letting light from the outside in. Paintings of rosy clouds on the ceiling are surrounded by deep brown and gold carved panels. Light-encrusted chandeliers hang from the sky in rows. Long shadows slant over the floors like fingers reaching from the windows to the books. Even the shadows want to grab the beauty and hold on. Some people sit at the tables, heads slumped over a thick book or a laptop, typing or reading or staring off into the distance.

I walk down the center of the room, trying not to disturb the stark silence in here. I breathe in the scent of paper and dust and wood—listen to the periodic turning of a page, the muffled click of a keyboard. My body thrums with adrenaline, as if it knows I'm not supposed to be here. I'm not a scholar. I'm not anyone. But the silence, the beauty, the proudness of this room make me pause, make it hard to leave.

Sam would've loved this.

I sit in a chair at an empty table, massaging my temple with my fingers as I breathe in and out, slowly, steadily. I don't know how long I sit here, but it's enough time that when I get up to leave, I don't feel like crumpling anymore.

I gather my things at my desk. Sal and most of the other conference people have left by now—turns out I missed the end of the session. Probably missed Henry too.

I duck my head low as I make my way toward the door, but his voice stops me.

"Bennet, wait." I turn around to see Henry hauling his bag over his shoulder, heading toward me. "You disappeared," he says. "I asked Sal where you went and he didn't know, so I waited."

My insides brighten a bit. "Why?" I ask.

"I wanted to see if you wanted to hang out," he says, adjusting the strap of his bag on his arm. "So . . . want to hang out?"

I'm shaken from the grief talk and tired from working, which normally would lead to an afternoon spent refilling my social battery at home by myself . . . but suddenly spending the day with Henry seems safe. Almost as good as being alone.

"Sure," I say, nodding, "okay."

As we step outside onto the busy sidewalk, the sun beats down on us. Sweat collects under my arms.

"It's gorgeous out," Henry says as he blocks the sun with his hand.

"We could go to the park," I suggest.

"I've got to stop at my apartment and drop off all this stuff, but it's right near my favorite spot." My stomach drops at the idea of his apartment. Going inside. Seeing if he's messy or clean. Seeing his shoes stacked up at the door. Knowing what kind of soap he uses.

"Your apartment." I shudder. "So intimate."

"Not for normal people," he says.

"Not normal, Henry," I remind him.

"True," he says. "Still."

Henry's apartment is in the nosebleeds of Manhattan, all the way up in Inwood. It's a small neighborhood, lined with corner stores and red brick. No tall buildings. It's nice.

"This is me," he says when we stop at his stoop.

"I'll wait outside," I say as I watch him dig in his pocket for his key.

"Come on," he says, jamming the key into the lock. "Two seconds. That's all you have to endure."

I roll my eyes. "Fine."

We head up a couple creaky, carpeted stairs to his apartment door. Inside is a tiny studio, jam-packed with heavy furniture and photography equipment. There's a full-sized bed with an olive-green comforter and two sets of pillows, a small bedside table, a dresser, and a desk with a monitor. On the other side, there's a tiny kitchenette with a microwave, minifridge, sink, and an oven next to a bathroom door that's slightly cracked open. The white walls are bare except for a framed picture of a mountain range. There's a pair of fuzzy slippers haphazardly tossed on the floor by his bed.

"These are cute." I compare one of the slippers with the size of my own foot. It's considerably larger. "They look like something my grandma would wear."

"I'd like to meet your grandma," he says as he digs in a dresser drawer for a change of clothes.

I turn my attention to a small pile of rocks sitting on top of the dresser. "Oh my god. You weren't kidding. You actually have a rock collection?"

"Mm-hm." He bends down to open another drawer.

I walk toward him and peer over his shoulder to view the collection of little rocks, which are more like pretty little treasures than pet rocks with googly eyes glued on. I let my eye wander briefly to the open drawer he's rifling through. He slowly turns his head toward me, raising a suspicious eyebrow. "Curious about my underwear drawer?"

My whole body gets hot. "I wasn't looking at that." *Lie.*

"It's okay, weirdo," he says, closing that drawer and opening the one below it.

I pick up a bright red rock. "Where's this one from?"

"Sedona."

I'm standing too close to him, and the blood in my stomach buzzes with energy. There isn't any space to breathe in this apartment. My apartment is small and stuffy and dark, but at least we have more than one room. Henry's is just a tiny cube, all for him.

"Does it have a name?"

He smirks. "Darth Maul."

I set it back in its place next to the others. "I'm embarrassed for you."

"If you keep making fun of me, I'm not going to show you my bug collection."

"You have a *bug* collection?"

He smirks, tapping his finger on the top of the dresser. "No. Although I did see a silverfish in the bathroom once."

I exhale, relieved. "When did you move in here?"

"When I came back from Denver."

"I'm surprised you live alone."

He shuts the dresser drawer with his hip. "Why?"

"I don't know, you seem like you like to be around a bunch of people all the time."

"Just because I like being around people doesn't mean I don't also like being alone." He tucks the clothes under his arm and heads toward the bathroom. "You can sit down if you want. I'll only be a minute."

The door shuts behind him.

There's a desk chair, but it's currently holding Henry's photography equipment, which leaves me with the only option of sitting on his bed. I perch on the corner with about a quarter of my ass cheek. My quads are on fire.

"Quite the commute to the restaurant," I call out.

"It's a pain in the ass, but I like it there," he responds from behind the door.

"I saw a movie with Sarah the other day," I say.

"No way." He bursts through the door in his change of clothes. His blue T-shirt is tight against his shoulders and highlights the contours of his muscles. I notice myself staring at him a second too long and snap my eyes away.

Muscles don't feel like a completely platonic thing to notice about someone.

"She's friends with my roommate's girlfriend, Jamie." I get up from his bed, hoping I didn't leave too big an indentation. "She said she knew you."

"You talking about me when I'm not around?" he asks, crossing his arms.

"No, I just—do you know her?"

"Jamie?" He scratches his chin, frowning. "I don't think I know a Jamie."

I tuck my hair behind my ear, feeling the heat rise in my body. "She said that you worked together before you moved to Denver. Remember? Jamie?"

Henry pauses, looking away as if he's collecting his thoughts. Then he returns to me. "Wait, Jamie Kiernan?" he asks, head tilted. "Short hair? Always wearing a leather jacket? I know Jamie."

"Yes. Jamie Kiernan." I squint at him. "How long did you work together?" I ask.

"Um . . ." He bites his bottom lip. "I don't remember. It was a long time ago. The staff is all different now."

"Oh." I reach for my bag on the floor, tossing it over my shoulder. But Sarah knew Jamie and Henry both, and so did Kevin, so the staff can't be all that different. "Should I tell her you say hi?"

"Sure!" he says, enthusiastic. "Yeah. It's been a while." He reaches into the fridge and grabs a couple of spiked seltzers and then hands one to me.

"Ready?"

Chapter Thirteen

We walk fifteen blocks from Henry's apartment down to Washington Heights, until we peel off and head down a looping pedestrian path through the trees, shading us blissfully from the sun. There's a low growl in the air and a faint fishy scent on the breeze—through a gap in the foliage I can see that the growl is from the rumbling of cars above us on the George Washington Bridge, and the fishy scent is from the Hudson River rolling out underneath it. I struggle to keep up with Henry like always, finding it frustrating that his only speed is way faster than mine.

The shaded footpath spits us into a long, narrow park with open patches of grass along the waterline. I take a big gulp of fresh air, tuning my ears to the sound of the city. A pleasant breeze presses my clothes to my body, and even though the park is full of people, I feel a sense of stillness, of peace.

Henry and I find a vacant spot under a tree next to a concrete wall that's crumbling a little bit, though the remnants of a spray-painted penis on its surface are still visible.

"Banksy?" I joke as we settle into our spot facing the water.

"You know, I hear he's moved on from political statements to phallic symbols." Henry sits with his back against the trunk, stretching his feet out toward the water.

"Shame the whole thing is crumbling off. I'd like to have seen it erect."

"I get the sense he's compensating for something."

"Banksy could be a woman, you know."

"You're absolutely right," he says as he cracks his seltzer open. "My internal bias got me on that one."

The George Washington Bridge is a giant, looming over the park—almost as its protector. I've driven on the GWB many times, but when you're on it, it's just a way to get from point A to point B—when you're under it, you're reminded of your size.

"It looks so big," I say.

"The penis?"

I snort. "The bridge, you idiot."

He crosses his legs at the ankles and follows my gaze to the ropy structure above us. It pulses with activity, yet remains steadfast, stoic.

"Big bridge, tiny lighthouse." He points to a little red lighthouse sitting underneath the bridge—I hadn't noticed it yet. It looks like a chess piece next to the giant structure. "It used to guide ships at night up the Hudson."

"It's cute," I say, watching a bicyclist swoop around the lighthouse's base.

"Now the light from the bridge makes the lighthouse irrelevant, but local legend says that the city couldn't bear to get rid of it and the people fought for it to stay."

I like that. A piece of history that might be overlooked by some, but celebrated by those who know its story.

I pull my knees to my chest. "I can't believe you were at my job today." I rest my chin on my knees. "So weird."

"People act like New York is this big, huge place, but it's really kind of small," he says, batting a fly away from his face.

"I'm starting to see that," I say. "Kind of."

"You just gotta carve out your place," he says. "You're on your way." He rests his head against the tree behind him and folds his arms over his stomach, closing his eyes. "Help me think of a passion to try next week. What did you want to be when you were a kid?"

"Nothing." I fiddle with the edges of my sock. "Everything."

"Did you go to college?"

"I dropped out in the last semester."

"I didn't go."

I turn toward him. "Why not?"

His eyes are still closed. "My family couldn't really afford school."

"Guess we're both hopeless, then," I say.

"Guess so." He takes his glasses off and cleans the lenses with the bottom of his shirt. I rest back against the tree, feeling the sleeve of his T-shirt brush against my arm.

I make a show of checking my phone so I can inch away from him without being obvious. Just a message from Sonya, nothing else. I click it shut.

"So . . ." I tuck my phone back into my pocket. "How did you know you wanted to be a photographer?"

His eyes follow a bird that flies from one tree to another, and then across the water out of sight. "It's a long story."

"I want to hear it."

He smiles halfheartedly and looks at me through the side of his eye. "Buckle up."

I mime buckling a seat belt.

He chuckles and shakes his head. "I had a speech impediment as a kid, nothing serious, but I didn't talk much because of it. My parents were worried I'd never develop normal language skills, and I was petrified of talking to people. So my dad started taking me out every weekend to parks and restaurants and any other public places he could find. He'd strike up a conversation with a stranger about anything. He told me he was practicing, that I should try too, so I started to do it on my own. It was hard for me at first, but I started to look forward to it."

He shifts his posture, bringing one knee up and draping his arm across it. "My speech started to improve, but I still wanted to conduct my interviews. I wanted to keep a record of all the people I talked to, so I started taking their pictures with disposable cameras. I liked that too, so I bought myself a real camera . . . and the rest is history. Or, sort of history. I'm still working on it."

He picks at a blade of grass beside him and pulls it apart with his fingers.

"That's really sweet, Henry," I say. "Your dad sounds like a great person."

"I've never said this out loud before," he says, almost as

quiet as a whisper. “But I think another reason I take pictures is because . . .” He swallows, looking away from me. “He doesn’t remember anything anymore. It’s like . . . he slips in and out. Sometimes if I show him a picture he gets it. Or he really tries to get it. If I show him an old picture of a neighbor, sometimes he can name them right off the bat. To me . . . getting that one moment of lucidity is worth it. I want to preserve it for him, to preserve it for myself. Because pictures are reality. Even if his reality is . . . changing.”

I realize just how different our experiences of grief are. Sam was gone in a second. Before I knew it, he was a memory. But losing someone slowly must be like having the person and the memory of them alive at the same time. He probably thinks about his dad every day. It makes me wonder why he’s here. Why he’s not at home.

“How is he doing? Your dad?”

He twists his mouth and tosses the blade of grass to the side. “Day by day.” I can tell he’s trying to keep it light, but I want to know about the dark.

“Why did you come back to New York?”

“You mean why didn’t I stay with him?”

I nod.

“My mom,” he says, almost smiling. “Practically kicked me out. Said I was getting in the way. I think she just didn’t want me to miss out on life . . . or whatever. I just never feel like I’m doing enough.”

I haven’t known Henry all that long, but I can tell the kind of person he is. I know he is absolutely taking care of them, even from afar. “You’re a good son.”

"I don't know if you're right, but thank you for saying that."

I return my gaze to the water. "Can I ask you something and you're not allowed to be funny when you answer?"

"Sure."

I take a breath. "Why did you *really* decide to help me? It's a lot of trouble to go through for someone you just met."

Henry sighs and shifts to an upright seated position. "I don't know." He taps the side of his seltzer can. "How much can I share without you being freaked out?"

"Depends," I say. "On if what you're going to say is freaky."

He chuckles and takes a sip. "Not freaky, just a little pathetic."

"Tell me, Henry," I say, watching him turn from playful to serious.

The side of his jaw clenches and relaxes as he gazes over the water. "There was a lot more going on when I went home. I mean . . . with me. Before I moved back to Colorado, everything in my life was go, go, go. Never stop. But then when I got to my parents' house, there was nothing. Being around all my dad's stuff, the medication, watching my mom basically become a nurse . . . it was a lot. And I was forced to sit still and really think about things. I moved home to help out, but I . . . I was useless. I couldn't bring myself to care for him. I couldn't bring myself to do much of anything. I felt like such a failure all of a sudden. I stopped wanting to take pictures because I couldn't find a moment worth capturing. You think it's noble that I moved home to help out, but really I just added to my mom's list of people to care for. I was not at my finest."

"I'm sure you were helpful."

"I absolutely was not. Hence my mother kicking my ass out and forcing me back on my feet. It was so hard to be here, away from them, at first. So hard. Sometimes it still is. But I didn't start to feel better until I started doing things again, going for walks, cleaning my apartment, small things at first, and then bigger things . . . like inviting a total stranger on a mission to find her passion." He laughs through his nose. "When I got back here, I knew that if I didn't keep things moving, if I didn't keep going, there was a chance I'd end up . . ."

"Feeling like shit."

"Yep." He scrubs his hand down his face. "Feeling like shit."

"So you were lonely," I say. "And you wanted to keep busy."

"I also like hanging out with you, Bennet. You're very charming when you're not vomiting in the men's room." He turns to me, smiling. "I could've picked anyone to be my adventure buddy, you know. You're very lucky."

"Yeah, right." I bite the inside of my cheek.

He returns his gaze to the bird, now flitting overhead. "Sometimes, when I meet people, I still feel like I'm out doing those interviews. Like all I know how to do is ask questions and collect stories and file them away on a shelf. My dad and I never talked to those people again, you know? After that first interaction, there was never any follow-up. So I sometimes find it difficult to get to know people on a deeper level, and they end up just being stories, sitting there on my shelf, making my life seem full, when really . . . it's not." He swallows, glancing down at the grass. "People expect me to be one thing, and I think they're disappointed when I'm not that thing all the time. I don't let a lot of people in, Bennet. I think maybe you and other people assume, because I'm like outgoing or whatever, that I must be good at being vulnerable, but the truth is, this is the most I've talked about my dad to anyone. It's too hard. I haven't felt . . . I haven't felt particularly safe to talk about it. But, I don't know . . . I kind of feel like talking about it with you."

I want to touch him, but I squeeze my hands into fists. "I'm really glad you told me. And I . . ." I clench my jaw, trying to get the scramble of words in my brain to form into sentences. "Anytime you want to talk about it, I want to hear it."

He smiles softly and nods. "Thanks."

"And you can put me on your shelf, or whatever. I mean, if you want to."

He laughs and returns his gaze to me—his luminescent smile cuts through the near-somber tone of this moment. "I think what I was just trying to say with the whole shelf thing is that I'm trying really hard *not* to do that with you."

We stare at each other for a fraction of a second, and I almost feel like I'm looking at a different person. He's not a simple optimist. His personality can't be explained away by calling him an extrovert and nothing else. He thinks about life, about people, and he misses his dad. He has a story—a sad, sweet story that plucks the few strings that are left in my heart. It makes me feel mushy and uncomfortable and curious and anxious all at the same time.

We break away to look out across the Hudson in front of us. The sun begins to tuck behind the buildings, turning the sky candy-pink. "I'll do my best too," I say.

We spend the rest of the afternoon making up life stories for the people in the park. We guess which pairs are married, which pairs are siblings, who wants to break up, who is the jealous one in the friend group. We make up voices for them and long, extensive backgrounds. We stay there under that tree until the park closes. I hug my arms to my body as Henry walks me to the train station.

When we stop by the subway entrance, the corners of his mouth bloom into a smile. "Saturday?"

I nod. "I'll be there. Wherever there is."

He steps toward me and opens his arms, but he freezes, realizing we don't usually hug goodbye. Laughing, he sticks out his hand instead. Without thinking, I bypass his handshake and wrap my arms around his waist. After a beat, he drapes his arms around my shoulders. I relax into him, muscle by muscle.

When was the last time I had a real hug? And one that feels this good?

I catch waves of spearmint on his shirt and close my eyes against his chest, breathing deep.

When I open my eyes, I realize that I'm . . . lingering.

I jerk away from his body, taking two steps back from him. "Sorry," I say, brushing my shirt in the front. I realize the reason it felt so wrong is because it . . . didn't really feel all that wrong.

He lets me out of the embrace and smiles, mercifully ignoring my brief panic. "See you later, Bennet."

Chapter Fourteen

Beads of sweat roll down the side of my face as I wrestle with my window air conditioner. June is here in all her glory and July is coming fast, threatening to swallow the city whole. It's not just the sun, it's the pavement, it's body heat, it's energy used to power the behemoth of a city. Everything is hot.

I balance the AC unit on my thigh and inch it closer and closer to the sill. I heave it into the opening and slam the window down on it, securing it in place. Turning it on, I feel relief for the first time since spring officially turned to summer. I let the air lap my face for a full ten minutes before I move a muscle.

I step over a pile of clothes and trip on an empty tissue box hidden underneath it, rolling my ankle and nearly falling on my face. I can't live like this anymore. Enough is enough. I pull the clothes onto my bed and sort them into piles. I strip the bed and throw the sheets and duvet cover in with the dirty laundry and take them to the basement to wash. I bring every glass to the kitchen, and wash and dry them by hand. I scrub every surface until it shines, wiping away caked-on dust and dead bugs. I take out the trash and vacuum everywhere, even under the bed. But I'm not done.

I wipe the countertop in the kitchen, return all the clutter to its designated places, and organize the drawers. I fold the throw blanket and dust the coffee table. I clean the fridge next, scrubbing at sticky juice stains and tossing out rotten vegetables. I fold the clean clothes and return the warm duvet to my bed. When I'm done, I collapse on the futon, the wooden feet wobbling under my weight. I'm sweaty and tired, but I feel good. I feel light.

I want to be this Bennet, the clean one, because the more trash you accept in your life, the more you feel like you deserve it. I don't want to feel like I deserve it anymore. This feels like Before-Sam Bennet, the girl who did her laundry every week and turned in assignments early. I can feel her close to me for the first time in a while. But then, as soon as she comes, she's gone. Clouds come back, as they always do, and I let them in. Welcome them, even.

Still, I have plans. I pull on a T-shirt, denim shorts, and white sneakers, and go to meet up with Henry all the way in Flatbush. He is waiting for me at the entrance of the Brooklyn College campus.

Together, we stroll through the campus, and it feels like we've walked into a bubble—bright green grass, red-brick buildings, students with backpacks. We're suddenly not in New York anymore, we're in a pocket of academia, tucked away from the rest of the city.

We stop in front of a brick building and Henry gestures to it and says, "Voilà! The Murray Koppelman School of Business!"

"*Business?*" I say to him as I scan the building. "How very traditional of you."

"It'll be good for us." He rests his hands on his hips, squinting through the sun.

"Good how?"

"As I found out recently," he says, shrugging, "neither of us finished college."

"Henry, I don't *do* math."

"I think there's more to it than math."

I cross my arms and pout. "Can't we do something fun?"

"Nope. They can't all be fun."

"I reserve the right to walk out the door if things get too boring."

"Martin would be so disappointed," he says.

Wait. "*Martin?* From the park?"

As if on cue, Martin from the park emerges from the glossy doors wearing another bright plaid shirt and khakis. Henry greets him by shaking his hand.

"Bennet, hi," he says as he notices me. "Henry tells me you're interested in studying business."

"Oh, does he?" I say between gritted teeth.

He smiles, revealing small, perfect teeth. "I've arranged for you to audit my summer class today. Follow me."

Martin opens one of the doors for us and we follow him inside. He leads us down an open staircase past water fountains and locked doors.

"Don't sulk," Henry whispers as we walk.

"I can sulk all I want. I was getting used to playing with puppies and learning to tattoo."

"Plenty of people are passionate about boring stuff. Who knows what doors it can open? And this will be good if I ever want to start a real business or something."

"Oh, so this one is for you," I tease.

"Give it a chance." He flashes me fake puppy-dog eyes, which just makes me think of the puppies I'm not going to be hanging out with today. "Pleeease?" he pleads.

"You can't sway me like that." I make my face as blank as possible. "I have a heart of stone."

"I don't believe that for a second."

I scowl. "Fine. But only because I want to see your pictures one day."

"Anytime you want." He nudges me on the shoulder, and then he forges ahead into the hallway. I pick up my pace to catch up.

Martin leads us into a small room full of kids who seem so much younger than we are. Henry and I spot two open seats in the back. We step over backpacks and textbooks and I try not to notice the students staring as we walk by. In here I feel ancient. I remember being them, feeling like the world is full of possibility as long as you do everything you're told, take every step laid out for you. Being resistant to learning, yet craving knowledge.

Martin stands at the front of the room and begins his class. Econ 101. I don't judge people for finding this kind of thing exhilarating, but to me it's about as interesting as a saltine cracker. My eyes glaze over as Martin drones on and on about

GDP until I can't handle it anymore. I grab a piece of notebook paper on a nearby desk as discreetly as possible. I tear off a corner and write *I hate you* on it and fold it as small as I can. I tap Henry on the shoulder and pass the note under our desks.

He opens it and smiles as he reads, but he immediately hides it under his hand and continues to watch the lecture.

Embarrassment fizzles through my body. Maybe he actually likes this and I'm totally raining on his parade.

My anxiety dissipates when Henry taps on my desk. He mouths the word *pen*.

I pass a pen under the desk and wait for his response. I feel giddy, passing notes like a kid in high school. When he hands it back to me, I don't even wait a second to unfold the note.

I don't believe you.

I scribble on the other side:

I don't think I'm meant to be a #girlboss :(

Henry taps his pen to his chin for a second and then writes his response.

Pay attention or I'll tell the teacher you have a theory you'd like to share with the class.

I hit him back.

You wouldn't dare.

He takes the note from my hand and looks at me devilishly. He raises his hand in slow motion. Oh no. *Do not draw attention to us, Henry, or I will kill you.*

"Yes, Henry?" Martin pauses the lecture.

Henry glances at me, an expression of demonic satisfaction across his face.

There's a big pause before he finally speaks. "Could you go back and explain scarcity again? I got a little . . . distracted." And then Henry flashes me the least subtle smirk I've ever seen.

Martin answers Henry's question and my heart slowly returns to a normal BPM. Henry passes the slip of paper back to me.

Next time you're toast.

Martin goes on for another mind-numbing hour.

After class, Henry and I sit down at a frothy pink boba spot across the street and order donuts and bubble tea. I take a bite out of a mochi donut adorably frosted to look like a kitten, and the spongy coconutty texture fills my mouth. Henry's panda donut is nearly gone already, with only one tiny ear remaining.

"Did you at least learn something?" I ask, licking my fingers. "Because I hated that."

"I did, thank you very much." He pops the last donut bite into his mouth and covers it with his hand while he talks. "And how was I supposed to know you'd hate it? You don't exactly reveal that much about yourself to me. I'm going off vibes alone."

"I have to work on the vibes I'm giving off, then."

He laughs, crumpling the donut paper. "You pick next week, then. By all means, knock my socks off."

"You know what? I will."

"All right. Ball's in your court. Next week it's all up to you."

I bring the boba straw to my mouth, chewing on the end. "It's gonna be amazing," I mumble before I slurp up some boba.

Henry raises an eyebrow. "I can see you panicking right now."

"No, you can't," I say, squinting at him.

"All the little factory workers in your brain are working overtime, I can tell."

I cross my arms and lean back in my chair. "Is there something wrong with my face?"

He shrugs. "Definitely nothing wrong with your face."

My cheeks get hot and I have to look away. I press my cold fingers to my neck to cool myself down. "Then how do you know what I'm thinking?"

"You scrunch your face when you're thinking too hard. Like this." He scrunches his face to mimic me.

I rub my chin, giving it a good thought. No one's ever told me that before, but—

"Like that!" he says, lighting up. "That's the face."

"Oh shut up," I say, relaxing my clenched jaw. "You have a face too, you know. It's like a smirky smarmy thing."

"Smarmy? Bennet, I'm flattered. Makes me sound like a pirate. And—oh wow, look!" he says pointing to my face with glee. "There's the face again!"

"If you don't stop teasing me, I'm going to take you to Times Square for the next outing," I say, a deadly threat.

"No!" he says, hand over his chest.

"I'm going to make you take photos with Elmo and the Cookie Monster."

"Agh!" he exclaims, sinking down in his chair.

"And then I'm going to make you wear one of those green foam Statue of Liberty hats. And when you're good and tortured," I say, bringing my voice low as a whisper. "I'm going to take you to the Times Square Olive Garden."

He gasps, eyes wide. "I think that might actually kill me."

I chuckle as I chew on the end of my straw. I won't bring him to Times Square, that's for sure. But I kind of feel like even if we did go there, maybe we'd have fun.

I stand still, balancing a tray of mimosas, but my mind is racing. Almost a whole week has passed and I haven't had a single good idea for the Passion Project. How can I pick an adventure for me and Henry when I haven't been able to do that for myself since moving here? The only places I know in New York are here at NYAC, the library, my apartment, and the places Henry has taken me.

My stomach grumbles at the smell of crispy bacon, scrambled eggs, and buttermilk pancakes. Would it be so bad to sneak a tiny piece of sausage? I banish the thought from my head as Mr. Kirk zooms in on me with those mean eyes. I make a note to steal a mini-box of Cheerios later just to piss him off.

At least I'm working the rooftop patio today, my very favorite of the NYAC event spaces.

The bartender places a final mimosa on my tray and I head back out onto the patio to unload them for the guests. Shortly after my tray is emptied, a man begins to give a speech. This is my chance to disappear for a minute.

I sneak away to the rooftop ledge. NYAC is at the very top of Central Park—from where I stand, it looks like someone took a scoop out of New York, and what lies beneath is a runway of greenery. Beyond the park, I can see the city's beauty, its intricate detail. From up here you can admire it without getting your hands dirty. I feel the warm breeze against my face and I inhale the fresh morning air. I find myself wishing I could get even higher—I wish I could fly over the city like a bird.

I want the city to give me some direction, some inspiration, some *something*, but it's quiet now. Or at least, it's quiet to me. I want to feel the connection I felt in the library, some tug in my soul that says I'm in the right place. "Come on," I whisper under my breath, watching cars move through the streets like Hot Wheels on a track. But it gives me no answers.

My moment of introspection is interrupted by a table that needs coffee refills. I make a fresh pot and fill everyone's cup to the brim.

When I get home, Sonya is on the couch splayed out like a starfish. She's wearing a tank top and tiny shorts and has an ice pack lying on her chest. She glistens with sweat.

"It's. So. Hot," she slurs when I come inside. Our apartment is like an Easy-Bake Oven, trapping the heat from outside into our living room.

"Why don't you go to your room? Did you set up your AC?" I open the freezer and bury my face in the cold.

"Because I wanted to make sure you're coming tomorrow." She sits up and grins.

I pluck an ice pack from the freezer and hold it to my neck. "Tomorrow?"

The happiness melts off her face like pancake batter. "I texted you."

I think hard. A text. What text? I bite my lip and divert eye contact.

"My party, Bennet. Because Harper & Jane is going to sell my earrings? I texted you, I sent you a calendar invite, and I told you about it at the movies. Ring a bell?"

I have no memory of this. None. I plaster a smile on my face. "That's incredible!"

"Yeah." She clears her throat.

"I'm sorry, Sonya," I concede. "I must've missed your text."

"Or ignored it," she says under her breath. Her eyes shoot bullets at me, which is really something coming from someone whose natural state of existence is "perky" and "chipper."

I've dropped the ball so many times with Sonya and I can't do it again. I want to turn her eyeball bullets back to eyeball rainbows. "I've been distracted. I'm sorry. I will be at your party. I'm excited!"

"Since I know you don't remember, it's tomorrow at three." She shifts her ice pack to her armpit. "The Frying Pan downtown."

"I'll be there. I promise."

She nods and shuffles into her room.

Tomorrow. Saturday. My Henry day. Maybe we can wait until next week. Can *I* wait until next week?

I shoot off a text.

> Something came up. Can we postpone our passion project to next weekend?

He responds:

> You just don't want to pick a place.

I type out:

> I did pick a place, but I devastatingly have to cancel our reservation at Bubba Gump Shrimp Co. I have *gasp* plans.

Henry replies:

> You have plans?? I feel like I barely know you.

I send:

> News flash, you do barely know me.

He volleys back quickly:

> I know you well enough to know you're joking about Bubba Gump.

He adds a winky face.

BTW we are totally calling it our
Passion Project from now on.

I smile at my phone like an idiot.

Corny.

He zips back with the corn-on-the-cob emoji.

I place my phone face down on the countertop.

It's fine. I can wait another week. It's for the best.

I don't let myself acknowledge the feeling of disappointment. Or the realization that without seeing him for a whole two weeks . . . I'm going to miss him.

Chapter Fifteen

The sun beats on my shoulders as I walk down a wooden path on Pier 66 toward the permanently docked floating barge-turned-bar—the Frying Pan. Two ships are docked on the barge to my left: the original *Frying Pan*, which the restaurant is named for, and a smaller red fireboat. I take a moment to breathe in the fresh summer air, the smell of fish and fry oil, the robin's-egg-blue sky above me clear as a coat of water color paint. The sound of gulls overhead and the bump of the loud music and voices from the restaurant ahead grow louder as I approach. I look back over my shoulder at the city behind me, the brown and gray buildings breathing down my back. I don't spend too much time in this area of Chelsea, but it's important to Sonya, so I brave it.

Sonya is my oldest friend, but sometimes it just feels impossible to get back to how we used to be together. We slipped away from each other when we went to different colleges, though Sonya did come visit once—it was before Sam and I got serious, but Andy and I were already best friends. I felt awkward about introducing my old best friend to my new one, but Sonya and Andy were quick to get along, even though they only had a couple days to get to know one another. The three of us spent the weekend drinking too much and watching bad movies. Sonya only visited that one time, and she never met Sam, a fact that I can't tell if I'm grateful for or deeply sad about.

In time, Sonya made art school friends and I lost myself in my relationship with Sam, and we just sort of drifted. It was pure chance that Sonya wanted to move to New York at the same time I did . . . and I only knew about it because she told my mom.

I get to the bustling restaurant area of the barge—a dining platform open to the air and big enough that you almost feel like you're on land. There are tables pressed to the rails on all sides, as well as picnic tables scattered in the center. I nod to the host as I spot Sonya and Jamie at a large table by the rail—they are with a whole bunch of people I don't know. Sonya waves at me, and I pivot on my heel, suddenly feeling like I should order a drink at the bar before I head over there to face a table full of strangers.

I order some kind of coconutty rummy drink and am shocked when the bartender hands me a neon-blue beverage. I cringe as I take a sip. I think I ordered the most obnoxious-colored cocktail on the menu. There might as well be rubber duckies floating in it.

I take a deep breath and center myself. Maybe I can use this opportunity to do what Henry did: practice talking to people until I'm not afraid anymore.

As I head to the table, I study each face, hoping to find a friendly one among the strangers. Sonya and Jamie are deep in conversation with their backs turned to me, talking to someone I definitely don't know. I don't recognize anyone else until I see a shimmer of blond sitting at the table, facing me. Sarah.

"Oh my gosh, look who it is." She stands as I approach her. Maybe this won't be miserable after all. I smile and open my mouth to say hello, but she walks past me, not even acknowledging that I exist, and greets someone behind me.

Oh my god. Embarrassed *is not strong enough a word for what I'm feeling right now.*

I pivot to make a beeline to the bar and smack right into a very broad, very sturdy chest. I spill my blue drink all over us both, soaking the front of his white shirt. The barge rocks and I lose my balance, almost falling backward, but the man grabs me by the arms and holds me upright. His thumbs press into my skin, firm but gentle. I know these hands.

"So, these were your big Saturday plans? Spilling drinks and making a scene?"

Of course Henry's here. Why wouldn't he be? He's everywhere. I would not be surprised if Henry had an army of identical siblings lurking around New York City, all on a mission to catch me in humiliating positions. But this is him. The one and only Henry. And I hate how my heart is racing just looking at him.

I let him keep hold of me, and I have to try to stop my body from moving closer. "What are you doing at a party for my roommate?"

He shrugs. "Sarah invited me." He guides me to a balanced

stance, and I get my sea legs back. He bends to pick up my plastic glass from the floor. The front of his shirt is dripping with my wreckage.

It's so random that he's here. But I'm too distracted to think about that for more than a millisecond, because the stain from my cocktail is spreading down his chest. Rapidly.

"Come on." He smiles and gestures to the soaked front of his shirt. "I think I saw a bathroom over there. Let's get cleaned up."

I glance behind me as Sarah watches us head inside, lips pursed. She definitely sees me now.

We find a single-stall bathroom with a lock. It's smallish and nautical, with shiplap lining the walls and a couple of porthole windows high above our heads. There's a tiny sink and an even tinier mirror above it.

My clothes are relatively unscathed—I mostly splattered the blue cocktail on my skin—but Henry's shirt is as good as tie-dyed. I blot my chest with a paper towel.

"Did you know I was going to be here?" I ask as I dab.

"No." He smiles. "I just keep getting lucky."

My blood feels hot in my veins. I press at my shirt with paper towels to keep my hands busy.

"I'm not trying to be weird, I promise," he says, "but I'm going to take my shirt off. Is that okay?" He gestures to his cocktail-soaked shirt.

I nod.

He peels the shirt over his head and runs the stain under the faucet.

I glue my gaze onto the wall, but a flash of skin in the corner of my eye is like gravity. I glance over, as if on an impulse, and then I can't look away. His body is different than I expected, much leaner. Trimmer. His skin stretches over the contours of his muscles, gentle as rolling hills. I spot a kidney-bean-shaped birthmark on his rib cage and trace my eyes to his bicep, but with the way he's standing I still can't make out what his tattoo is.

He catches me staring.

"What?" He raises an eyebrow.

"Nothing." My stomach flips like pancakes on a sizzling griddle. I try my best to avoid making eye contact as he vigorously scrubs at the shirt, his muscles tensing and relaxing under his skin. My throat goes dry.

I don't know what's coming over me, but remembering his hands around my arms, the way he saved me from falling on my ass, his vulnerability in the park . . . I'm *sweating.* I'm realizing that I haven't been in a room with a shirtless man in way too long. The fact that it's Henry is making me short-circuit a bit.

"Henry?" I crumple my paper towels into a wad and toss them in the trash.

"Yes, Bennet?" He glances over to me out of the side of his eye, and I feel a flood of nerves in my gut.

"I was just wondering what your tattoo was."

He tosses his shirt over his shoulder like a rag and stretches his arm out to show me. "It's a mountain range." A drop of water trails from his wrist to his elbow. "My dad and I used to hike a lot."

I study the jagged edges of the mountains laid over his inner arm. I want to swipe the pads of my fingers across it, feel his taut arm under the ink.

"I noticed his dementia for the first time when we were on a hike, actually. He couldn't lead us back down the trail. One we hiked like a million times."

He bunches his shirt up and holds it under the hand dryer, turning his back to me. "I'm sorry," I say.

He shrugs and brushes it off, like he always does. "It's okay."

I watch his shoulder blades move, the way his spine curves and slopes toward his hips. I wonder how warm his skin would feel if I were to brush against him.

Every time I've noticed something in Henry's physical appearance I've been able to shake it away in two seconds. But now . . . it's sticking to my bones. I press my palms to my eyes, trying to drive the image of him out of my head, but when I open them again, he's still there, his back to me, half-naked. It's not like I hadn't known that Henry was attractive. I just didn't really register it until now.

He pulls his shirt over his head and smooths it across his torso. The wet spot clings to his chest.

"Henry"—I swallow—"I'm going to give you a compliment now."

He rakes his fingers through his hair. "You saw me with my shirt off and now you want to give me a compliment?" He raises an eyebrow. "You're full of surprises, aren't you?"

My skin burns. I shouldn't, but I'm feeling reckless in this terrible bathroom. I swallow. "That tattoo . . . is hot." *Jesus fuck, what am I doing?*

Henry's face flickers with surprise. "Bennet. Are you flirting with me?"

"No!" *Shit.* "I shouldn't have said anything. I just like the damn tattoo. Are you happy?"

"I can't believe what I'm hearing."

I cover my face with my hands. I can't even look at him. "It's just that you're all clean-cut, and then you have a tattoo, and it's just . . . unexpected." I wince under my palms.

His lighthearted laugh fills the tiny room. "I am genuinely flattered."

"Oh god." I peel my hands from my face. "You're never going to let me live this down, are you?"

He shakes his head, smirking at me. "Never."

"I regret telling you. Pretend I don't exist."

"Yeah. Like I could do that." The playfulness in his eyes flickers into something else when he looks at me now, something different. We're so close I can smell the soap he uses in the shower. It's different from the spearmint. Sweeter. My pulse races in my neck, and I feel weak.

I could bottle up the way he's looking at me and take shots of it. I could get drunk on them. The heavy eyelids, the spearmint aftershave. I feel bigger, brighter. I feel shiny in his eyes.

I swallow, allowing myself to glance at his slightly parted lips. "Henry?"

"Mm-hm?"

We're standing so close, water from his shirt drips down the front of my leg. "Your shirt is still soaking wet."

"Oh." He looks down at the spot on his shirt that is clinging to his chest.

"Let me get it." I grab a stack of paper towels and dab the wet spot on his torso. His body tenses when I touch him. The paper towels soak through one by one until we've gone through the entire stack.

"There." I lay my palm flat against his stomach when it's mostly dry. The fabric is damp, but not soaking. "Better."

He looks down at my hand on his torso, then back up at me, his eyes wide, his jaw tense. I can tell he's thinking what I'm thinking—that this feels charged. It feels electric. I glide my hand up to his chest, feeling his erratic heartbeat under my palm. He doesn't move, doesn't take his eyes out of his locked-in gaze on mine.

For once, I don't want to break eye contact. I want to stay exactly where I am, studying Henry. Studying his expressions, discovering what they mean. This is one I haven't seen yet. One I've yet to learn.

We hover like this, each baiting the other to make a move or break away, but neither of us will budge. He finally moves, placing a palm on the side of my neck, just above my collarbone. I want him to touch me even more.

I inch toward his mouth ever so slightly, letting my eyelids flutter closed. My heart is thudding and my fingers are shaking, and I can't even think thoughts.

"Bennet," he whispers, gently pushing back on my shoulder, stopping my advance.

"What?"

He slides his hand down my arm. "No."

All the air leaves my lungs. "No?"

He shakes his head. "I'm not going to kiss you."

"Oh," I say. I bring my lips together when I realize my jaw is hanging open like a stunned fish.

"I'm not going to kiss you," he says, dropping his hand from my arm. "Because you told me you want to be friends. And I believe you. You're caught up in the moment. This isn't what you want."

"I don't know what I want." I reach again for the wet spot on his shirt. He flinches when I touch him.

"Yeah, but . . ." He takes my hand and squeezes it once before pulling it away from his body. Our skin against each other is slick with water and cocktail. "*I* do."

What does that mean? What does he want? I open my mouth to ask, but an angry knock on the door snaps us apart.

"One minute!" Henry turns away, dabbing his shirt.

"Fuck." I cover my eyes with my hands.

"We'll be out in a second," he calls.

"Oh my god." I wince, feeling the smallness of the bathroom get even smaller around me. The reality that I just tried to *kiss* him comes crashing down around me. And the reality that he rejected me makes me wish I could turn to dust. "Oh my god."

"It's okay," he says.

"I just tried to . . ." I cross my arms and slump down onto the toilet, wishing I could shrink to the size of a urinal cake. When I close my eyes, I see Sam frowning at me, shaking his head. My heart lurches into my throat. It's even worse than I thought. I wanted hands on me. A man's hands. Hands that aren't Sam's. It's a whole new level of screwed up.

"Don't freak out about this, please," Henry says, his eyebrows coming together to create a tiny concerned wrinkle in the middle of his forehead.

"How can I not freak out about this?" Now it's going to be weird. And he was right. I'm not ready for anything to happen. Not when I still feel so guilty about Sam every single day. Why did I compliment that stupid tattoo? I don't know what came over me. Why would I assume he wanted to kiss me anyway? Sure, we have fun together, but maybe I'm having more fun than he is? Maybe it's just been platonic fun the whole time? It was naive of me, presumptuous to think that something could happen between us. That someone could see beyond the mess and want to take it on.

His eyebrows furrow as he frowns. "Do you want to talk about it?" I look up at his pretty, angular face, walnut hair, the kindest eyes on planet earth, and the humiliation washes over me again. He didn't want to kiss me. I thought he did, and I was wrong. I don't think I could articulate to him what I'm feeling even if I wanted to. I wish time travel were a thing, and I could delete the last ten minutes of my life. Actually, the last ten years would be better.

"No. I don't want to talk about it," I mutter.

Technically nothing happened, so why does it feel like I've just committed a crime? A betrayal of myself. Of Sam. Of Henry.

"Let's just get out of here and forget this," I murmur.

"Bennet—"

"Please, Henry. I'm serious," I snap.

"Okay." He raises his hands in the air, as if to say, *I surrender.* "Fine."

We burst out of the bathroom to Sonya waiting impatiently, tapping her foot.

Caught.

"You've got to be kidding me." She grits her teeth, eyes flicking between the two of us. "I've been looking all over for you."

"We weren't . . . um . . . we weren't doing anything," I say.

She crosses her arms. Her mouth is tight.

"She spilled on my shirt." Henry gestures to the wet splotch. "We were cleaning it up."

"It's fine," she says, nudging her way between us.

"Sonya, wait—"

She whips around. "You know what? No. It's not okay. Ever since we moved here, I've been begging you to hang out with me. Begging you to be my friend again, and you finally come out with me, and what do you do? You lock yourself in the bathroom with a guy. You must really loathe spending time with me."

"I don't—"

She zeroes in on Henry. "Did you know that Bennet is my oldest friend? Now she can't even be bothered to say hi to me at my own party."

Henry shoves his hands in his pockets, dodging my eye.

Sonya returns her attention to me. "And you can't even remember the most basic details about my life, like the fact that I design jewelry."

"I'm so sorry," I sputter, "I have a lot going on—"

"We all have a lot going on, Bennet, and I'm done pretending you're not hurting my feelings. Jamie tells me to give you a pass because you're going through a tough time, but it's not an excuse anymore. Just because you keep everything locked up in a cage doesn't mean the rest of us have to. Just because you think you're all alone doesn't mean you are. People care about you. People want to care about you. Stop pretending we're the enemy. It's really tiring." She slams the bathroom door behind her, and my heart feels like it's caving in on itself.

"Oh my god," I whisper. I had no idea she felt that way.

"So that's Sonya . . ." Henry says.

I pushed the nicest person I know to her breaking point. I've never heard her say a bad word about anyone. I glance over to Henry, who's stunned.

"I don't know what to say," he says.

"Don't say anything." It comes out terser than I mean it to.

"I . . ." He scratches his chin. The last time I saw this expression on his face was at the restaurant the first time we met. When he was licking his wounds. He runs his hand through his hair and stares at the floor. "Maybe I should give you some space for a little bit."

He looks at me, expecting me to say something, but I can't.

Don't go, I think. *Say it, Bennet: Don't go. Don't let him walk away.* Maybe I've just humiliated myself, and maybe I'm confused, but I know I don't want him to leave. I want things to go back to normal.

But I can't. I stand there frozen.

"Okay," he says, nodding softly. "I'm going to go." He turns, heading toward the massive city that for once feels far away, shaking his head as he walks.

Tears sting the corners of my eyes as I catch my breath. I let

Henry get too close. I pushed Sonya too far. In one day, whatever fragile relationship I had with each of them is shattered.

I consider trying to make amends by heading back to the party, but I realize I don't know what that would even look like. I don't know what I would say or do, and I just want it all to *stop*.

I watch Henry until he is far enough away that I can't see him anymore, and then I follow the same path he took to get off the barge, desperate for solid ground.

Chapter Sixteen

The baby shower is going to be football-themed." Sal vibrates as he speaks. "I got little football-shaped cupcakes from this bakery in Jersey. Chocolate and vanilla marble. I sent you and Henry a picture. Did you see?"

Sal has been pinging Henry and me in our Facebook Messenger group chat constantly—photos of ultrasounds, baby clothes, everything. I honestly love hearing from Sal, and I love the way Henry always beats me to answering him, but the last message Sal sent us has gone unanswered—mostly because Henry and I aren't talking.

"It's adorable," I say, smiling. I try to stay engaged in conversation, but my brain is in so many other places. It's with Henry, rejecting me. It's with Sonya, slamming the bathroom door on me. How have I been so insensitive to her feelings? I took advantage of her cheery nature and finally she snapped, that's how. I fucked things up, like I always do.

". . . And look at this backdrop for photos! They make it

look like you're standing at the goalpost. Look!" Sal zooms in on Amazon on his phone. "Oh! And these streamers . . ." He scrolls down in his Amazon purchase history to show me the metallic streamers he ordered.

"What if he grows up and doesn't like football?" I ask.

Sal shrugs. "He can like whatever he wants," he says. "The baby shower is mostly for us, anyway."

Talking with Sal at the library has saved me over the past week. Without him, I think I'd be a puddle on the ground 24–7. Instead, for the lucky hours I sit at a desk next to him, or get to sneak away to other magical corners of the library, I don't feel like I'm on the verge of tears.

"You're right, Sal," I say, packing up my things. "He's a lucky kid."

"I'm glad you've been around so much this week, sweetheart," Sal says, tossing his backpack over his wide shoulders. "Don't tell the others, but you're my favorite one at Carlyle."

"I don't deserve that," I say as we walk toward the door, incapable of stopping the events at the Frying Pan from flickering through my mind like a film. A horror film. With me as the villain.

"Doesn't make it any less true." He winks. "I'm off to pick up some more stuff for the shower," he says as we exit the library onto the busy sidewalk. "What about you?"

I check my watch. "I'm going to be late for catering if I don't leave now." I hike the tote bag with my NYAC uniform higher on my shoulder. "See you later, Sal," I say as I dash away. If Sal is the antidote for my emotions, NYAC is the poison.

I rub my temples on the subway up to Columbus Circle. It's been a week and four days since I've seen or talked to Henry. The humiliation of that day is raw. I feel like such an idiot, and I don't know how I'll ever face him. Sonya is avoiding me by spending every night at Jamie's place, and when she's in the apartment she makes herself scarce. I fill up my time working two or three shifts a day. I don't give myself a second off to let the loneliness catch up. Today that means back-to-back shifts at the library and NYAC.

Just because you think you're all alone doesn't mean that you are.

Sonya was wrong. I had my chance. I had my one person, and ever since he went away, I knew I wouldn't get another. This whole mess is proof of that.

Sam was it.

I get off the train and rush into the loading dock at NYAC, swallowing any lingering emotions. Who cares if there's no passion here? Passion makes things messy. It can break your heart.

NYAC is having their annual hall of fame induction, where they honor a handful of their members. All it really means for me is lots of expensive champagne and high-profile guests. I don't pretend to know who any of them are, but I'm not there to schmooze anyway. I'm there to pass out food as quickly and quietly as possible.

Even though I try to keep them in check, my emotions are dangerously close to the surface, and I'm afraid that at any moment they will spew like a geyser.

I can't believe I wanted something—I don't even know what—to happen in that bathroom with Henry. I don't know how to explain that to him. How to explain myself. I want him to be with me all the time, and simultaneously am not ready for anything beyond friendship, but I also basically attacked him with my mouth. *God, I'm even confusing myself.*

All I do know right now is that I miss him. I miss Sonya. And I miss Jamie. I miss what little shaky community I had with my friends, but I don't know how to face them.

I change into my catering uniform and Dansko clogs in the bathroom and scurry onto the floor for Mr. Kirk's pre-shift meeting. He gives me a death glare when I join the group at the back of the room, but doesn't say anything. He can't. I'm three minutes early. Suck on that, *Mr. Jerk.*

I give myself a mental high five for that sick burn, and then listen to the rest of his spiel. Easy plated dinner, three-course meal. I can do it in my sleep.

When I approach a table with a bottle of champagne for the toast, a man with speckled skin around his neck grabs me by the hand to tell me how beautiful I am. I smile and try to get away as fast as possible. When I return with the salads, he grabs me by the elbow and tells me that I smell good. I smile and try to get away as fast as possible. When I return with the filet mignon, he grabs me by the waist and tells me to smile more. I smile and try to get away as fast as possible.

Just before dessert, I find Mr. Kirk in the kitchen.

"Sir?" My voice shakes. "Can I switch sections for dessert?"

"What is it this time?" Kirk doesn't look up from scooping ice cream onto molten lava cakes.

"One of the guests at table six is making me uncomfortable."

He looks up to me and glares, annoyed. "How?"

"He's . . . grabby."

"Bennet," he says, setting down the bottle of chocolate syrup. "You think you're the only person who's had uncomfortable run-ins with guests? That's the way it is in the service industry. If you can't handle it, I suggest you leave."

"No one will notice if I switch—"

"It's too late in service to change. You'll have to deal with it." He goes back to scooping ice cream, apparently done with this interaction.

I grit my teeth and try to bite back my anger.

I fill my tray with lava cakes and hoist it onto my shoulder. My pulse is fluttering faster and faster as I approach the table one more time. When I reach the final seat, the man grabs me by the ass and squeezes. He tells me I'm too beautiful to work at a place like this. I do not smile. I do not try to get away as fast as I can. I dump the entire tray of lava cakes in his lap and top it off with a full glass of champagne from the table.

Then I walk away.

Obviously I'm fired. Mr. Kirk screams at me for twenty minutes, spit flying everywhere. He's not the only one who's angry. Rage burns through me like a fuse. I throw my uniform at him and book it out of the building.

As soon as I hit the fresh air, my rage dissolves into a sobbing fit. I double over on the street, hyperventilating into a subway grate. I let the shame and anger and frustration and embarrassment wash over me. My emotions swallow me, and

I welcome them. The world goes in and out of focus as I try to regain control.

"Hey." I jerk my head in the direction of a stranger's voice. A woman stares at me, an expression of concern and annoyance across her face. "You all right?"

Embarrassment courses through my body as I try to put a lid on my emotions. "I'm fine," I say, wiping my eyes.

"You need help getting somewhere?" the stranger asks, cocking her head, and I realize her expression isn't *annoyance*. It's the expression of someone who's in a rush and took time she didn't have to ask if I needed help.

"Um." I look around me at the city swooping by, the still-busy sidewalk full of people rushing around us. No one's ever looked twice at me on the streets. "No. I think I'm okay."

"Okay," she says, smiling sweetly at me. "Whatever happened, it's not worth it."

And then she walks off faster than she came.

The interaction shakes me—I'd come to expect a level of anonymity on these sidewalks, assuming that no one would notice or care for a stranger crying. Or if they did, it wouldn't be to offer help. New Yorkers don't have time for that bullshit. But clearly they do . . . sometimes.

As soon as she's gone, I feel my lip start to quiver as I try to hold in a sob. As much as I want to believe her, that it's not worth it, I know that it is. It so is.

There's only one place I can think of going right now.

When I arrive, the door is locked. They must've closed early. I peer through the window into the warmly lit restaurant. Henry is alone, wiping the bar down with a rag. He moves with such grace, and I admire how the orange light from the candles flickers against his outline.

I tap on the window and he pauses. Slowly he turns, throwing the rag over his shoulder and squinting at the window, cupping his hand over his eyes.

I watch him decide whether or not to let me in.

Please, I think. *I don't want to be alone.*

He scratches his chin, walks to the door, and unlocks it.

"Hi," he says, twisting the rag between his fingers.

When I see him, the wells of tears in my eyes start to spew. I turn away. "Sorry." I wipe my cheek with my knuckle. "I'm sorry. I shouldn't have come here."

"What's wrong?" He tucks the rag into his pocket.

The muscles in my stomach squeeze as I feel my emotions come from deep inside. I hug my arms around me, trying to keep myself from breaking.

Henry seems unsure of what to do, unsure of how to approach me. "I'm sorry," I say. "I'm a mess."

Tears blur my vision as Henry inches toward me. "Bennet," he says. "Are you okay?" He puts one hand on each of my shoulders, squeezing gently.

I close my eyes and focus only on his hands. The way they feel on my shoulders. I feel the warm summer air brush against my face, dry the wet splotches on my cheeks. After a few deep breaths, my heart rate begins to decrease, my throat loosens up.

I open my eyes to him, wiping under my lashes and sniffling. "Sorry," I say. "I'm good."

I wish I could see his expression, see the details of his face, but he's backlit from the restaurant. He steps inside. "Come on," he says as he holds the door open for me to follow. He leads me to my barstool from the first night and pours me a glass of wine. He doesn't make me talk, he doesn't make me feel embarrassed. He cleans the rest of the tables in silence.

Then he pours himself a glass and sits down next to me.

"What happened?" His expression is sincere and concerned, but not one of pity.

I blow a breath out through my lips. "I got fired and got reported to my temp agency because some old guy groped me and I poured champagne on him, and Sonya won't talk to me because I suck as a friend, and you're mad at me, and I just feel like I'm making one colossal fuckup after another." I sniffle, and it's not a dainty one. "Every time I feel like I'm a smidge closer to getting my life together, I take a million steps back, and I just don't understand why it's so easy for everyone else and not me." My chin twitches as I try to bite back the tears that want to come to the surface again. "I don't know how to do this."

"Let's deal with one thing at a time." He swivels on his stool to face me. "One: I'm not mad at you. A little confused, maybe, but I wanted to give you some space. That's all."

"I don't want space." My throat tightens at the realization that I want just the opposite.

"Me neither." He smiles, and the relief I feel is overwhelming. "Two: no one knows what the hell they're doing, they're just good at hiding it. Do you think I want to work here instead of starting my own business? Of course not. You can't beat yourself up like this. You're amazing and you're brave and smart and you're funny as hell. You need to give yourself some more credit."

My skin flushes and burns, and although there's no mirror nearby, I assume my cheeks have turned cherry-red.

"Three: Sonya cares about you. No one goes on a rant like that if they don't care."

"I let her down. I'm always letting people down."

"It's what people do. We're imperfect. We hurt each other, but I don't have any doubt in my mind you will make it right."

"I want to." My voice quakes. I will.

"Last." He grips the edge of the bar tight, his knuckles turning white. "I cannot believe someone touched you tonight, and if I were there, he would have ended up with a lot more than some champagne on his head." The muscles in his jaw clench. "Are you okay?"

I nod, wiping my eyes. "It's fine. It was stupid. I'm okay."

"Okay," he says, releasing his grip. "And . . ." He scratches at his collarbone, dodging eye contact. "About the Frying Pan . . ."

"I'm sorry," we blurt at the same time.

"You don't have to be sorry," I say. "I'm mortified."

He laughs and crosses his arms, rocking back on his stool. "How about I keep my tattoo hidden from you from now on?"

I cringe. "I'm not sure I can laugh about it yet."

"Sorry." He takes a gulp of his wine. "We'll get there."

My chest feels hot and tight. If I knew in that brief moment in a nautical bathroom that I'd never feel him that close again, I might've tried to remember it better. I'm not the type of person who can just do stuff like that. Even if it feels good. Not that Henry wanted it anyway. I got a clear message: *No.*

"Henry," I say, squeezing my eyes shut. "You were right. I . . . I have no idea why I . . . I keep embarrassing myself in front of you."

"Don't be embarrassed. That bathroom was really sexy. I can't blame you."

I groan. "Can we please just go back to normal? I need to be normal."

"Of course," he says. But I have a terrible feeling that we can't. That we have to find a new normal, because now I feel different around him—a little less guarded and so incredibly nervous about it. "Okay?" he says, nudging me on the shoulder. One nudge, and my pulse is triggered.

"Okay," I say.

A crooked grin spreads across his lips. "Now that that's out of the way, we need music."

He disappears into the kitchen. After a few moments of silence, Dolly Parton's "9 to 5" blasts from the loudspeakers.

Henry bursts out of the kitchen's double doors wearing a pink cowboy hat pulled low over his eyes. "Oh my god!" I shriek through laughter. "Where did you get that?"

"Bachelorette party last week," he says, tipping the hat to me. "Miraculously, none of them got drunk enough to puke in the bathroom."

"Hey!"

He shrugs. "What? We can't laugh about *that* either?"

I scrunch my nose. "Fine."

"Good." He grins. The chorus rings out over the speakers,

loud and bright. Henry points in the air. "This is the best part!" he says.

He sings every word of the song, hips swaying like Elvis, and my tears turn to laughter. He grabs my hand and leads me to the middle of the restaurant between the empty tables. He places the hat on my head and swings me around, spinning me in circles until I'm dizzy and choking with laughter. When the song ends, I'm out of breath and sufficiently slaphappy, and Henry's face is flushed pink.

"I needed that," I say, collapsing to the floor as "Hush-a-Bye Hard Times" starts to play over the speakers.

"Everyone needs a little Dolly sometimes," he says as he joins me. We sit facing each other, crisscross applesauce. "Feel better, cowboy?"

The kindness in his face cracks me open, and I find myself wanting to say something I've been feeling for a long time, but have been too ashamed to tell anyone out loud.

I clear my throat, flicking my hair back off my shoulder. "You know how when you get a piercing or a new organ or something and your body recognizes it as a foreign object and starts to reject it? Even if it's harmless or if it's saving your life . . . your body just expels it."

He nods as though this is a totally normal analogy.

"I think New York is doing that to me."

He shakes his head, his chest rising and falling from dancing. "I think everyone here feels like that to some degree."

"Do you?"

"Of course," he says, laughing. "You think it's natural for a guy from the mountains to live here?"

"I guess not."

He looks at me under a furrowed brow. "I hope you at least know that I'm happy you're here."

I rub my fingers against my chest, trying to massage away the erratic beating of my heart underneath it. I dig in my brain for the words I want to say in response, but nothing comes to the surface. Instead, I use his. "I'm happy you're here too."

He smiles, sincere and kind, and claps his hands together. "Good."

"Can we keep doing the Passion Project?"

"As long as you still pick the next place." He steals the hat back, tips it over his face, and leans back against a nearby chair like a sleepy cowboy.

"I can do that."

Chapter Seventeen

NYAC reported the incident to Carlyle Staffing Solutions, who then called me in to have a "reassessment." Which means I'm probably fired. Not just from NYAC. From the whole Carlyle operation.

If I lose this job, I'll have to move home to Pennsylvania, no doubt. A couple weeks ago I might've looked at this as an excuse to take the plunge back into the womb, but today the thought of returning to my hometown doesn't fill me with relief, it fills my head with alarm bells.

I wait for the meeting in the Carlyle office. The room is so bright that it's giving me a headache. The floors and walls are stark white and almost every piece of furniture is neon. Neon-purple desk, neon-green chairs, neon-orange picture frames with photos of neon-blue fish. I wonder how anyone gets anything done in a place like this.

I close my eyes and try to imagine how this meeting will go, but when I press my lids shut, all I see is Henry dancing to

Dolly Parton in the dark restaurant, how he turned my entire night around with a pink hat and a goofy smile.

I have no idea where to take him for the next Passion Project outing. I try zeroing in on things that have made me happy. The things that used to make me happy before Sam. Maybe I can trace the feeling of joy back to a single act. I felt good when I got into college because I had accomplished something. I felt good when I helped Fred get adopted at the adoption event. I felt good with Henry in the bathroom at the Frying Pan. . . .

I shake my head as if I can knock the thought right out of my ears. *What is wrong with you?* We're just friends. That's what I want.

I felt good when I made dinner for my parents after my grandma passed. We were all devastated, but my mom was inconsolable. Doing a small task for her, even if it was just making terrible mac and cheese, was the best way I could show my love.

It's not much to go on, but an idea starts to form in my head. I text Henry the address of a Home Depot in the Bronx. I know what we're going to do.

As I'm clicking my phone off, a smallish woman wearing a polka-dot blouse approaches.

"Bennet?" When I stand, I'm a full five inches taller than her. I feel like Godzilla. "I'm Anna. Right this way."

We head into a small office with a yellow door. She gestures for me to sit. I oblige. She clears her throat and smiles at me from across her desk. I can't believe I'm about to get fired by this adorable person who looks way younger than me.

"So, I hear that the catering jobs aren't going so well," she says.

I shake my head. "It's just NYAC. I can cater anywhere else."

"John Kirk was very upset when he called us. He threatened to cut ties with our services. This is serious, Bennet. They are our best client."

"I understand." I cross and then uncross my legs.

She cocks her head, her lips thin. "Do you still wish to work with us at Carlyle?"

"Yes," I say. The truth. I want to stay in New York for a little longer. I want this organ transplant to take.

"Okay." She sighs, clicking her pen. "We'll continue to work with you on a probationary basis. You won't be allowed to do any catering shifts."

"Okay." I crack my knuckles in my lap.

"However," she continues, "the team at the library would like to keep you on a semi-regular schedule. Sal Thomas, as you know, left the city to support his daughter through a medical emergency. He recommended you personally to fulfill some of his duties."

Eggplant baby. Oh my god.

"Sorry." I blink. "What happened with Sal?"

"I can't discuss personal details of our contractors with other contractors."

"Right." I tap my fingers on my knee. *Come on, lady. Throw me a bone.*

She clicks her pen again. "Do you think you could do what I asked?"

"Yes, of course. The library. Semi-regular. No catering. Got it."

"Great." She flashes pearly white teeth through her pink-lipstick-stained lips. "Then we're done here. You know how to get out of the building, right?"

I nod and dash out of her office, heart racing.

The first thing I do when I'm in the tacky green elevator is scroll Sal's Facebook page. Nothing since the 3D ultrasound. No news is good news, right? If there was a tragedy there'd be some trace of it online, surely. A boulder drops into the pit of my stomach. Of course not—if there was bad news they'd keep it private.

I type out a quick message in the Facebook chat with Sal and Henry, but question if that's the right thing to do. What if I'm not supposed to know about his daughter's health problems? What if he wants to keep this all hush-hush? I delete it.

Instead, I text Henry.

Have you heard from Sal? His group chat messages have gone quiet . . . I think something is wrong.

I know it's a long shot.

The blue dots pop up right away.

Haven't heard from him since the baby shower messages.

And then another text.

Want me to see if I can reach him?

No. It's okay. I just worry.
I'm sure it's fine.

I don't want Sal to feel like we're crowding him in a difficult time. When I was grieving, I didn't want anyone to reach out to me. I know Sal is a different person than I am, but it's so hard to know what's appropriate, what's going to make a hurting person feel better.

But, boy, am I worried.

I need to shake this fear out of my body, so I start to formulate my Passion Project plan. I do some preliminary research on my phone to see if it's even possible, and then I open my calculator app to try to figure out how much it'll cost. By the time I've planted my butt on the subway seat, I realize that with the extra money I made from working overtime the past couple weeks, and with the very small skill set I have for design, I think I can pull it off. I think *we* can pull it off.

The excitement of coming up with the plan and the thrill of not knowing how it'll turn out is not enough to stop me from thinking about Sal and his daughter the entire way home.

Chapter Eighteen

I'm wearing a pair of denim overalls, a yellow tank top, white sneakers, and a pair of sunglasses I bought at Duane Reade when I meet Henry at the Home Depot. A pool of sweat has formed on the lower back of his pale blue shirt.

"You stumped me. What are we doing here?" He takes off his glasses and wipes the lenses with the bottom of his shirt.

"We're doing something nice for Sonya," I say.

"Are we remodeling your apartment?" He looks concerned. "It might not be sexy to admit this, but I'm not super-handy."

I grimace. "Um . . ." I press my sunglasses up the bridge of my nose and bite back a joke about Henry being sexy, which leaves me with absolutely nothing to say. All I can hear, ricocheting around my brain, is the phrase *Henry Sexy* and a very loud fart noise. "Yeah . . ." I wince at my sheer inability to form words.

He makes a pained face. "I didn't mean to suggest that I . . . um . . ."

"Um . . ." I glance down at my shoes, cutting him off. "Sorry, I lost my train of thought."

"Well," he says. "You brought me to Home Depot for some reason, and then I said the word *sexy* and everything got weird."

"Stop saying it," I blurt. "I mean . . . let's go." We head toward the outdoor section. I grab five yards of fake grass, a roll of double-sided Astroturf tape, and two folding lounge chairs. Henry pushes the cart behind me as I pick out a small portable misting machine and a lawn flamingo. I throw two potted cat palms and a string of twinkle lights into the cart and run through the checkout line.

Henry calls a car for us and I punch my address into his phone. I haven't had a friend in my apartment . . . maybe ever. No one except Sonya and Jamie. And now Henry.

It takes us three trips to bring everything up the five and a half stories to the roof, but we finally make it, sweaty and pink with exhaustion. Our roof is a mess. It's not meant for people. There are empty bottles, dead birds, and strange graffiti on the hip-height walls around the perimeter. It scares me that the only thing keeping us protected from falling off the side of the building is a puny parapet, but like I said, this roof is not meant for people.

Yet.

We leave our haul on the roof and head into my apartment for cleaning supplies, garbage bags, and a drink of cold water.

"So, this is your place?" He explores, studying a piece of HomeGoods art.

"Complete with a bunch of broken furniture found on the street."

"It's really . . . nice." He collapses onto the futon, his arms spread across the top.

"No it's not." I fill up two glasses of water with extra ice. "The futon is falling apart, the paint is scuffed, and it's so dark in here it might as well be a dungeon." I hand him one of the glasses, which he presses to his neck immediately.

"Those things aren't the problem with this place—you know that, right?"

I take a big gulp of water. "Oh really? What's the problem, then?"

A splash of water tips out of his glass, rolling down his neck and soaking a little spot on his shirt. I try not to remember the last time Henry's shirt got wet—the way it felt pressed against my palm. "It just doesn't seem very you," he says, pulling the cup from his neck.

I pry my eyes away from him and survey the room. The pictures on the wall are abstract in a hotel art way. I always viewed them as placeholders for when we decided to *really* decorate, but we never did. The futon was the cheapest, lightest one we could find, and the decor is a collection of random things we didn't have the energy to scrutinize before putting on display. He's right. None of this is curated to Sonya's or my taste at all.

"I think we never put effort into our space because we didn't know how long we'd be here. We never put down any roots or anything."

"Well," he says, setting his glass on the coffee table. "We're putting them down now, aren't we?"

I smile. "We are."

I throw some garbage bags, disinfectant, sponges, rubber

gloves, and paper towels into an IKEA bag, and we head up the stairs.

We pick a corner of the roof that has a little bit of shade. I scrub the floor and parapet while Henry collects trash. I think I see him pick up an old needle at one point, but I ignore it. I come across a dead bird, and Henry slaps on the rubber gloves and picks it up without flinching. I mime a gagging noise.

"I used to feed Falkor silkworms for dinner. This is nothing."

When everything's relatively clean, we measure out the Astroturf and cut it to fill the spot. Henry lifts the roll and I try not to stare at his muscles flexing as he heaves it into place. When the grass is secured, I place the cat palms in the two farthest corners, flush to the parapet. I put the flamingo under the shade of one of the plants and the two lawn chairs in the middle. Henry strings the twinkle lights along the parapet and I place the mist machine at the edge of the Astroturf facing the two chairs, so that whoever is sitting there can turn it on and get relief from the oppressive heat. It's not much, but we created a little garden oasis on the roof.

I collapse into one of the chairs. Henry lies on the Astroturf, his body stretching out flat.

He cups his eyes to block the sun, which is slowly beginning its descent. "Is this your way of telling me you want to be a landscape architect?"

The mist from the machine sprays us gently. "Not exactly. I just wanted to do something nice for Sonya."

Henry rolls over to face me. "Mission accomplished."

"I've just gotten a little too lost in my own head to let her know I still care about her."

"She'll love it," he says, flopping onto his back.

"Henry," I say, squinting down at him splayed out on the grass.

"Mm-hm?" he mumbles.

"Should we get some rum?"

He props himself up on both elbows and lets his head droop back. "Absolutely."

I run down to the corner bodega and grab a can of pineapple juice and some sunscreen, and then to the liquor store across the street to buy a bottle of rum. When I return to the roof, Henry is asleep on one of the chairs. I take a moment to look at him, not wanting to disturb his peace. He's not often still and quiet, and seeing him like this is strange, but nice. I find myself wishing it could be simple, that I could be normal, that he didn't reject me . . . that I could admire him in my solitude. Because when he's sleeping, I don't have to pretend I don't feel soft around him. I don't have to pretend that he doesn't confuse the shit out of me. But I can't stare at him forever. If I don't get sunscreen on him he'll burn.

"Henry," I say, tapping him on the shoulder. "Get up, I have rum."

He smiles at me before he even opens his eyes. "Thank god."

"I also have sunscreen. You're burning."

He squints up at me through lazy eyelids. "You trying to take care of me?"

"Take the sunscreen, smart-ass." I hand him the tube. He haphazardly squirts some into his palm and slathers it on his face, leaving white streaks all over his cheeks and nose.

"You look ridiculous."

"It's fine," he says, smearing it over his forehead. By the time he's done, he looks like he just got a pie in the face.

"It's not fine," I say. "It's all over you."

"Where?" he asks, rubbing his cheek with the back of his hand, which is also covered in sunscreen.

"Everywhere," I say.

He rubs the extra sunscreen onto his arms and wipes his hand on a towel. "I give up."

"Ugh," I moan. "Here. Let me." I kneel next to him and press my fingers to his cheeks. I massage the sunscreen into his skin, which feels warm and soft under my fingertips.

Henry's eyes flutter closed and I admire the slope of his nose, the way it's turning pink, with a couple of spots that might become freckles tomorrow. I notice the way his eyelashes spread across his lower lids like a fan.

Slowly, his eyes open, locking on mine. In the sun, his pupils shrink, the lush green and gold of his irises becoming more vivid.

"Sorry," I say as I finish evening out his sunscreen and sheepishly back away. I rub the rest of it into my palms.

Friends don't put sunscreen on friends like that.

"It's okay." He tosses his head back against the chair. "You don't have to freak out every time you touch me. We're supposed to be acting normal around each other, remember?"

I cringe. "Shut up. This is normal."

He snorts. "Okay. Sure."

I plop into the seat next to him and pour us each a rum and

pineapple juice. After a couple sips, I begin to feel drowsy, and my muscles scream from hauling equipment. Henry's eyes are closed next to me, so I do the same.

I must have fallen asleep, because the next time I open my eyes, it's dusk. Twinkle lights hang above us like stars. The sounds of the city are dim and distant.

I turn to face Henry, whose chin has drooped to his chest, his legs outstretched on the grass. I smile and turn back to the sky, letting myself doze off next to him.

I'm wearing a ridiculous Party City Hawaiian shirt, bright pink sunglasses, and a dollar store lei. I make two pineapple Bellinis with the rest of the juice from last night, loop an extra lei for Sonya around my elbow, stand alone in our living room, and wait for her to get home.

The sound of a key opening the front door stops my heart. "Sonya?" She comes into the apartment with a tote bag full of clothes and a pile of mail. "Where've you been?"

"I slept at Jamie's." She tries to scoot past me, a move I've done many times around her.

"Sonya, I want to talk, but first I have something to show you." I do my best to emulate Henry's wide, open smile as I offer her a Bellini.

"Bennet, I'm tired." She flops the bag on the couch.

"You don't have to talk to me ever again, but I think you'll like what I'm going to show you." I extend the olive branch cocktail toward her one more time. "Please?"

She frowns as she takes the drink from me. I lead her up the stairwell to the oasis, where I've already got a speaker playing "Dancing Queen."

Sonya tilts her head, a blank expression on her face.

"I figured since our apartment is so hot, why not turn it into a tropical paradise?" I gesture to the Astroturf with a pathetic little jazz-hands ta-da. "There's a mist machine to cool you down, and you can't tell right now, but those twinkle lights are really pretty at night. Oh, and these are real plants over here, but I promise to take care of them, you don't have to worry about that."

She bites her lip. "Why did you do this?"

I take a deep breath. "I haven't been the best friend to you in a really long time. Actually, I haven't been a friend to you at all recently. And I'm sorry."

She looks away from me over the horizon. I continue. "I think sometimes I assume you and Jamie don't want to spend any time with me because, frankly, *I* don't want to spend any time with me."

She presses her lips together in a thin line. "When you said you wanted to move here with me, I was shocked—but I was also so excited to have you in my life again. I thought maybe we could reconnect, but you haven't even let me try. You act like you don't want me around. And then I saw you with Henry . . . a stranger. You're more comfortable with a stranger than with me."

"I know," I say. "I love you, Sonya. There was just a time when . . . when everything went down I kind of lost it and I didn't know how to let anyone in anymore. And, if I'm being honest, I think it's a little bit easier for me with newer people because they don't know who I was. They don't know me as anyone but who I am now. There are no expectations, no memory of me before Sam or during Sam or anything. But you know me. You know me better than anyone else in the world, I think, and that scares me so much because I feel like I'm not that same person anymore. I want to be, I want to be so badly, but I'm not, and you can see right through me. It's marginally easier for me to be with someone like Henry than you or Andy, because he . . . he's new. And believe me, it's been so hard for me to be comfortable around him too. I'm honestly not even there yet."

She furrows her brow, staring down at her feet. "I get it," she says. "It's just hard to feel like my best friend is a stranger and barely wants to get to know my girlfriend."

"I like Jamie!" I say. "This is as much for her as it is for you. I figured the two of you could come up here and enjoy the weather and drink tropical cocktails. It's not much, but I do hope you like it. And even if you never forgive me for how I've treated you, even if you want to never talk to me again, I hope you understand and believe how sorry I am. I'm trying to be better." I shake my head. "I'm not trying, I *am* going to be better."

She takes a slow sip from her cocktail.

"Okay," I say. "I'll leave you alone now. There's more drinks downstairs, and if it gets too hot just flick that machine on. Again, Sonya. I'm sorry." I turn to walk toward the stairwell. At least I tried.

"We're going to need another chair up here."

I pause, almost to the door. "Another chair?"

"For the three of us. Me, Jamie, you."

I turn around to see a big grin plastered across her face. I could cry.

"Of course I loved the old you," she says. "I mean, she was my best friend. She helped me get through coming out to my parents and going on my first horrible dates with girls who didn't like me. She snuck my paintings into coffee shops in hopes that someone might notice my work and want to buy it. She cried in my arms when we went to schools in different states, and she introduced me to her new friend Andy, who I know loved that Bennet too. But what I think you don't understand is that, yes, I loved that Bennet, and yes, you've hurt me, but I don't see you any different than I did when we were sixteen. You're still you, you just have more colors, more depth, and, yeah, more pain. And this whole time I only wanted you to let me in and let me love you as the entire person you are. Old Bennet, new Bennet, it's all the same—different parts of a whole. You're not some scary person," she continues. "You're funny, you're caring, and you feel everything deeply. Don't rob people of that because you can't see it yourself."

"I want to know all the versions of you too," I say, my fingers trembling. "And I'm so sorry."

Sonya laughs, slicing through the emotions in the air. "Okay, I forgive you. Can we hug now?"

I throw my arms around her small frame. She's stiff for a moment, but eventually she wraps her arms around me. "I miss your hugs," she says.

"I miss them too," I admit.

She squeezes me, one little pulse. "You still have to buy my earrings, though. Three pairs at least."

I pull away and smile. "Deal."

"And if you forget I design jewelry again, I'm moving out," she says.

"Deal."

She flicks her long dark hair off her shoulder. "Good."

"I'm so sorry, Sonya. I'm so sorry I pushed you off for so long. I didn't know how to be anything, so I gave you nothing. No more. I promise, no more. That ends today."

She hugs me again, and I breathe in her familiar scent. "I forgive you. Of course I forgive you."

Downstairs, I rifle through the mail and find a heavy card-stock envelope. The official invite to Andy Chase's wedding. My ears start to buzz as I tear open the envelope.

If I've let Sonya's friendship wither away from lack of sunlight and water, I murdered Andy's friendship with gardening shears.

I grip the card stock in my hands until it feels too heavy to hold. I shove it to the bottom of our silverware drawer without opening it.

Chapter Nineteen

I meet Henry outside Penn Station. He has a big black bag slung over his shoulder and is carrying a smaller one in his fist, dangling near his thigh. The sun is hiding behind a thick haze of clouds, so he's more bundled than usual in a crewneck and jeans, and his long body is leaning to one side, sinking into his slim hip. When I'm close enough to see his eyes he winks, and it's a straight shot to my nervous system.

Ugh. *Why does he have to look like that?*

"What are we doing this time?" I ask, eyeing the bags.

"I have a shoot," he says, smiling down at me. His dimple makes my stomach drop. "Figured you could be my assistant."

"Not outside, I hope." I point to the sky, which is as deep as a bruise. It looks like it could turn into a thunderstorm any minute.

"Not outside." He hands me one of the bags. It's so heavy I nearly drop it.

"Oh my god." I heave it off the sidewalk, but it takes a great effort.

"Fine, you can take this one." He trades bags with me. This one is lighter by ten pounds at least.

"I see, you were trying to pawn the heavy one off on me."

He smirks and glances at me out of the corner of his eye. "Something like that."

We head into the station, buy our New Jersey Transit tickets, and maneuver through sweaty bodies to board the packed train. We find two seats across the aisle from each other in different rows. Instead of being next to Henry, I'm seated next to a woman with fluffy white hair whose perfume assaults the membranes of my lung tissue with every breath.

I sneak glances at Henry three rows ahead of me. From here, I can see the outline of his left arm on the armrest, flexing every time he checks his phone. He turns around to look at me, as if he can feel the weight of my eyes on him. I snap my eyes shut and pretend to be asleep. I hear his laugh from across the train.

After a couple of stops, Henry gets up and gestures for me to follow.

"Maplewood, New Jersey." I eye the sign on the platform as we step off the train. "Are you going to tell me what we're doing here?" I say through a yawn.

"Told you. I have a shoot." He scratches his jaw and glances at the parking lot.

"Maybe I'll discover my passion is being a photographer and I'll take all your clients."

"Yeah, right. You could never steal my clients."

"What?" I cross my arms. "Are you underestimating me?"

"No. I think you'd like me to *think* you'd do something like that, but I think you like me too much to take my clients."

My stomach twists and I freeze. I open my mouth to respond, to quip back about how I don't like him *that* much, but the words turn to mist in my mouth.

His eyes bear into mine, his smirk dangerously taunting me. "You're blushing," he says.

"Stop looking at me," I say, feeling my cheeks with my hands. They're warm.

"Where am I supposed to look?"

"I don't know," I say, glancing at the tracks, spotting a large, fuzzy mass scurrying across the metal. "There's a rat. Look at that."

"You're so weird," he says.

A car honk breaks the moment. "Sweetheart!"

A man is standing in the open driver's-side door of a beat-up blue sedan, waving at me like a maniac. I squint my eyes to get a better look.

"Sal?"

Henry nudges me in the ribs with his elbow. "Told you you'd like it."

"Oh my god," I screech as I run down the stairs toward his car. I throw my arms around him, without thinking about how weird it is to be hugging Sal, my work friend who I didn't realize had become a real friend. "I was so worried."

He pats my back. "Marjorie gave us a little scare, but she and the baby are doing great."

Henry gives Sal a chummy handshake. "Thanks for picking us up."

Sal's purple face lights up. "This guy." He buries Henry in a bear hug. Henry makes eye contact with me as if to say, *He's crushing my lungs.*

"We should get to the house before it starts to rain," Sal says, releasing Henry from the death grip. "Here, put your stuff in the car." He pops the trunk, and I am shocked at the display. There are boxes of diapers and wet wipes, a mobile, and a baby doll that looks like it was made in the 1920s and is haunted by ghosts. There is absolutely no room for the photography equipment. We have to pile it in the backseat. Henry insists that I ride shotgun, so he sits in the back with all the crap. His tall body scrunched into a C position.

"I'm so glad everyone's okay," I say to Sal, who's behind the wheel. "What happened?"

Sal lets out a grumbly laugh. "Marjorie was diagnosed with preeclampsia, which basically means her blood pressure was too high. It got a lot worse pretty quickly. Right after the last time I saw you, her husband called me and told me they had to induce her labor early. Mary and I dropped everything and left the city to take care of her."

His voice is coarse and tight. "Anyway, while the baby was in the NICU, Mary and I were doing all the cooking and the cleaning and taking care of stuff, so I didn't have time to let anyone know everything was okay. To be honest, I wasn't even checking Facebook at all, so I didn't read any of your messages. Wasn't till this guy tracked down Marjorie's home phone number that I realized I'd left you hanging."

I whip my head to the backseat to look at Henry, who's dodging my gaze. "How did you do that?"

He keeps his eyes trained out the window and shrugs. "He wasn't that hard to find once I got my hands on an old football article, which led me to Marjorie's LinkedIn and an old office she used to work at, and . . . I got there eventually."

My jaw hangs open as he casually taps his fingers on his knee. "Henry, that's . . . you're . . . that was so nice of you."

"I thought they might want a newborn photo shoot." He modestly smiles and finally looks at me. "Pro bono, of course."

A wave of affection cracks open in me like a can of fizzy soda that's been shaking ever since we met. I look back at him, crumpled into a ball in the backseat so that I could take the front. This is the essence of Henry, the thing I've been trying so hard not to trust. I don't know if I have the strength to suppress it anymore. Don't know if I even want to.

We pull up to a small white house in a cul-de-sac. A couple of wilted balloons hang in the air attached to the mailbox. Henry hauls the bags out of the backseat and hands me the lighter one while Sal unlocks the front door.

"Why do you have to be such a good person all the time?" I sling the bag over my shoulder. "You're making the rest of us look bad."

"Maybe I'm actually a terrible person." He slams the car door shut. "And I just have a soft spot for you."

Oh god. Also, when did he get so tall? Was he always this tall? My fingertips buzz with the urge to reach up and touch his face.

"Ready to meet the little guy?" Sal shouts from the stoop.

"Ready," Henry and I say in unison.

Sal takes us through the house and out to the back porch, where Marjorie and her husband, who introduces himself as Pete, are sitting, glued to a baby monitor. Pete is a huge dude, nearly seven feet tall with a shaved head. He looks like Vin Diesel on steroids.

Marjorie, on the other hand, is tiny. She's got chocolate-brown eyes and pin-straight hair that stops halfway down her back. She hugs me with the same vigor as her dad.

"It's so nice to meet you two!" Marjorie moves on to hugging Henry, who gives me the same look of pain as when Sal hugged him earlier. "Thank you sooooooo much for doing this for us." She must be used to speaking to the baby, because she's talking to us adults in baby-voice. She releases Henry from the death grip and turns to me. "Did you know Dad calls you his work daughter?"

Pete sets the baby monitor down on the arm of his Adirondack chair and takes a hefty gulp of lemonade. "We appreciate you coming. It's been a rough month," he grumbles. He looks exhausted.

"It was Henry's idea," I say.

"How long have you been together?" Pete grunts.

"Oh no—it's not like that," I stammer. "We're just friends. He's helping me with something."

"We're working on a Passion Project together," Henry says, awkwardly scratching his chin.

"A *Passion* Project. I get it," Marjorie says, trying and failing to wink.

Henry laughs.

"Not that kind of passion," I add sheepishly.

Sal's wife, Mary, interrupts the moment with two lemonades for Henry and me, and we settle into our own Adirondack chairs facing the others in a circle. Even though the temperature has dropped significantly and it seems like rain is inevitable, the fresh air still feels nice.

I watch, tight-lipped, as Henry charms the pants off these people. He's magical to observe, and seeing him through this family's eyes is like seeing him for the first time. The more they love him, the more I feel a pull toward him. Sam was nothing like Henry. Sam was bookish, shy, understated. Henry is none of those things. He's charming, adventurous, dynamic.

I don't know why I'm comparing them to each other.

Somehow, we've moved on in topics from the baby to the grim weather forecast and then to whatever politician got caught sending dick pics this time. I never find the perfect time to chime in with a witty response or fun fact. The sky gets thicker and thicker, tucking the sun behind a curtain of gray.

Sal enters with the baby swaddled in a powder-blue blanket. All I can see from where I'm sitting are tiny little hands stretching out and reaching for Sal's nose.

"Meet baby Michael Paul Alexander," he says, beaming.

Henry eyes me from across the deck and holds up three fingers. He mouths the words *three first names* with a glint of glee on his face. I bite my lip, hiding my smile.

"You want to hold him?" Sal asks, approaching me with the child.

I've never held a baby before. "What if I break it?"

"Come on." Sal presents the bundle of joy to me, dangling

him over my lap. I panic. Henry must sense it, because he springs to his feet and swoops in.

"I'll hold him!" He taps Sal on the shoulder and peers down at the little bundle. "We're gonna have to get to know each other if I'm gonna photograph you, aren't we?" Sal gently hands the baby to Henry, who cradles his neck perfectly and lovingly and oh god I hate what this is doing to me right now. *Fuck.*

"Normally I'd say we should shoot outside for the natural light, but . . ." Henry squints at the sky right as a couple of drops start to fall. "I think we better stay inside. No worries, though, I'm prepared for an indoor shoot. I brought some props in case you were interested." He gestures to me to open the lighter of the two bags. I unzip it to an explosion of plush. I pull out a furry onesie and a tiny gold felt crown. A Max from *Where the Wild Things Are* costume.

"Henry?" I raise an eyebrow. "Why do you have all this?"

"I asked my cousin to send some baby stuff." He looks up at me through his rain-splattered glasses and shrugs. "Is it weird?"

"Not at all." I hold up the Max costume. "We have to do this one."

He smiles, satisfied. "Absolutely."

The air cracks around us and the sky finally opens up, pouring down a barrage of raindrops. Sal opens the sliding door and ushers us in.

Once Pete gets Michael dressed in his costume, Henry is more or less set up in their living room to take the pictures. Pete sets baby eggplant Michael on a blanket, and Henry stands over him, clicking away on the camera.

"Hey." Henry waves me over. "I have a job for you." He

hands me a colorful ring of keys. "Dangle these up here so Michael looks up at the lens. Try to get him to laugh if you can."

The keys are wet and sticky with what I hope is just water from the rain, but I know deep down is some form of unidentifiable baby liquid. I try not to visibly cringe.

"Hey, Michael." I do my best baby-voice. It's totally unnatural. "Look what I got!" I shake the keys. I stick out my tongue, but the baby is unamused.

A clap of thunder pierces the air, stunning the baby. He looks like he could cry any moment.

"Quick, try singing," Henry says with his eye pressed to the camera.

Singing? Michael looks like he's on the verge of exploding. I spit out the first words I can think of to the tune of "Daisy Bell," a song my mom used to sing to me as a kid, all the way up through elementary school.

Eggplant baby, give me your answer, do.
I'm half crazy, all for the love of you.

A bubble of laughter comes from Michael's little mouth. I continue while shaking the keys like maracas.

You look so sweet, good enough to eat,
In the grocery aisle for two.

Michael's face lights up and beams with joy. Henry pounces on the opportunity, taking picture after picture. It's cute, I have to admit.

Marjorie sidles up next to me, clapping her hands together with glee. "You have to write down those words for us. I haven't seen Michael laugh before!"

"Here," I say, handing her the keys. "I'll go write it down." As I exit the living room into the kitchen to find a pad of paper and pen, I can't keep my eyes off Henry at work. So serious, so grounded. It's a side of him I haven't seen before, a side I want to see more of.

The rest of the evening is spent changing costumes and backdrops. All the while, I hand Henry various lenses, help him adjust the lights and frame the shots. I like being his partner for the day, working as a team. It feels nice.

When the baby is sufficiently tired out and the rain is hammering on the roof, Mary pours us all a glass of wine and makes a cheese board. I feel toasty from the inside out, like I spent the day with my own family. Or even with the Chases. There's something magical about being in a warm house during a storm. Something safe.

I duck away to the bathroom, taking my phone with me. I sit on the closed toilet, opening up my mom's contact.

Hi.

It takes her all of half a second to respond.

Everything okay?

It breaks my heart that in my desire to keep my family from worrying about me, I've cut them off enough that they think the only reason I'd reach out would be because I was in trouble.

Just miss you, that's all.

Miss you more.

Can we catch up tomorrow?

Of course. Love you to the moon and back, Benny.

Love you too.

I smile at myself in the mirror, feeling a zing of something almost resembling contentment in my body. I tuck my phone back into my pocket and return to the kitchen, where the rest of the crew is hanging out.

I feel the kind of soupy tipsy that starts at your toes and creeps up the rest of your body after I polish off my second glass of red, leaning on the kitchen counter under a sign that says HOME IS WHERE THE WINE IS.

"The big man's out like a light," Mary says, pointing to the living room.

Sal's chin droops down to his chest, and he is snoring in front of a *Family Feud* rerun.

"We should go," Henry whispers to me, glancing at the clock. It's ten thirty. Way later than we planned on staying.

"Do we have to?" I pout.

"Yes. You're tipsy, and while it's very cute, something tells me you'll want to get home and sleep." He leans down to my level. "And you're taking the heavy bag this time."

"No way, I'm so dainty." I bat my eyelashes. "I can barely hold a pencil, I'm so weak."

"Uh-huh." He rolls his eyes. "We're going to head out," he says to everyone.

"Oh no you don't," Marjorie interrupts. "We've all been drinking. None of us can drive you to the train station. You'll stay here."

Henry and I lock eyes.

"Oh no, we'll get a cab. It's no big deal," I say, a little too forcefully.

"Yeah, it's really not. . . ." Henry trips over his words. "We can get an Uber."

"No need for that when we have a spare room with a double bed."

"Oh . . ." I search for an excuse. Any excuse. "Um . . . it's okay. We wouldn't want you to have to change the sheets or anything."

Pete's been awfully quiet this whole time, and I suspect that's how he survives in this house. I look to him to save me, pleading with my eyes. But he nods and says, "It's no problem. We did the sheets last night."

Chapter Twenty

Before we know it, Marjorie has stuffed us in the spare bedroom and given us each a clean pair of pajamas.

The room is tiny, with a pink-and-yellow quilt over a double bed. Did double beds get smaller? It looks smaller than normal.

What's even scarier than the tiny bed is that every surface in this room is covered in dolls. Antique dolls, American Girl dolls, Barbie dolls. It's . . . truly nightmarish.

Henry and I sit on opposite sides of the bed. He holds up Pete's enormous New York Giants T-shirt. I get the short end of the pajama stick as I examine the MAY CONTAIN WINE tank top and the booty shorts that Marjorie picked for me. They say JERSEY GIRL on the butt.

"This is horrifying," Henry says—about the dolls or the pajamas, I'm not sure.

"Which one do you think is most likely to come alive and kill us in our sleep?"

"Hmm." He scans the room before settling on a doll. "That one. Definitely." He points to a particularly terrifying doll sitting at a vintage school desk. She's got cherry-red hair and lips to match.

"Don't upset her. I'm not interested in getting slaughtered tonight, thank you very much."

"Oh well." He stands up and pulls his sweatshirt over his head, his perfect stomach staring right at me. His gentle ripples of muscle slope toward his belly button, his skin taut around them. When he looks at me, I notice his chest start to turn red in splotches.

"Sorry," he says. "I can go change in a different room."

I swallow, but my throat is dry. "It's fine," I say. I try not to stare at his body, but it's addicting looking at him. I can't look away.

So I don't.

He cocks his head, intrigued. "Okay," he says. "I'll change here, then."

He steps out of his jeans, revealing a pair of plaid boxers, and I watch, drinking in his movements. His legs are toned and sinewy. Does he work out? He's never mentioned working out. He looks up under his mop of hair and chuckles at me staring as he pulls on Pete's sweatpants. But he doesn't comment on me watching, he just lets me.

He pulls Pete's shirt over his head, and it lies across his body like a curtain. Obscuring the ridges and divots that I've just sunk my eyes into.

"You were really good today," I say. The words drip off my lips like silk.

"I told you." He adjusts the huge waistband of Pete's sweatpants, tying it tight around his hips. "I'm a professional."

"Yeah, but you didn't tell me you were freakishly good with babies."

"What? I'm not freakishly good with babies."

"Better than me," I say, flopping back on the bed, staring at the ceiling.

His body weight shifts the bed as he sits down next to me. "Low bar," he teases.

"Hey." I shove him on the shoulder.

He laughs as he burrows back into the pillows. "Please get ready for bed," he says. "I'm tired."

It's now that I realize it's my turn to change into pajamas.

I'm mortified at the idea of him seeing my body, naked, in a room full of dolls. I shoot up to a seated position. "I'm going to the bathroom."

I scoop the clothes into my arm and head across the hall. To my horror, the bathroom door is locked and the shower is running. I wait around for a minute, which turns into two, which turns into five. Is this the longest shower in the world?

Defeated, tired, and ready to go to sleep, I head back to our room and find Henry on the bed, scrolling through his phone. "I'm going to change, and you can't look."

He lies back and covers his face with a furry pink pillow. "Go ahead."

I pull my shirt over my head and unclasp my bra, exposing my chest to the air. Henry being in the same room makes this painfully erotic. He's not looking, but even existing in the same space makes it feel dangerous. Sexy. I slide my pants down my hips, standing there in my underwear for a second too long before I pull the tiny shorts over my thighs. The hem of the shirt lands a centimeter above my belly button, and the fabric presses flush against the contours of my breasts. I pull it down as much as I can, but it springs up every time I let go. I'm basically in a Hooters costume.

"I'm done," I say, wincing at the thought of Henry's seeing this. He opens his eyes, settling his gaze on my hips. "It's terrible, I know."

"It's not so bad," he says, stretching his arm behind his head.

I shoot him a squinty face. "No funny business."

"I can control myself." He grins, pulling up the sleeve of his shirt to reveal his tattoo. "Can you?"

Oh god. We're flirting again. We're flirting again. *Help.*

"Shut up." I roll my eyes and slide into the bed next to him. I take one of the throw pillows from behind my head and tuck it between our bodies. He looks at me like I'm crazy.

"What?" I say, shoving another pillow between us.

He gestures to the barrier. "Are we in junior high?"

"I don't want to"—how do I put this delicately?—"touch butts."

"You're a child."

He leans over to turn off the bedside lamp. As my vision adjusts to the darkness, the doll eyes start to come into focus, almost glowing neon-white against the backdrop of black. The soft sound of rain patters against the windows. The anxiety and playfulness settles between us into a quiet comfort. We've been joking around, but being in bed alone with Henry doesn't feel very silly.

I swallow, hugging a pillow close to my chest, facing him. "Henry?"

"Yeah?" His voice is low, hushed.

Silence lingers between us as we listen to the soft dance of the rain. Henry's face softens and my heart beats faster and faster with every second that passes.

"I'm . . ." I start to speak, not really sure where it's going. "Thank you," I say.

"For what?"

I gesture to the room. "This."

"I'm glad it worked out," he says. "I like Sal." He sucks in a breath and shifts in bed, letting his eyelids flutter closed for a moment.

"Also . . ."

He opens his eyes. "Yes?"

"I'm glad you made me be your friend," I say through the quiet static of the rain. "Even if I sometimes make a fool of myself in bathrooms with you."

"You didn't make a fool of yourself, Bennet."

"I did," I say, twisting my mouth, making eye contact with a particularly nefarious-looking doll, whose beady eyes shine bright in the glow of the moon. "Twice."

"Neither time," he says, blinking in the dark.

"Especially the second time," I say quietly. I put my mind into that bathroom, how I leaned in, eyes closed, to make a move I wasn't ready for. How he stopped me. His firm no.

"You have to let that go," he says.

"I know." I close my eyes. "You made it clear that that's not what you want."

He stills, breathing slower. "I never said that," he whispers. "I said I *know* what I want."

My heart bumps my chest, faster and faster, as the rain spits on the roof. "What do you want?"

The side of his jaw flexes and his mouth opens to say something, but whatever that something is, it remains unsaid. "Another time," he says.

I clutch the pillow close to my chest. "Another time," I repeat.

A streak of lightning bites through the air, illuminating his face for one sliver of a moment. A tiny flicker of green eyes, a millisecond of walnut-brown hair. Before I can really register his expression, it's dark again and all that's left is the sound of the outside world, the motion of our steady breathing on the mattress.

I press my teeth into my bottom lip, feeling the blood move through my veins. Slowly, I grab the pillow between us and pull it away, letting it fall onto the floor. Then I shed the second one, so there's nothing between us anymore. Henry doesn't move, doesn't surrender any thoughts in his head.

"One more question," I say, snuggling down under the comforter.

"Sure," he says.

"Marry, fuck, kill: Princess Leia, Queen Amidala, or R2-D2."

"I'm not doing this with you right now." He rolls onto his back on an exhale.

"You're no fun."

"I am so much fun." He reaches over and palms my face in the darkness. He sticks his finger in my ear. I bat him away.

He rolls away to face the wall. "Good night, Bennet."

"Good night, Henry," I whisper.

I don't feel the least bit tired.

I focus on the sound of the rain on the window, listening to nothing but that quiet static and the sound of Henry breathing. Usually, when I can't fall asleep, I count my breaths. It doesn't seem to work tonight. I keep my eyes on his back, watching it rise and fall. I count his breaths until my body evaporates into a light, tense sleep.

My eyelashes press against something as I blink them open. I shift a little in bed, but am restricted by the weight of an arm around my shoulders.

Henry.

One of his arms holds me close to him, and my chin rests on his shoulder, my eyelashes brushing his jaw. My leg is slung over his hips, and I feel the contours of him stiff against me. His heart beats under my arm, strong and slow. I close my eyes, trying to abate my panic, and I wonder how we got here. The way I'm flung on top of him tells me that my sleeping body initiated this, not his.

I instinctively run my hand across his arm, dipping my fingers in the fabric of his sleeve. His sleeping body pulls me tighter against him, his mouth moving slightly in his sleep. He doesn't open his eyes, he just melts back into a sleeping heap. My heart is going to explode, it's beating so fast.

As slow as a turtle, I slip out from his grasp and replace my body with a pillow. He adjusts, clutching it in his arms, but he doesn't wake up.

I pick up my clothes from yesterday and lay them out on the bed. With one eye monitoring Henry, I pull the booty shorts off and step into my jeans, clasping the button. I pull the tiny shirt over my head, once again exposing my chest, and right when I toss it on the floor, baby Michael lets out a bloodcurdling scream from somewhere in the house. Henry jolts awake, opening his eyes, which settle directly on my naked breasts. I rush to cover myself with my hands.

"Oh my god! Close your eyes!"

We both lower our gaze to the spot on the bed where the comforter tents upward. He shoves a pillow on it, his face reddening. "Oh god. Sorry," he chokes.

I turn away from him. "Pretend you didn't see that. Please."

He claps his hands over his eyes. "Why would you face me when you're changing!"

"I wanted to keep an eye on you in case you woke up! I realize how terrible that plan was now!"

"I didn't see anything," he spits. "The dolls, on the other hand, are blushing."

"Ha. Ha." I stare at the wall. "Keep your eyes closed while I finish getting dressed, please?"

"Fair enough," Henry says. "But I can't promise the dolls will."

I pull my bra and shirt on, my head racing, heartbeat pulsing between my legs. In the bathroom, I swig a mouthful of mouthwash and splash some water on my beet-red face. When I get back to the room, Henry's in his normal clothes and has made the bed.

"A gentleman."

"I can never leave a bed unmade." He folds the gigantic pajama shirt and flannel pants he wore last night. I look over at the wad of Marjorie's clothes I left in the corner of the room and, embarrassed, I pick them up and start to fold them.

"An unmade bed is so much cozier. Like the comforter is saying, *Here I am, come inside me.*"

Henry lets out a disturbed laugh. "Come inside me? Bennet, I'm starting to think you might be a secret perv."

"I wasn't the one staring at your naked body this morning."

"Nope. Just last night," he says, and it feels like little firecrackers are going off in my stomach.

"I wasn't . . ." I say, squeezing my legs together. "I mean—"

"There you go again, being so easy to tease," he says, grinning.

I feel like I need to fan myself with my hand, or squirm out of his line of sight, because it's so vivid and intense. "We should get going," I say.

"You're right," he concedes. I avert eye contact with him by looking at a Kit Kittredge doll on the dresser. "I need to get the hell out of this room before my body gets possessed by demons."

We reject an offer for coffee and pancakes and say our polite goodbyes before Sal drives us back to the train station. Henry takes the back once again, and Sal shouts stories about Michael over the sound of the radio.

At the train station, the car rolls to a stop and I unclick my seat belt. Sal gently grabs my wrist.

"I can't tell you what it means to me that you came to check on us. This guy disguised it as a photo shoot, but I know it's because you care. Come back anytime," he says. "You're always welcome here."

I give him a quick hug over the console and promise him that we will visit, and then head to the platform.

Henry and I buy our tickets at a kiosk and wait for the next train. We find a lonely bench under an awning and stake out. It's that purply blue time of morning, when the sun is almost fully risen and the light plays tricks on your eyes, blurring the edges of the world around you. Our knees touch as we sit on the platform enjoying the peace of the morning.

"Hey." His voice is soft and cautious as he brushes my knee with his hand. "When are you going to tell me about him?"

Chapter Twenty-One

It's a story I've told many times before, so many times that it's almost callused over. Sam died in a car accident.

It's *almost* the truth.

The only two people who know the entire truth are me and Sam . . . though I suppose that leaves only me. And Henry in a few minutes.

I take a deep breath. "You really want to know?"

"Only if you want to tell me."

"It's melodramatic." I squint, following the path of a cloud in the sky.

"I can take it."

"Like soap-opera-level melodramatic."

"I love soap operas." He raises an eyebrow.

"You're not going to let this go, are you?"

"Bennet," he says, resting his arm on the top of the bench behind me, "if you don't want to tell me, I'll drop it right now and never bring it up again."

My instinct is to guard and protect the frayed nerve of the truth deep inside my chest, and that instinct has kept me from talking about it at all, but I can't hide it from Henry. Not sincere, straightforward, openhearted Henry.

I keep my eyes on the horizon. I can tell the truth if I don't have to look at him.

Breathe.

"Sam was my college boyfriend. I don't remember if I've mentioned my best friend Andy to you, but she and I met freshman year during orientation. We ended up living in the same hall, and . . . I don't know. She and I just loved each other instantly. Not like we had much in common, but we just had this soul connection right from the start. We spent all this time together, Andy and me, and one day she introduced me to her brother Sam. It was like she knew I'd love him too. In a different way . . . but . . ."

I clear my throat, rubbing at my chest.

"He played baseball, but he wasn't like the other athletes. He was quiet, but his mind went like a mile a minute. Constant thoughts, constant theories about the world." I smile. Sam still makes me smile after all this time. "We could keep ourselves entertained for hours, just the two of us in his apartment playing board games or watching *Jeopardy!* If it were up to us, we'd never leave." I flip my gaze to Henry, who's listening intently. I look away quickly. "I loved him so much. *Too* much."

Henry lets out a puff of air.

"Like, really. Too much."

"I believe you," he says, his voice soft and gentle.

"When he graduated, he moved back with his parents in Jersey, not too far from here. I was still in school, so we were doing long-distance. It wasn't ideal, but we wanted to stay together. He wanted to teach English in the city, live on the Upper West Side, and raise our kids as Yankee fans . . . but I didn't know what I wanted. I was just a kid myself. I didn't even know what *my* dreams were." My throat starts to sting. I close my eyes for a moment to center myself, willing myself to be strong. "When I say that I loved him too much, I mean that I stopped thinking about me when I was with him. It wasn't his fault or anything, but I stopped planning my future outside of him. The plan was always to graduate and move to New York together. I didn't consider anything else. So when he graduated and I was alone for the first time since we got together, I started to freak out a bit. Graduation was coming fast, and I hadn't made any decisions beyond what Sam wanted. I started to panic." I curl my toes in my shoes, knowing what I have to say next. "This is the really sad part. Buckle up."

He mimes buckling a seat belt like I did when he told me about his dad. Perfect.

"I started to apply for internships in other cities. Mostly as a test, you know? It wasn't serious. I wasn't going to get anything. But the more I did it, the more I wanted it. I couldn't tell Andy because she's Sam's sister, so I didn't tell anyone what I was doing. I just sort of did it. I figured it would be a sign from the universe. If I got an internship, I'd take it. If not, New York was where I would end up."

"You got one, didn't you?"

My eyes start to burn, but I nod and push through. "I was going to intern at a marketing agency in Chicago. It's not like I was passionate about marketing or anything, but . . . but it was mine, and I wanted it. I wanted to explore, to try new things. It feels so stupid to say."

"It's not stupid." His voice is even and low.

"I told him on the phone when I'd already accepted it. I wanted to keep trying long-distance, but he got so upset that I had sprung this on him. It got out of hand so fast, and suddenly we were fighting and saying awful things." My voice cracks. "All of a sudden this person that I wanted to spend my entire life with and I were breaking up because of a choice I made. A decision I made."

I turn to look at Henry to take in his reaction. He looks at me with an expression of sadness, but not pity.

"He, um . . ." My breath shakes. I pause, finding the words. Henry pauses too, following my lead through every word. "He got in his car. He didn't tell me he was coming. I guess he wanted to talk it through in person." I shake my head, hoping it'll help this story get easier to tell. It won't. "It was Saturday night in a college town, people were out drinking, and I guess Sam wasn't paying attention and a million things went wrong and he . . ." The words stick there, like they're caught in honey. I can't. I thought I could. My hands start to shake. They do this every time I talk about him.

"It's okay." Henry pulls me into his chest. "It's okay. You can stop."

"I want to tell you," I cry into his shirt.

"Shh." He strokes the back of my hair, rocking me gently. "You told me. It's okay."

"I couldn't look at his family. I couldn't talk to Andy about it. The guilt was eating me alive. I don't know why I did what I did. Why I pushed him away like that. I wish I didn't. Every day, I wish I didn't."

"It wasn't your fault. How could you have known? Bennet, please tell me you know it wasn't your fault."

"I've spent every day since then trying to convince myself of that, but the truth is if he never met me . . . if I didn't try to put myself first . . . he'd still be . . ." I clear my throat. Henry tightens his grip around me. "I dropped out of school after that. Andy and I canceled the trip to Europe we were planning. I bailed on my internship. And then I moved here to honor him, to live out the life he wanted. But I'm so stuck. I never explored. I never found myself. I watched everyone around me grow up and flourish, but I stayed where I was, as close to Sam as possible. Every day I'm failing him. Every day I'm letting him down."

Henry pulls me away from his chest and cups my face in his hands, wiping my tears with his thumbs. "You are not failing. You're doing a hard thing."

I shake my head. "I'm so scared all of the time. Of everything. Of *you*."

"You moved to a new city with no backup plan. Do you have any idea how brave that is?"

"It feels terrible."

He folds me back into his chest, tucking my head underneath

his chin. "Being human is terrible." He laughs, a shallow chuckle. The vibrations of his chest under my ear calm me down. "Listen." He strokes my arm. "You've become one of my favorite people very quickly, and I know that's scary to you, I'm not trying to scare you, but I need you to know that. You're not letting him down. You're not letting anyone down. It hurts me knowing how much you're carrying. I can't explain it, but I wish . . ." He taps against his sternum. "I wish I could take it from you and put it here. I wish I could make it better."

"You are." I pull myself closer to him, my cheek pressed to his shirt. "It'll never be better. But with you, with the project . . . I feel for the first time like I'm honoring that version of me. I feel . . . almost normal again."

He laughs again. "Almost?"

"Almost," I snort. "Getting there." I wipe a tear with the back of my hand. "I'm sorry I keep breaking down like this. I keep staining your shirts." I poke a splotch of mascara on the front of his chest.

I've built up this thick wall that keeps me from feeling the pain, but it's also kept me from feeling *anything*. Something inside that wall rattled loose when I met Henry, at first a slow trickle, then a stream, now a tsunami.

I don't know if I can do it, get lost in the tidal wave of life. I could drown again. I could lose myself again. But it's hard to be guarded with Henry. It's hard to be closed off when he's holding me as if he cares. Part of me wants to dive in, and part of me wants to stay safe on land.

"Looks better that way, anyway." He smiles, rubbing at the stain with his thumb.

I feel soft, safe, seen. I lift my gaze to meet his, letting go of my tight grip on him briefly.

"Hey." I smile.

"Hey." His eyes are so sincere I might kiss him or vomit.

The part of me that wants to dive wins out, and, tentatively, I dip my toe in the water.

I squeeze his shirt in my fist, clearing my throat. "Andy is getting married in L.A. in September and they gave me a plus one." He smiles down at me like he knows what's coming. "Will you go with me?"

"Absolutely. I love weddings."

Chapter Twenty-Two

What the hell did I do?

I invited my new friend whom I sometimes want to kiss to my dead ex-boyfriend's sister's wedding. Oh, and by the way, the dead ex-boyfriend's sister is also my ex–best friend whom I've basically ghosted since his death. *That's* what I did.

It was a spur-of-the-moment thing. An impulse that felt right. I didn't think, I just spoke. Henry is incredible with people, and I thought having him there would help me through it. Because I can't face that wedding alone. But now my mind is racing with thoughts of what this all means.

I panic as Sonya, Jamie, and I lie out on the roof.

Sonya's neon bikini blinds me as she rubs sunscreen on Jamie's shoulders. "So . . . do you like him?"

I pull my baseball cap down over my eyes. "I don't know."

She closes the lid on the sunscreen bottle. "Do you want him to be your boyfriend?"

I wince. "I don't know." I glance down at my chest, which is either breaking out in hives from the stress or burning. "Pass me the sunscreen."

"She's avoiding the question," Sonya chirps as she passes the bottle to me. "You *do* want him to be your boyfriend."

"Don't pressure her, Sonya," Jamie pipes in from behind her round black sunglasses. She rubs in a patch of sunscreen on her legs. "This drugstore sunscreen is so greasy. I feel like I jerked off a dolphin."

"Horrendous joke, Jamie." I do laugh, though. A little laugh.

Sonya slaps her on the shoulder. "That's the most disgusting thing I've ever heard." Her disapproval makes it even funnier.

I decide to take Jamie's side. "It's true, I feel like I fell into a vat of lube."

Jamie chortles, lying back in her chair.

"Classy." Sonya scowls, but I think, from the corner of my eye, I see her crack a smile. "I hate you both."

"No, you don't," Jamie says.

Our laughter settles as Sonya squints at both of us. "I know I said I wanted you to be friends, but I take it back. You two are getting a bit too chummy," she says.

"Don't be jealous, baby," Jamie says, grabbing Sonya's hand. "You know I'm yours."

"And Bennet is Henry's," Sonya teases. I cringe with embarrassment.

"Baby steps," Jamie says, shushing Sonya. She turns to me. "We don't have to talk boyfriend or anything. Let's start small. Do you enjoy spending time with him?"

I look forward to every second with him. I scrunch my face, willing this conversation to end. "Yes. Okay? Yes. I enjoy it very much. Please don't make a big deal out of it."

Jamie pushes on. "Okay, that's step one. Step two: What do you like about him?"

"He's kind." I lean back in my chair and close my eyes. "He's outgoing. He's sort of a nerd, but you wouldn't expect it. He's smart, he's artistic, he's funny, he doesn't make me feel like I'm a mess." I take a deep breath. I adjust my bikini bottom over my stomach. "I like his smile."

"Awwwwwwwwww!" Sonya squeals.

"Sonya, we're not making a big deal out of this, remember?" Jamie scolds.

"Sorry. You're right." She slurps her iced coffee. "Carry on."

"My favorite part about being with him . . . there's this sincerity to him. It's like it would be impossible for him to be jaded. He's just . . . he's just Henry."

"Are you attracted to him?" Jamie asks.

I sink down farther in my chair. "I mean, I tried to make out with him at your party, Sonya."

"Oh!" Sonya sits up. "I was right! Something *was* going on in that bathroom!"

"Yeah, well, not really." I frown. "He rejected me. So this might be a pointless conversation anyway."

Jamie shakes her head. "He was probably just worried you were drunk or something. You did spill your entire cocktail on him."

I squeeze my eyes shut. "He's the first person since Sam that

I've even . . . that I've . . . felt anything for. Even if it is confusing. I just can't be rejected again. I think I'd evaporate."

"You won't evaporate," Jamie says, reaching to my chair to squeeze my arm. "Tell him you like him. He likes you back. I promise."

"How do you know that?"

She clears her throat and retreats to her chair. "I just . . . I have a feeling. Based on everything you've told me."

"Okay. But say we *do* cross that line. What then?"

"Um . . . you live happily ever after?" Sonya says.

I shake my head. Happy-ever-afters and I don't work out. "What if we're just too different? He's so . . . positive. And I'm . . . not."

"Ever heard of opposites attract?" Sonya says, gesturing between herself and Jamie. "I mean, hello."

I tilt my gaze to the sky, watching a cloud roll over the sun. "I'm afraid that . . ." I close my eyes. "I worry that because he has such a positive outlook, he might not be seeing me right."

Jamie crosses her arms. "What do you mean?"

"What if he is seeing what he wants to see and not what's right in front of him? What if I mess things up, say the wrong thing? What if I'm not ready for all of . . . it?" I gesture aimlessly to the air, trying to communicate to them the strange pit I feel developing in my core.

Jamie whips her sunglasses off and sits forward. "Bennet, I mean this in the absolute kindest way possible, but you need to get over yourself."

"What?"

"It's not some inconceivable miracle that someone might like you. I like you. Sonya likes you. It's not out of this world that Henry might like you too. I know you think you're some black hole of sadness and you hate your job, but having your shit together is not a prerequisite for love."

Having your shit together is not a prerequisite for love.

Wow.

"And you clearly like him. I'm not putting pressure on you, but you invited him to a wedding across the country when you easily could've just brought Sonya or someone else. You need to listen to yourself here. You deserve love, Bennet. You deserve to be happy. Don't keep punishing yourself."

"Good lord." My jaw hangs open at the way Jamie just laid into me. "Sonya, you have the dopest girlfriend ever."

"I know." She leans over and plants a kiss on Jamie's lips.

Warmth prickles into my fingertips. "I love you guys."

They respond almost in unison, in the sweet syrupy way that couples do. "We love you too."

I sink back into my beach chair and slide my sunglasses up the bridge of my nose as I take in the view over our little slice of Harlem. I can see the roof of Yankee Stadium, the top of my bodega, and some taller buildings across the Bronx River. But I always find myself wishing I could be higher, wishing I could see more. If I saw everything, if I took in the whole view of this city, maybe it wouldn't feel so big, like it's swallowing me whole.

An idea bubbles to the surface as the sun blankets me in warmth. I know where I want to take Henry next.

Chapter Twenty-Three

Henry and I walk through Hudson Yards, weaving among tourists clamoring to get a picture of the Vessel, the honeycomb-like structure at the core of this area of Manhattan. I haven't told Henry exactly what we're doing here, mostly because I want to surprise him, and partially because if I say it out loud, that means I'll actually have to go through with it.

"I know you threatened me with Times Square," he says, sidestepping a woman taking a selfie. "But this isn't much better."

"We're playing tourists today," I say. "I'm practically a tourist here, anyway. Figured we might as well go all out."

He shrugs good-naturedly, plunging his hands into his pockets. "Are we going up in the Vessel?"

I shake my head.

"Walking the High Line?"

"No." My pulse quickens. My heart feels like it's trying to wrestle its way out of my chest.

He twists his mouth in thought. "I'm stumped."

I squint up at a tall building, one of the many skyscrapers that make up the skyline. Jutting out from the side of this particular building, almost at the top, is a triangular platform—an observation deck a hundred stories high. It's as tiny as a tortilla chip from where we're standing.

"Oh no." His face goes white as realization blooms across it. "Oh no, no, no."

I nod slow-motion. "Oh yes."

He looks grim, his ashen complexion replaced by an unsettling green. "We're going up there, aren't we?"

"Surprise!" I say, wiggling my fingers like jazz hands. "We're going to strap ourselves to the outside and climb all the way to the tippy-top like King Kong and that lady in the pretty dress."

After my rooftop conversation with Sonya and Jamie, I realized that I needed to really push myself. Really take a leap of faith. So I thought of the scariest things I could imagine: bear attacks, Henry, scaling a skyscraper, Henry, drowning, Henry. The only scary thing that I could actually, feasibly do was scale the side of a skyscraper, so I booked an appointment.

"Oh god." His breathing quickens. "Oh man." He rakes his hand through his hair once. Then twice. "We're going to *what*?"

"They harness us to the building so we don't fall, but yeah. We're climbing that baby."

"Holy shit," he says, rubbing his forehead.

"Are you scared?" I grab his free hand, prompting him to relax a little.

"Maybe," he wheezes. "Oh man." It would be a good time

to admit that I'm also scared shitless, but seeing Henry freak the hell out makes me want to be the positive one, for once.

I turn to face him, placing both of my palms on his arms, rubbing up and down to try to calm him.

"Henry," I say. "It's okay."

"Bennet, I'm afraid of heights." He rakes his fingers through his hair, keeping his head low. I didn't even imagine Henry being scared. Henry is fearless. I feel terrible that I picked something that would petrify him like this.

"You helped me through my fears, now let me return the favor," I say in the most calming voice I can muster.

"Your fear was talking to people. Mine is falling to my death from the top of a skyscraper."

"Both of those things are equally terrifying. And besides, don't you climb mountains?"

"That's different. That's nature. Mountains are meant to be like that. This . . . this is completely man-made and completely *un*natural. . . . We're not even meant to be that high in a building, you know. People just decided to keep going up and up and up. How high is too high? Oh god."

He's rambling. He's actually rambling.

I take his face in my hands, forcing him to look at me, feeling the gentle prickle of stubble on my skin. I breathe in deep through my nose. Henry follows suit, breathing in with me.

"You can do this," I say. "It's going to be the coolest thing you've ever done, and you're going to love me forever after the fact." The look on his face is that of unbearable fear and desperation. "And also I'll buy you an ice cream after."

He blinks slowly and clenches his jaw. "Rainbow sprinkles."

"Deal."

It takes some coaxing to get Henry to the actual building and up the hundred stories in the elevator, and he can't even look out the windows when we get to the check-in area. As we sit and listen to our instructor, Roscoe, give the safety demonstration, Henry's leg is bouncing up and down like a jackhammer. I put my hand on his knee to steady him.

"Has anyone ever died doing this?" he blurts.

"You'd be the first," Roscoe grunts through a mouth shrouded in facial hair. His partner, Matthew, is much scrawnier, with red hair and a freckled face. "If you slip off the side of the building," Roscoe says, holding up a thick cable, "the harness will catch you."

Henry shifts uncomfortably in his seat. "What if it snaps?"

Roscoe shrugs. "You go splat."

He was trying to be funny, but Henry turns almost green.

Roscoe notices Henry's grim mood and follows up. "It is perfectly safe. We've got a one hundred percent success rate."

Henry's knee starts jerking again. "It doesn't comfort me knowing that one mistake ruining that one hundred percent success rate would mean a one hundred percent chance of falling out of the sky and being flattened out like a pancake."

Roscoe scratches his beard. "Look at your girl. She's cool and collected. Be like her."

Your girl. A small smile creeps onto my face. I bite the inside of my cheek.

"When I did this the first time, I pissed my pants," Matthew chimes in.

"Lovely," Henry says flatly.

"But I loved it so much that I kept coming back. Now I work here. Best thing I ever did."

Henry takes a shallow, gravelly breath, like there are stones in his lungs.

"Hey." I swivel to face him. "If you don't want to do this, we won't."

He takes another shaky breath, toes still tapping on the floor. "I want to."

"I'll be right there the whole time," I say, trying to keep my tone light and fun. "I will not leave your side."

He stops jerking his knee and unclenches his jaw. I watch his face morph back into the man I know through a series of deep, steadying breaths. Finally, he smiles weakly.

"I can't promise I won't piss my pants."

We get zipped up in jumpsuits, strapped into harnesses, and buckled into helmets. We are clipped to a railing by safety cords, so that if we god forbid slip and fall, we'll dangle off the side of the building instead of plummeting to our deaths. I test the cord by pulling, hard. Henry smiles at me, as if he were thinking the same thing. He looks like he's about to pass out as Roscoe and Matthew guide us to climb up a metal staircase. We're still inside the building, but the boundary of danger and safety already feels paper-thin up here.

We climb, one by one, up the winding stairway. Henry follows behind me. Light pours onto my face as we come to a door that opens out to the side of the skyscraper, completely exposed to the world, no safety net, a thousand feet above the city.

"Here she is, folks," Roscoe says, stepping out onto a teeny platform. "Stop one on the journey to the top."

My fingers are sweating as I clutch the railing as tight as I can. My throat tightens and my breathing gets shallow, and I find it difficult to take a step forward out of the safety of the stairwell, but I think about Henry behind me, how terrified he must be, and I take a tentative step onto the metal platform.

The wind whips my face as Henry comes up next to me. I grab his hand, clinging to his trembling fingers as we look out onto the Hudson. Henry, I notice, is barely able to look at the view, so he keeps his eyes locked on me.

"Almost to the top," I say to him. He blows air out through his lips and nods as Roscoe points to another set of steep stairs, this one on the outside of the building, that will lead us to the highest platform. "We can do it," I say, squeezing Henry's hand.

The buildings below us get smaller and smaller as we climb the metal stairs—they remind me of risers at a high school football game, except way freaking higher in the air. My thighs and lungs burn as I try not to look down through the slats on each step, only up. The sun hangs low in the sky, reflecting gold off the windows of the buildings around—and below—us.

My entire body is shaking when we get to the final platform on the building, perched so high in the sky I feel dizzy.

Slowly, I turn toward the horizon and open my eyes. It takes every molecule of breath out of my lungs, being able to see everything so high up, no barrier between me and the world. I glance to Henry, whose eyes are closed as he continues to breathe steadily, calming himself.

I brush my fingers along the sleeve of his jumpsuit. "Want me to describe it to you?" I ask.

He nods without opening his eyes.

I scan the horizon, the sun gleaming on all the buildings I couldn't name if I tried. "It's gray," I say. One edge of his lip curls up into a tiny smile that flickers away as soon as it comes. "The city is . . . god, it looks like teeth, or like stalagmites or something. The buildings look close together, like they're one thing. And I suppose they kind of are, one big massive thing made up of a bunch of littler things. It looks like I could reach out my hand and smooth all the buildings over. Like if I stretched a finger out I could prick it on the top of the Empire State Building." I turn to face him, my nose stinging from the wind and from the view. "The sun is so gold, Henry. It's one of the most beautiful things I've ever seen, and it's so scary and it's so powerful and I really want to share it with you. You should look."

Slowly, he opens his eyes, but keeps them trained on me, still not daring to look at the view. I take a breath and tell him the truth. "Being up here makes me feel small, but being with you makes me feel significant."

We stare at each other, zeroed in, his green eyes glittering. There's something between us in this glance. Something electric, something that says, *You are safe with me.* He takes one last shaky breath before turning to the skyline and taking it in. I know he feels the same way I do, because his eyes start to well up.

"Holy . . . wow," he says.

"I know," I say, looping my fingers through his.

Roscoe and Matthew explain that we can lean over the ledge if we want, letting our harnesses hold our lives more than a thousand feet in the air. Henry is smiling now, and I know he wants to do it too.

We step up to the ledge, our toes right at the line where the building meets air, and we slowly lean over the city, putting all our weight in the tiny piece of rope holding us up. I don't know if the air is thinner up here or if I'm just losing my mind, but I feel drunk and loopy and so *light*.

Tears begin to flow down my cheeks and I start to laugh. I open my arms wide, like wings, and I scream at the top of my lungs, feeling true freedom for the first time in such a long time.

I'm hanging over the city, bearing my heart to her, and for once, I'm not afraid.

I wipe my face, unable to stop laughing or shaking. I imagine a tear falling off my nose and evaporating before hitting the street below.

Henry lets out a whoop beside me, and when I look at him, he's downright goofy with glee—face full and bright and so painfully gorgeous, I no longer feel like looking at the view. We slowly reel ourselves in and retreat back onto the safety of the platform.

Henry looks at me, his eyes as wide as saucers, his cheeks pink from the wind. He closes the distance between us, enveloping me in his arms, clutching me as if I'm the solid ground and safety he craves.

"Oh my god." His fingers dig into my back.

I cling to his neck, pulling him closer. "I'm so proud of you," I say.

His arms tighten around my waist. "I never would've done this without you. My whole life, I never would've." We breathe deeply against each other, letting our hearts race. Maybe it's the adrenaline, maybe it's the sunset, but I'm not afraid of this. Not right now. He loosens his grip on me and I lay my head against his racing heart. "Thank you for making me do this," he says, still holding me against him.

Normally one of us would pull away. One of us would remind the other that we're just friends. One of us would say this is too much. But neither of us do. I let him hold me, drenched in the golden summer sun at the very top of the world, for once not thinking of the consequences of that action. I let it be.

Chapter Twenty-Four

The next few weeks fly by like a trash-scented New York City dream. Henry and I have started to meet up multiple times a week for a new adventure. One day, I helped him with an engagement shoot in a sculpture park in Astoria. The next, we took a sommelier class in Little Italy. Henry described a particular Sangiovese as tasting like "the inside of a leather jacket after being sat on by a sweaty mall Santa," and now I can't help but chuckle whenever I have a glass of red wine. We went to the Rockaways and had cheap hamburgers and slushies on the beach. We walked the Bronx Botanical Garden at night, the dark sky cocooning us inside a warm greenhouse with the most beautiful orchids I'd ever seen. We went to a speakeasy in the back of an art gallery after spending the day in the Museum of Natural History gaping at dinosaur bones.

When we realized we hadn't been to Staten Island yet, we took the ferry across the Hudson and crowded against the railing to see the Statue of Liberty. Jokes were made about how we truly were acting like tourists, but what's wrong with that? The funny thing is that the more I act like a tourist, the less I feel like one.

We saw a one-woman play that was so terrible it made us both pee our pants with laughter afterward, at the bodega across the street from the theater. One week we walked across the Brooklyn Bridge and my sandals rubbed a blister in my heel the size of a quarter. Henry carried me piggyback the rest of the way and then took me to a discount shoe store to buy the most ridiculous Hello Kitty sneakers I've ever seen.

Every day I notice a new feature of Henry I like. A mole on his neck, the dip in his cupid's bow, the way his glasses lie slightly crooked across his face, the tiny specks of yellow in his green eyes, the way his walnut-brown hair appears reddish in the sun, the way he laughs so loud, unafraid of causing a scene. I admire the way his voice catches when he talks about his dad, the way he cleans his glasses with the bottom of his shirt, leaving them even more smudged than before. I watch him when he moves, his broad shoulders and long limbs seeming to take up exactly the right amount of space in every room. I start to notice myself touching him on the arm, sitting an inch closer to him than I would have even a month ago. I notice myself wanting more contact, more laughs, more, more, more.

I suspect we both know I'm not looking for my passion anymore, but we keep the Passion Project title as a guise to protect whatever is happening between us. Because I told him I only want to be friends. At the time it was true, but now everything in my body is screaming at me to try. Just try.

Having your shit together is not a prerequisite for love.

That sentence spins through my brain at the bodega, at the grocery store, at the library. It ricochets through my bones when I meet Sonya and Jamie at happy hour, and when I visit Sonya at Harper & Jane. It swims in my veins when I hear from Sal or Marjorie, or when I call my mom to tell her about something we did that week, or when Henry shows me the edits on his latest shoot. I refuse to believe I'm not enough. I won't do it anymore.

Today we take a lazy walk through the Cloisters, taking our time silently studying fifteenth-century art, gaping at stained glass, and exploring the arched walkways and impeccable architecture. Like the library, the Cloisters makes me feel like I'm suspended between yesterday and today, standing next to historical artifacts with an iPhone in my pocket, walking through floors built a hundred years ago in a pair of sneakers and denim shorts that would cause the architects to spit their tea out if they saw. I imagine myself as the thing being studied, rather than the art. *Look, a twenty-five-year-old woman, see how she stands so close to that brown-haired man with a camera around his neck. What do you think she's thinking?*

When we finish our walk through the museum, we stroll through Fort Tryon Park. It's the perfect backdrop for Henry to take free portraits of people going about their daily lives, enjoying the gardens and the beautiful weather. I hang back to watch him snap pictures, happy to take him in. Watching him when he's calm, quiet, focused, is one of my favorite lenses to see him through.

We find a stone bench with a bit of shade and settle in, shoulder to shoulder. Henry skims through the photos on his camera, sometimes smiling a bit to himself at ones he particularly likes.

"Hey." He clicks his camera off and puts it in his bag.

"Yeah?"

"I, um . . . I've been thinking." He gazes out over the garden, not looking at me.

"Yeah?"

"I know we agreed to be friends, but lately it feels like . . ." He glances down at me and then quickly looks away. He's nervous. "It feels different. I don't know."

I expect panic to rise in my stomach, but it doesn't. I'm cool, calm. He continues. "I could be reading it wrong, but if something's changed . . ." He clears his throat. "If something's changed . . . do you want to go on a date with me?"

I pull away slightly, just so I can get a better look at him. Is this real? He looks serious, but he was the one who rejected me. I think back to the bathroom at Sonya's party, to the bed at Marjorie's place.

I never got clarification as to what he meant when he said he knew what he wanted, but maybe Jamie was right. Maybe in the bathroom, he just wanted to be sure I was ready, that I knew what I was doing. Maybe now he can sense that I'm inching closer and closer.

He swallows. "I mean . . . let's redo our first date. Let me take you out for real."

I pick at the edges of my frayed denim shorts as I consider.

This is a chance to restart. To not be so scared. To actually go for it. Of course, it's also a chance to make a fool of myself in a hundred new and even more humiliating ways.

It's a chance to get heartbroken again.

What if I'm not ready?

He taps his knee lightly. "You don't have to answer now. Let's just say I'll be at Rosencrantz & Guildenstern on Friday at five thirty."

I look out over the gardens, pink roses and gladiolas swaying in the breeze. Maybe this thing between us is already different, already changed, despite my efforts to keep it in control. Maybe the train has left the station and I either have to grab on or let it leave me on the platform. Maybe if I can admit that I want something bigger and better than just friendship . . . maybe I deserve it.

I don't want to be left at the station. I swallow, closing my eyes to the warmth of the sun and leaning my head on his shoulder. "I'll be there."

Every time I check my phone, the clock hasn't advanced. Not even a minute. I tap my foot under my desk and bite my lip. Now it says four fifty-six. Four more minutes and I'm off. And then . . . Henry.

I woke up at six this morning, unable to sleep. I tore my closet apart looking for something to wear, which was silly, since he's seen me in all my clothes already. But I needed something special. *First-date* special. In desperation, I knocked on Sonya's door. She was more than happy to help. Actually, she was euphoric. She blasted ABBA, she swiped makeup across my lids, she dressed me head to toe. I ended up with a gorgeous deep blue dress that Sonya wore on her first date with Jamie.

Now I'm shivering at a brand-new Carlyle assignment as time ticks by, waiting until I can be released for my date. Carlyle needed someone to fill in at this stuffy corporate event space, and though I've been assigned to the only library since Sal left, they insisted they needed me to work the front desk.

Why am I nervous? This is what Henry and I do. We hang out. Nothing is different. But also, everything is different. I fight the urge to check my bag to make sure Sonya's blue dress is in there where I left it and it hasn't decided to spontaneously grow wings and fly away.

I've straightened up everything at the desk three times, I've checked that the conference rooms are empty twice, and I've locked the keys in the safe box so no one can get in overnight. I have to leave right at five to make it to the restaurant, and my phone is almost dead. Would anyone mind if I slipped out early?

I haul my bag over my shoulder and make a beeline for the door.

"Bennet," a voice calls from one of the offices. "Going somewhere?"

I whip around to see Anna, clutching a Carlyle Staffing Solutions clipboard to her hip. Memories of her firing me from NYAC flash through my eyes.

"Hi, Anna," I say, and my stomach drops. This must have something to do with why they suddenly needed me to switch locations today. "My shift just ended. What do you need?"

She twists her mouth into a frown. "Probationary checkup."

Fuck.

I glance down at my phone. Four fifty-nine. Of course, now time is moving quickly.

"Can we do this another time?"

Anna tuts. "These are always a surprise, Bennet. We can't make an exception for you."

Text Henry. Tell him you're running late. He'll understand. I open my messages and start to type.

Caught up at work. Wait for m— |

But as my thumb hovers over the key, the screen turns black. *No.* My spit goes sour. *No, god, no.*

"Bennet?" Anna clicks her pen.

I hold the power button on my phone hoping it'll come to life, but it's dead. "Oh god, not now," I mumble under my breath, pleading. I look up at her, desperate. "Can I please borrow your phone?"

"Miss Taylor," Anna says in a powerful, clipped voice. "I need to conduct this check-in now or you won't be able to work any shifts with Carlyle."

Run. Just go. Who cares? Just do it, Bennet. Go.

But . . . I can't. If I don't have this job, I won't eat. I'll *have* to leave the city.

"Of course," I say. "I apologize."

I follow her into a small office, where she asks me a series of questions about my shifts and my coworkers. Any incidents? Nope. Any difficult guests? Nope. Any life-changing dates you've potentially missed due to work? Yes. Then she reads a lengthy report by the library manager, which, thankfully, is positive.

There's no clock in this room, otherwise I'd be studying it, watching every second tick by. Every second Henry sits alone at that bar is pure torture. A cruel repeat of our first date. I wish I could telepathically tell him, *I'm coming. I'll be there.*

Finally, Anna clicks her pen and smiles. "Everything looks great. Good work."

"Thank you," I exhale as I dash to the door, turning back to ask, "What time is it?"

She glances at the watch on her wrist. "Five thirty-seven."

I sprint to the train station, tapping my phone against the paypad on the gate only for the turnstile to slam into my gut, unmoving. Right. My phone is dead. I can't pay for the train this way.

Come on.

I dash to the kiosk and insert my debit card. The machine spits it back out.

A sign scribbled on top of the machine says CASH ONLY.

The next machine takes my debit and, after what feels like an hour, delivers a new MetroCard. I swipe through the gate and run down the stairs in enough time to see the train race away, carrying with it the last shred of hope I had of making it to the bar before Henry throws in the towel. *No. Don't give up.* I haul ass back up the stairs to the busy street, but I can't call an Uber because my phone is dead. I see yellow cabs zoom by in the intersection, not stopping long enough for me to call one.

God, this is so stupid. I've never called a cab before, and I don't really even know how. The train is my only option. I scurry back down to the subway, pay again, and race to the platform praying that a train is coming. It's torture waiting here, and my dreams of changing into the pretty blue dress or even making it to dinner are dwindling away bit by bit. I've never felt time move slower. Never in my life. By the time a train comes, it's six fifteen, and I'm forty-five minutes late already. I catapult my body onto the train and hope Henry hasn't given up on me.

Sonya's blue dress is in a wad in my bag. Her makeup job is smeared. I don't care.

Just get there.

The train turtles along the whole way down to Delancey Street. I zoom out of the subway station, practically plowing people down on the way. My lungs hurt and my forehead is dripping wet.

I yank open the door at Rosencrantz & Guildenstern and make a beeline to the bar.

No Henry.

I fumble through the dining room, checking every table for him. He's not here. He's nowhere.

I head across the street toward L'italiano. I'm sure that's where he'll be. Just like last time.

I grasp the door handle and take a deep breath. But when I see who's sitting at the bar, I'm confused. It isn't Henry. In fact, it's one of the last people I expected.

"Jamie?"

When she sees me, she jumps to her feet. "Bennet! Where have you been? I've been calling you."

"Caught up at work. My phone died. Is Henry here?"

I look around the dining room, checking every table.

"No. Sarah said he came by after you didn't show. But he's gone."

"Oh! Sarah!" I walk back toward the bar and see her polishing glasses. "Do you have Henry's number in your phone?"

She frowns as she scrubs the rim of a glass. "Why? So you can ghost him again?"

"I didn't mean to," I say. "I got caught up at work and the train was slow."

"Why don't you ask Jamie? Since she's the one that asked him to go out with you in the first place," she says.

Jamie looks at Sarah with daggers in her eyes.

I shake my head. "Sonya found him on a dating app. Jamie didn't have anything to do with it."

"You really think it's a coincidence that Jamie happened to work at the same restaurant as the guy her girlfriend set you up with?" Sarah cocks her head.

"Sarah, stop," Jamie interjects.

"No." Sarah sets her polishing cloth on the bar. "A half hour ago, someone I really care about came into this restaurant after being ghosted by her for the second time, and he was miserable. I don't like to see my friends miserable. Especially Henry, who's, like, always happy."

I feel the floor shift under my feet. Henry was miserable. Jamie somehow set us up. I'm so confused.

"Jamie, what is going on?" When I look at her, she's dodging my eye.

She takes a deep breath and finally looks at me after a long moment. "Don't be mad," she says. "But I might have lied about how well I know Henry. We worked together before he went back to Denver. Sonya wanted to find some way to get you to stay in New York. When she thought about sending you on a date . . . I . . . I reached out to him."

"You reached out and . . . and what?"

"I asked him to go on a date with you," she says, cringing. "Cheer you up."

"What?"

"Yep," Sarah says. "He owed her a favor for all the shifts she covered when he was in Denver."

"Oh my god." I step back, away from Jamie. "It was a pity date?"

"No—" Jamie insists. "It was never a pity date. But, yes . . . he knew."

"What did you tell him? Did he know about . . ." My throat tightens. "Did he know about Sam?"

Jamie shakes her head quickly. "All I told him was that you were in a tough spot, and I wanted you to have some fun."

"How did you even match us together on the app? I saw his profile. He liked my photo."

Jamie swallows, uncomfortable. "I had him make a profile, and then I swiped on his phone until I found you. It didn't take too long once we narrowed the search range and the preferences."

My mind flashes to the moment Sonya saw Henry's like on my photo. She talked a mile a minute about how gorgeous he was—how pretty his green eyes were. The realization that it was Jamie on the other end is humiliating.

"Fantastic. This is . . . this is really great. It feels great to know that I was such a sad, pathetic bummer of a person that you had to ask someone to go on a date with me and pretend to like me and take me on adventures so I wouldn't mope around the apartment." I'm suddenly more embarrassed than I have been in my entire life. "Did you tell him that? That I'm a depressed mess and need to be saved from myself?"

"No. It was all very . . . informal," Jamie says, nervously stepping toward me. I jerk away, prompting her to stop. To not touch me. "It wasn't a conspiracy. He was just trying to help."

This changes everything. Everything about the past few months. Every time I asked why he was hanging out with me, he lied. Every time I asked what was in it for him, he lied. What else has he lied about? Henry didn't find me on an app and choose to swipe right. He was asked to. As a favor. I doubt he would have even wanted to go on a date with me in the first place if Jamie hadn't convinced him to do it. What must he have thought of me, that first night in the bathroom? *Wow, everything Jamie said was right. This girl* is *a disaster.* How bad must he have felt to insist on the Passion Project? Was I that obviously desperate?

I feel a bit of bile rise up from my stomach.

"That is so fucked up," I say as I step backward, inching toward the door.

"If you're mad at anyone, be mad at me," Jamie says. "Sonya told you the truth up front about why she was setting you up, and Henry was just being a good guy. He's a really good guy, Bennet. And he likes you so much. And you seem happy together. I've never seen you so happy. And Sonya says the same thing. She says she hasn't seen you smile like this since before Sam."

"I can't . . ." I say as I take another step backward, my fingertips buzzing. "I can't even look at you."

I stumble through the door to the street. It all makes sense. Henry pushing me away when I tried to make a move. Henry constantly saying that we should stay just friends, insisting that *I'm* not ready. That *I'm* confused. He was doing Jamie a favor.

But then why would he even ask me out a second time? Just a cruel extension of this whole fucked-up favor? I imagine him telling Jamie that I'm still depressed and maybe if we go on another date I'll finally turn the corner. Suggesting that if we take it to the next level, I'll finally be happier. Or . . . oh god. Jamie told him about our talk on the roof. He asked me out because he knows everything I said about him. That I started to have *feelings* for him.

I felt hope for the first time in years. I liked myself for the first time in years. And it's all fake? I wasn't wanted. I wasn't considered. I wasn't desired. I was a favor.

I rush to the subway as fast as I can, hoping I can outrun this feeling. I think I hear someone call after me, but I don't stop. I don't stop until I get home.

Chapter Twenty-Five

Sonya strokes my hair as I lie across her lap.

After what Jamie told me last night, I should be mad at Sonya. I should slam my door on her and never talk to her again. But once I saw her standing in her bedroom doorway when I got home, I couldn't be angry. I couldn't shut myself off from her.

I needed my friend.

She apologized over and over again for her part, but I'm not mad at her. I'm only mad at Henry. And myself. And a little bit at Jamie.

Sonya was trying to help. Henry was a stranger who agreed to fool a poor grieving mess of a girl.

"I know you don't want to hear this," Sonya says as she squeezes my shoulder. "But you have to talk to him."

"He lied to me," I say.

"He might have a good reason."

I cover my eyes with my hands. "I feel so stupid." Stupid for thinking I was anything more to him than a charity project. Stupid for every time I felt something for him, and stupid for how guilty it made me feel.

"You're not stupid," Sonya says. "You're just mad."

I grind my palms into my eye sockets to keep from crying. I'm more than mad. Much more than mad.

"Do you want to do something today?" Sonya goes back to stroking my hair. "Get your mind off it? I asked Jamie to stay away. Give you some space. So I'm all yours."

I shake my head and roll from my side to my back, eyes trained on the ceiling. "No."

"Want to sit around and do nothing?"

"No."

"Well, those are the only two options," she says.

I sit up and turn to face her. "Go be with Jamie. I'm not ready to talk to her yet, but I still don't want her to feel like she's a bad person."

She bites her lip. "You sure?"

"Yeah," I say. "It's fine. Go be with your girl. I need to be alone."

"Okay," she says, standing up and adjusting her shorts. "But you're both my girls. Just so you know."

"Go be with the girl you kiss," I say. "Is that more specific?"

She grabs her keys off the coffee table. "Yes. And for the record, I'm only going to see Jamie because she feels terrible about all this, and I know how she gets. I'm worried."

"You don't have to explain. Go. I'm fine."

She leans down to give me a hug, holding me tight.

"Call me if you need me," she says as she heads out the

door. When it shuts behind her, it dawns on me that I'm alone for the first Saturday in months. Without Henry. I open my phone to his contact, swallow a lump in my throat, and hit block. For real this time.

I'm so mad at him I could hit something. The sadness I felt last night has transformed into something rougher, something aggressive. I'm not sad. I'm not depressed. I'm pissed.

I remember all those nights in college at the batting cage. Andy encouraging me to swing harder. Sam trying to help me with proper form, but I didn't care about that. I just wanted to get it out.

I jerk off the couch, marching myself to the subway station toward the second-best thing to a batting cage I can think of.

The Devil's Rage Room is exactly what it sounds like: a place in Hell's Kitchen where you can pay to whack shit around and make a mess.

The guy at the desk takes my card for an hour alone in the room and leads me toward the back. He shoves a bat and some goggles into my hands and plops a helmet on my head.

When the door to the rage room closes behind me and I'm alone, I almost don't know what to do. I feel the bat in my hands and grip it tighter.

Tentatively, I set an empty beer bottle on the table in front of me, snap the goggles over my eyes, and think of how Sam taught me to swing. I bring the bat to my shoulder, take a breath, and *smack*.

I hit the bottle square in the center. It flies off the table, hits the wall, and shatters into a million pieces.

I take my bat to the front of an old TV, cleaving a line down the middle of the screen. Again and again I hit it, until I'm losing my breath. I smack a lawn flamingo, knocking its head clean off. I smash my bat on the table, sending bits of plaster and wood flying. I whack a glass vase, and another one, and another one, before moving on to an old toaster. With every hit I feel adrenaline spike through the nerves in my body, and I let out a guttural scream as I unleash myself.

When I'm done, I stand in the middle of the room and survey my wreckage. I've done a pretty good job, in my opinion—every square inch is covered in debris, and I have a body that feels siphoned of my anger. Exhausted, I surrender my weapon. It hits the floor with a metallic clink.

"God, that felt good," I whisper to myself. My body is shaking all over. My heart pounds against my ribs as I catch my breath.

I feel dizzy as I pour out onto the street. I realize that half my anger was directed at Henry, and the other half at myself for falling for it. For being so naive. I know deep down that I'm not meant to fall in love again, so why did I buy into it anyway?

Another thing this excursion has taught me is that I don't need Henry to do the Passion Project anymore. I can do it all on my own.

I hoist my bag of groceries higher on my shoulder as I hike the five floors to the apartment. A bead of sweat trickles down my sternum. It's so hot today, I feel like I'm in a pot of ramen noodles. I could barely put clothes on this morning, just an airy black spaghetti-strap dress and a claw clip for my hair. Still, it feels like too much.

This week, I've been operating on cruise control. Eat, sleep, go to work, try not to think about Henry, repeat. This is my new normal.

I turn the key in the door and open it to Sonya and Jamie standing in the living room. I also haven't spoken to Jamie since our fight a week ago.

"Hi," she says, dipping her head low as I enter.

She has red eyes and clumpy eyelashes. I set my grocery bag on the floor and kick off my sandals. "Hi," I say.

"I'm so sorry," she says. "I shouldn't have lied to you."

She looks terrible, like she's been crying all week. "You were just trying to help," I say.

"I just . . ." She takes a moment to regroup, glancing at Sonya for support. "I just know what it's like, you know? The sadness. And, loving Sonya . . . it made me feel less hopeless. I wanted that for you too. It was naive and stupid."

I shake my head. "I'm not mad at you anymore, Jamie," I say. "I understand why you did it."

"Still . . ." Jamie looks down at her feet. "It was so wrong."

Sonya takes both of us by the hands. "We shouldn't have meddled in your life," she says. "All I really wanted was for you to stay in New York. You never gave it enough of a chance. And, I don't know . . . I thought if there was a guy here maybe you'd try to love it."

"It's okay." I squeeze her hand. "Who else gets to say they have friends who'd go through all that just to make them feel better? I'm pretty lucky."

"We love you," Jamie says. "Enough to meddle from time to time."

"I know," I say, taking Jamie's hand so we're in a circle. "I love you both too."

Sonya throws her arms around us, collecting us in a group hug. I laugh as Jamie sniffles. "I'm still so mad at Henry," I say, a quiet confession. "I can't get past it."

Neither of them say anything in response, so I just let them hug me until it's too hot to bear the physical contact. I pull out of the hug and fan myself with my hand. "God, it's hot in here," I say. "No more hugs until we get central air."

"In your dreams," Sonya says as she picks up the grocery bag. "About the hugs and the central air."

Someone buzzes to enter the building. Sonya hops to press the button to let them in. "I ordered Sweetgreen," she says. "How about we have lunch on the roof? Enjoy the weather outside."

"Now?" I ask.

"Yeah," she says, plucking a head of lettuce from my bag. "Jamie will unpack your groceries and bring up the salads. Right?"

"Sure." Jamie shrugs as she grabs the lettuce from Sonya and puts it in the fridge.

"Let's go." Sonya tugs me toward the door, where I barely have time to slip my shoes back on before we're out in the hallway.

She leads me up the staircase, pulling me behind her. "What is going on?" I ask.

When we get to the top of the stairwell and face the door to the roof, she stops and drops my hand. "Please forgive me for this, but I had to meddle one more time."

She pushes the door open, and standing there in the middle of our rooftop garden is Henry.

Lightning shoots through my bones.

"No." I take a sharp turn and head back toward the stairwell, but she's already closing the door on me.

And now I'm alone on the roof with Henry.

We stare at each other, the sun beating down on us both. His lips are slightly parted, and his eyes are sad. The wind ripples through his messy hair and presses his clothes to his body. I hate looking at him. I hate that it still does something to me.

"Bennet . . ." He takes a step toward me.

I step back. "No."

He stops. "Let me explain," he says.

I shake my head, clenching my jaw. "No."

"Please," he pleads.

"You lied to me," I say. "I asked you a hundred times why you were helping me, and you lied to me every time."

"No." He twists his mouth into a frown. "I lied to you the first time. Everything I told you since the night we met has been the truth." He stops in front of me. He looks as if he wants to reach out, but wouldn't dare.

"Truth built on a foundation of lies is still a lie," I say, brushing past him toward the garden. "I can't believe I was never anything to you but a pity date. An arrangement."

"That is not true. It wasn't some devious *arrangement*," he says, exasperated.

"Maybe it was a social experiment. To see if you could manipulate a sad girl into doing whatever you wanted. I was just another story you wanted to collect."

"It wasn't like that!" He takes a microscopic step toward me. "I swear. I didn't tell you because I knew it would hurt you, and it doesn't reflect how I feel about you. It wasn't like that."

"Well, then tell me what it *was* like."

He looks away, scrunching his face in the sunlight.

"The truth," I say, stepping close to him. He swallows, still dodging eye contact. "If you just felt bad for me the entire time, Henry, I want to know."

"The truth." The sides of his jaw flex and he finally looks me in the eye. "Jamie asked me to go out with you, yes. That much is true. And maybe, at first, I agreed because Jamie is cool and I'm always happy to help a friend." I shift uncomfortably, waiting for the other shoe to drop. "But all of the reasons I gave for initiating the Passion Project were true. I was lonely, and I was treading water trying to keep busy so I wouldn't go under." He knits his brows together and shakes his head. "The night we met, the first night, when Jamie set us up, I was pretty nervous, actually. All I knew about you was that you were Jamie's girlfriend's roommate and you needed cheering up. I know why she asked me specifically. Because I never let people see me upset and I'm outgoing, or whatever. But I was worried I couldn't actually do what she was asking because of everything I had going on in my own life. But when you came back to get your wallet . . . when we actually met . . . I wasn't nervous. You made me laugh. You threw me off balance. And, yeah, maybe I saw an opportunity to keep my promise to Jamie, but, Bennet, you have to believe me. It got real, real fast."

He clears his throat and lets out a sharp breath. "You know what? Fuck it. Cards on the table." He steps toward me, a new intensity painting his face. He's so close I feel the heat off his body. "It has been absolutely addicting getting to know you. And when I'm with you, I'm not worrying about my family or anything. I'm present. You're funny, and weird, and you're so beautiful that sometimes I want to smack myself for ever using the word *friend* in relation to you. I have wanted you for longer than you think, and I couldn't risk losing you by telling you about what Jamie asked me to do."

"You rejected me in the bathroom," I say, my voice wavering.

"I thought you weren't ready for anything to happen," he says. "You were still guarded. Still wrestling with yourself. I didn't want to be a mistake. I didn't want you to regret anything. I wanted to do things right with you. If I was going to kiss you, Bennet, it wasn't going to be half-drunk, half-confused in a nautical bathroom. I wanted you to be fully sure that it's what you wanted."

I feel my heart in my throat. "Why should I believe you?" I ask.

"You should believe me because it took everything in my power not to kiss you, like, a thousand times since meeting you. You should believe me because when Jamie told me you might have real feelings for me, I did an actual happy dance. Like, a real, embarrassing happy dance. And it still took me weeks to work up the courage to ask you out again. You should believe me because I could've stopped hanging out with you at any moment this summer. If I didn't care about you, I could've fucked off into oblivion after that first weekend, but I've found an excuse to spend my entire summer with you. Jamie didn't ask me to do *that*. No one did. I made that choice myself because

I wanted to be near you. I wanted to be around you all the time. I still do."

I swallow. It's still so complicated. "Do you ever think that maybe . . ." I clear my throat. "That maybe you should like someone who's a little easier? Less messed-up?"

"No." He shakes his head. "Not for a second."

My heart is pounding out of my chest. I'm afraid he can feel it. I'm afraid everyone in New York can feel it.

"You have to believe me," he whispers. "There is nothing I want more than this." His thumb traces my jaw, inching toward my mouth.

He hesitates, freezing before he grazes my bottom lip.

"But it matters what *you* want, Bennet. If you're not ready, or if you just want to call it quits, I'll understand. If you say you just want to be friends, I'll never mention this again. But you can't flirt with me and touch me like you want me and then pull away like you're not sure. We can't do that anymore. It's too hard for me. I don't want to keep this hope inside me if nothing is there. You just have to tell me, Bennet." He brings his hand to my forehead, brushing a strand of hair out of my face and then resting his palm on my cheek. "What do you want?"

The backs of my hands brush against the fabric of his pants. My legs are like noodles and my body is completely out of control. *Say it. Spit it out: I want you. I believe you.*

His hand moves from my neck to my shoulder; his thumb presses into my collarbone. "It's okay, either way."

Every instinct in my body is telling me to reach for him, to grip him with both hands and not let go, so I step in to him, wrapping an arm around his torso, pulling him flush to my body. We're nose to nose again like we were in that horrible bathroom.

"I want to be more than friends," I whisper.

He presses his forehead to mine, and my nose brushes against his cheek. If I move one millimeter toward him, our lips will touch. I know he's not going to do it. It has to be me.

All I have to do is move one millimeter, and close the gap.

I tip my chin up to him, feeling his lips brush against mine, so light it's almost a tickle. His hands slide down my neck and arms, gripping me tightly. He smiles against my mouth. "Yeah?"

I nod, unable to stop the grin from spreading across my lips. "Yeah."

He kisses me. A real kiss, the kind that makes my skin prickle, slow at first but with the momentum of a speeding train. He slips his tongue between my lips and I hook my arms around his neck. We've been holding off on this for so long that now that it's set in motion, I don't think I can stop it.

He tastes like sugar and smells like spearmint, a spicy sweet combination that aches. His lips guide my mouth open as he draws his hands up my body, brushing past my chest to my hair. His tongue gently presses against mine, not too much, not too little.

"Can I kiss you here?" he whispers as his mouth glides down my neck. My head falls to the side for him.

I feel frenzied—lightheaded and hungry. All my defenses down in an instant. "You can kiss me anywhere," I say, somewhere between a laugh and a groan.

So he does. His lips skate across my eyelashes, my cheekbone, my chin, my mouth. My mantra come to life in front of my eyes as he touches me.

My cheeks are real. My chin is real. My lips are real. I am real. I reach for his face, his neck, his skin rough under my fingers. I let my hands trace his body down to his torso, relishing in every muscle, every contour, until my thumbs slip through his belt loops. *Henry is real.*

He wraps his arm around my waist, pulling me even closer. It's not enough. How could anything be enough when I'm kissing Henry? His hands slide down my body, taking their time on the way as if he's savoring every inch of me. He glides his touch all the way down to my thigh, where he guides my leg around his hip. I throw my arms around his neck, clinging to him, needing his lips. Our bodies move together, breathe together until I trip on one of the beach chairs on the turf.

"Shit." I start to fall backward. Henry hugs my body against his and holds my head to his chest as we fall together. He softens the blow with one arm, protecting my head from hitting the hard surface with the other.

And now he's on top of me.

I brush his hair off his forehead as he looks down at me. "You good?" he asks, surveying my body for bumps and scratches.

"Henry," I say, cupping his face in my hands. "I'm so good."

I flip us so I'm on top, my legs spread across his hips, straddling his lap, and I pin him down by the shoulders.

"You sure you're good?" He laughs, his hands resting on my thighs.

"Yeah, why?"

"We're in public," he says, craning his neck toward the door to the roof.

"It's a private roof," I say, pressing my lips to his neck. "And I don't really care who sees." Because I want more.

He grabs both sides of my face, kissing me deep and hard. "I can't believe I'm kissing you," he groans.

All the times I stopped myself from touching him are rushing through me, and I'm releasing them all right now.

I rock my hips back and forth against his. "Fuck, Bennet," he growls.

I grab handfuls of his hair as he cups my hips and ass, his fingers pressing into my soft flesh. A strap from my dress falls off my shoulder and Henry presses his lips to the spot where it used to be. I reach down for the bottom of his shirt and pull it up over his head, finally feeling the warmth of his skin on mine. I let my dress fall under my chest.

He traces the outer ridge of my nipple. "Beautiful."

He kisses between my breasts, gentle and tender. I moan, feeling him move and grow beneath me.

"This is my favorite Saturday," he says.

"You're just saying that because I'm half-naked." I kiss his chin.

"No." He hugs my body close to his and flips me onto my back. "I'm not." He lowers his body on top of me. I squeeze my legs around his hips and he groans. His fingers trickle down, and he gently caresses my inner thigh.

"This okay?" he asks as he inches his fingers between my legs.

"Absolutely." I fall open for him, knees spreading.

He slips a finger beneath my underwear, stroking up and down. He dances around me, until he finds a spot that makes my body go rigid. "There?"

I nod, concentrating. "There."

He grins as he presses into me, stroking that spot. I maintain focus on the feeling, the pleasure. I let out a microscopic groan as he edges me closer and closer.

I arch my back as he continues his blessed ritual between my legs. I don't want to tip over the edge just yet. It's too soon. "Henry," I gasp. "Do you have a condom?"

He reaches into his back pocket and pulls out a brown leather wallet. *Faster, faster, faster.* I want his weight back on me as soon as possible. He fishes for a moment before he pulls out a silver-wrapped condom and hands it to me. I inspect it.

"This expired last year."

The excitement drains from his face. "Do you have one?"

"Yeah, the depressed girl and her lesbian roommate definitely have condoms lying around everywhere."

"Shit." He lays my skirt back down over my hips.

"Shit, indeed." I stretch out on my back. Henry rolls off and settles beside me.

"Of all the ways I imagined this happening," he says, "*that* was definitely a surprise."

"How'd you imagine it happening?"

He laughs, inching closer to me and brushing his hand against mine. "In most of my fantasies we weren't on a roof."

"Most?" I nudge him with an elbow.

"Well, there was one where I kissed you on top of that skyscraper."

My heart melts like ice cream doused in hot fudge. I turn to face him. He's already looking at me.

"I'm sorry I missed our date." I tap his lower lip with my fingers. "Both of them."

He guides my leg over his hip, tangling our feet and legs together. He kisses me long and slow before he speaks. "I'd wait for you at that bar a million times if it meant I got to be here with you."

I place a palm on his cheek. *You're safe with me.* That's all I see in his eyes when he looks at me. That's all I feel in his lips when he kisses me. *You're safe with me.*

He blinks, and I can feel his eyelashes glide against mine. "Want to go to my place?"

Chapter Twenty-Six

We try to keep it PG on the subway but I can't stop touching him. I pull him into a corner seat and drag my lips up his neck. He squeezes my knee and gives in to me, crashing his mouth against mine, pulling my hip closer to his. This kiss is dizzying and deep and like a black hole, sucking me in. I forget we're on a subway, I forget where we're going, I forget my freaking name. After a moment, he pulls away, his lips pink and hair messy, and buries his nose in my neck. "If we don't stop this right now," he whispers, teeth scraping behind my ear, "I might come before we even get to my place."

I ride with my hands in my lap for the rest of the trip to Inwood.

When we get inside his apartment and shut the door behind us, it's like the frenetic energy settles between us. It shifts into a moment of electrified, focused silence as we stare at each other. He presses me against the door and kisses me softly, taking my bottom lip between his teeth. His hip bones move and grind against mine. I grab fistfuls of his shirt, pulling him closer and closer.

"Is this how you treat other girls?"

He gently nips the side of my neck, brushes his other hand across my chest. "Is this you trying to get me to admit there are no other girls?" He scoops me up, jolting me, making me feel wanted, needed. I wrap myself around him, letting him carry me to his desk. He sets me down gently, his body between my legs. "Because there are definitely no other girls. Not since I laid my eyes on you."

I bite my lip and raise an eyebrow at him as he studies me.

"What?" He smiles. "What's that look for?"

I reach my hand low, skimming my fingers across his hip, just above the band of his pants. With careful concentrated focus, I tug it up past his stomach, rib cage birthmark, chest. . . .

He raises his arms in the air, helping me undress him.

I press my fingers into his tattoo, pleasantly feeling the hardness of his muscles beneath the ink. I kiss him there, up and down the jagged peaks and valleys, then I let my kisses travel up his arm to his collarbone to his neck to behind his ear. My hands greedily stroke his body, each divot, each valley. I'd kiss him everywhere he'd let me. His birthmark, his tattoo, his forearm, his hands, anywhere.

"Don't ever get any more tattoos," I say as I kiss his chest. "I'll explode."

"Note to self," he says as he tangles his fingers in my hair. "Get more tattoos."

I return my focus to his face, the way I feel shiny when he

looks at me. In his eyes, I'm confident, brave, larger than life. I dip my hand to his zipper, gently caressing him end to end.

"I want you to feel good," I whisper into his neck. I reach for the button on his pants, popping it open with one hand. Slowly I drag the zipper down. So slowly, he winces.

"I feel fantastic," he groans.

I slip my hand under the waistband of his boxers and stroke him back and forth. He stiffens, guided by my movements. He brushes my strap off my shoulder and cups my jaw with his hand. His eyes flutter open as he tosses his head back.

I used to like watching him sleep. Watching this is so much better. I wrap my legs around his hips and pull him closer.

He grins, reaching into a drawer next to us. He pulls out a condom, holding it up to be inspected. "How's the date?"

I squint at the foil, praying for something usable. *For the love of fuck. Thank god.* "Perfect."

I hop off the desk and kick my shoes off. Henry steps out of his pants, and slides his glasses off his face, tossing them on the bedside table. My heart beats faster and faster. He returns his attention to me and watches intently. I hook my thumbs under the straps of my dress, letting it fall to the floor.

He drinks me in, his hair even messier over his forehead than normal. He scans my whole body as I scan his.

I hear nothing but my heartbeat in my ears, feel nothing but air on my skin.

He walks toward me, and plants his lips on my neck. His fingers hook around the band of my underwear and he tugs them off my hips in a swift and gentle motion. They fall to the floor around my ankles, and I kick them to the side, finally fully exposed to him. He starts leading me backward toward the bed, and lays me flat. Still standing, he brushes his fingers against my inner ankles and traces them up my calves, knees, inner thighs, spreading my legs apart. He crawls over me and plants both hands on either side of my head, his face now above mine.

"Hi." He smiles.

"Hi." I glide a finger down the front of his chest, and then I wrap my legs around him, pulling him down on top of me.

"Easy," he says as he stretches for the condom on his nightstand. "Don't forget why we came all this way."

He tears it open and hands it to me. I reach between his legs to roll it onto him. And now there's nothing in our way.

"Ready?" he asks, kissing my cheek. I nod, situating myself underneath him.

He presses into me slowly, and I breathe, letting all the air escape my lungs. I moan as he thrusts inside.

He kisses my throat, making my skin activate red-hot as I arch my back. His hands cup my breasts as he dips farther and farther into me. I lay my head back, grabbing handfuls of the sheets to cope with the pressure of him between my legs.

"Oh my god," I groan.

I hook my arms around his neck and angle my hips so he can move deeper.

"Oh my god, Henry," I gasp. It feels like he's scratching the edges of my soul.

"You okay?" He pauses. He lies inside me like a dagger. "Need to stop?"

I shake my head and a laugh escapes my lungs. "For the love of everything good, Henry. Don't stop."

He smiles, a smile dripping in thirst, and he begins to move gloriously into me again.

My legs shake around his body, weakening with every sharp movement. I can't control myself around him, I can't keep it in, and it feels good not to have to. Here, I'm broken, but in a beautiful way, in a way that all my pieces reflect light and color, not darkness. He glides into me; every movement, every breath, I feel flooded with him.

"You're so beautiful," he says, lips brushing the shell of my ear in a half-dazed, half-crazed sort of way. "You're so beautiful," he says again, this time looking at me, almost as if it slipped out the first time, but he's making sure I know he means it the second. I pull him back over me, claiming his mouth so that he knows just how beautiful I think he is too. He moves into me like a rainstorm, and I want no shelter.

When we're done, my body buzzes from him all over me. We lie together, an exhausted heap of sweat and fire. His fingers skate across my cheeks, tapping gently on each freckle. As close as we can be. For someone who relishes her personal space and keeps everyone around her at an arm's length, if I could crawl inside his chest and take a nap there, it wouldn't be close enough.

I close my eyes, only for a moment, and I already miss his face. When I open them again, he's smiling at me, ear pressed to the pillow. My body throbs everywhere. It may tingle forever.

I touch his cheek, just under his eye. "I'm not used to seeing you without glasses."

He laughs. "I'm not used to seeing you without clothes."

I lay my palm on his rib cage so I can feel him breathe. "What do you think?"

His hand settles on my ass, pulling me close. "A feast."

I roll my eyes. "So dramatic."

He laughs and pokes me in the ribs. I squeal, burrowing deeper under the covers until I rest my head on his chest, listening to the slow thud of his heart. My own heart is racing, pumping so fast I know it's not *only* caused by my feelings for him. It's anxiety and fear and panic and whatever else my nervous system will throw in there as a hookup party gift.

"What are you thinking about?" he asks, sensing my withdrawal. I take a deep breath and I tell him the truth. "I have this impulse to overthink everything all the time, and it's a bit exhausting. I was thinking about you and how wonderful you are and how I can't wrap my head around my life changing so fast, for the better, when I've been stuck for so long. And I was anxious that you might see me as something I'm not or that I won't be able to live up to whatever you expect. And I just . . ." I move so my shoulders are over his, my hair falling in a curtain around his face. "I wanted you to know that I'm happy we did this, I'm also just freaking out a little bit."

He tucks my hair behind my ear, cupping my cheek. "Is there anything you need from me?" he asks.

"Patience," I decide, as I place my palm on his bare chest, feeling the heat of his skin on my hand. "And sex."

"That, I can do," he says, gripping the back of my neck and pulling me down to kiss me. I crawl on top of him, spreading my legs over his hips. He kisses me deep, and I cup my hands around his jaw.

"What do you want to do today?" he asks, his fingers scraping up my spine.

"This?" I say.

"It's Saturday," he says, his hands now traveling down my waist, settling on my hips.

"And?"

"It's our Passion Project day," he says, pausing to look at me, eyebrow raised.

"And?" I ask again.

"And, as much fun as it's been finding a . . ." He preemptively winces. "Uh . . . new kind of passion—"

"Booooooooooo." I cringe.

"Sorry, I know that was awful." He grins, knowing his cheesy jokes actually do work on me. "Don't you want to try a passion today?"

"Doesn't this count?" I brush his hair from his forehead. "Can this count?"

He lets out a sigh and lays his head back against the pillow. I press my lips to his chest, feeling his heat against my mouth. "I had a whole thing planned," he says. "A food convention downtown. Taste your way around the world."

"We can order takeout," I say. "Let's order takeout and do our own tour of the world through the restaurants in your neighborhood and not leave this apartment for one second. Come on. That totally counts."

He grins, his hands trailing from my hips down my thighs and back up again. "It would've counted anyway even without the takeout."

"Good." I lean down to sink my teeth into him again.

"Fantastic," he says, peeling the comforter off my back, exposing me to the air.

"Amazing," I say. "Now get another condom."

He laughs and kisses me on the nose. "I like you so much."

My skin tingles. "I like you too," I say.

I like you. It's something most people have no trouble admitting. Schoolchildren yell it at each other from across the monkey bars. People send love letters to serial killers in prison. But for me, this is a step I didn't think I'd take with anyone again.

He swipes another condom from his bedside table and adjusts himself under me. I sink slowly on top of him, letting myself fill up with him. It's an exhale, a release, a shared moment of relief.

"Yeah," he says, sucking in a breath. "This definitely counts."

I snort a laugh as I start to move over him. His fingers curl into my thighs, guiding me. "I knew you'd come around."

"Mmm," he hums in agreement. "You're very convincing." He tugs me down so my chest is pressed against his. This is only our second time, and the thought that there could be, there *will* be more of this makes me flush all over. He looks at me through his long eyelashes, wraps his arm around my waist, and flips us, pinning me to the pillow in a swift, playful maneuver. It steals the breath from my lungs. He drinks my mouth in, soft and gentle sips of joy. Kissing him gives me tunnel vision, like suddenly his lips are the only thing in the world, and I'd do anything to fall farther into him.

I can't stop thinking about how much fun this is, how I never want to leave this tiny apartment, how passion can feel a lot like joy if you let it.

We sweat together, laugh together, breathe together, until

the sun is deep below the horizon and the moon hangs proudly in the sky. When we stop for a break, we sit on the floor wrapped in sheets and try some lumpia from a Filipino spot on the corner, birria tacos from a hole-in-the-wall taco shop, french fries from McDonald's (yes, they count as international because they're French), and a soft pretzel and schnitzel from the biergarten a couple blocks away. For dessert, we Postmates banana pudding from Magnolia Bakery and drink wine Henry stole from L'italiano.

I tell him about the time Sonya and I got caught texting each other during math and got our phones confiscated by the principal, and Henry tells me about how his mom and dad met, how they always wanted to be parents but weren't sure it was in the cards until Henry came along. I spill some consommé on a shirt Henry let me borrow, and when I loudly proclaim what a mess I am, he tells me, "Stop saying that about someone I like so much."

I agree never to say it again.

It feels like I'm returning to him after a long journey, like I've met him in a past life, rather than mere months ago. It's a kind of familiarity that lives below my skin, warming me from the inside out. I wonder if Henry feels it too.

Sounds of New York rumble below us. Sirens pierce through the air. A car stops at an intersection and I can feel the vibrations of their music thrum through the walls of Henry's apartment. I breathe in the scent of Henry, letting it fill my lungs, invading my body—my life. For the first time in a very long time, in this exact place with this exact person, I feel like I'm right where I need to be.

Chapter Twenty-Seven

I let the door slam behind me as I enter my apartment. I want Sonya to know I'm home. I *want* her to burst out of her room like a cuckoo clock.

Like I hoped, her door handle clicks and she pads into the living room.

"Excuse me, where have you been for the last two days?" she asks, raising an eyebrow. "And in the same dress I last saw you in?"

I drop my bag on the couch and grab an ice pack from the freezer.

"Is Jamie here?" I collapse onto the futon, ice pack resting on my chest.

"No dodging the question. You've been gone since I snuck Henry on the roof. That was two days ago. Are you upset?"

"No." I cover my face with my hands and burst into hysterical laughter. "I'm definitely not upset."

"Bennet, did you finally do it?" she squeals. I laugh even

harder. It's a nervous laughter, but I can't stop it. "Bennet! Oh my god!"

"It's so ridiculous." I wipe a tear from my eye.

"Did you sleep together?"

I peek out from between my fingers, unable to hide the shit-eating grin spreading across my mouth. "Maybe."

"I'm so proud I could cry." She curls up on the couch next to me. "I've never seen you like this. At least not since Sam."

"Like what?"

"I don't know." She folds her long hair up into a twist and fans her neck. "Giddy."

I know she's right. I've been in a committed relationship with my misery ever since I moved here, and Henry has made me a mushy pile of hope.

"Yeah." I smile. "Maybe."

"I'm serious. Ever since he came into your life you've been laughing more. And you've come out of your shell."

I shift the ice pack to the other side of my chest.

"Is it anti-feminist?" I ask genuinely.

"What?"

"That a man makes me this happy?"

She snorts and rolls her eyes. "Jamie makes me that happy, and she is definitely *not* a man."

I bite my lip. "It feels . . . wrong."

She kicks her feet over my lap. "I think it's just love."

"I didn't say anything about love."

"You didn't have to." She smiles like a demon.

I cringe. "Gross."

"I know. It's the worst."

"Henry just can't be my only source of happiness. I can't rely on him for that."

"Think of it this way." She crosses her ankles in my lap. "Imagine your soul is made up of a bundle of matches. They're not on fire or anything. They're just sitting there. Do you follow?"

"So far."

"Each one represents something in your life. A match for love, a match for family, a match for career, and all the other stuff that fulfills us. Still with me?"

"Mm-hm."

"You've been pouring water over your matches to keep them in perfect order because fire is scary and you can get burned, but matches don't want to be wet, they want to be on fire. All it takes is one thing to happen, one tiny match gets lit, and it's like a domino effect, lighting all the other matches. All you have to do is light that first match."

I scrunch my face and immediately have to stifle a smile at the memory of Henry calling me out on my scrunchy faces.

"Henry could be the thing that lights you up," Sonya continues. "And so could a million other things. But you have to stop pouring water on your matches or nothing will ever happen, and you'll stay in a cycle of sadness until you die alone sitting in your own waste."

I cringe. "Horrifying. When did you come up with that analogy?"

"One hundred percent off the cuff. You impressed?"

"A little bit, yeah."

She swings her legs off my lap and stands. "I'm going to

visit Jamie at the coffee shop." She grabs her purse from a hook by the door. "Think about it, okay? Light a match."

"Tell Jamie I say hi."

"Can I tell her you finally fucked the hot guy you've been flirting with since May?" she shouts back at me from the hallway.

"Sonya, volume!" The door slams before she can respond.

I open the freezer door and stick my head in. Matches burn bright, sure, but don't they also snuff out quickly? What happens then?

The past still looms over my life, a shadow I can't cast off, even with Henry's light. I could lose him at any moment. After all, isn't that what I do? Push people away? Look for what could go wrong? Didn't I do that with Sam? With Andy? With Sonya and Jamie?

I know I want to be happy. I know that deep down, every fiber of my being wants to experience good things again, wants to love again. And yet. And yet there's something stopping me from giving in to it all. Something messed up in my brain chemistry that focuses on the hurt and the pain. As if I don't deserve to live any other way.

I crawl into my bed, my clothes smelling like Henry's detergent, and I try not to think of the million ways I might fuck this up.

Chapter Twenty-Eight

I see Henry every day.

Now that everything's out in the open with Jamie, Sonya, and Henry, it's like a sigh of relief. Henry fits in with us. He sat through all of *Mamma Mia!* and *Mamma Mia! Here We Go Again*. Here's the kicker, though: he liked it.

I feel myself getting deeper and deeper in this. Wanting him more and more. We took a trip to Arlene's Grocery to see Terrance play with his band, the Curtanas, and I couldn't get Henry off the dance floor. He swung me around, clutching me close to him as we rocked back and forth to heavy-metal guitar. We went back to the dog shelter to see Fred get officially adopted by his new owner, and we both got misty-eyed as they trotted down the street into the crowd. Henry whistled "The Way You Look Tonight" the whole way up to his place, an ode to our old friend Fred on his journey home. We walked arm in arm at the Queens night market, smelling the kettle corn and dumplings and kebabs and smoke from the charred grills of the vendors.

Our Passion Projects have become nights together, kisses between subway stops, lunches at L'italiano. They've morphed into morning sex and afternoon coffee. Lazy days learning each other's bodies, our likes and dislikes. How I can make Henry come apart in my hands, how he can do the same for me. He tells me stories about Denver, about hiking with his dad, and I show him pictures of my family, of Andy, the Chases.

I've also been going on adventures alone now. Last week I took a pottery class in Queens. The week before I took a pasta-making class at Eataly all by myself. I Rushed a Broadway show and sat in the back row, crying softly to myself at the end. I read a poem in front of everyone at a coffee shop. I spent half a day getting lost in the bookshelves at the Strand, and then had my aura read by a woman in Chinatown. I actually tried a street vendor pretzel . . . and it honestly wasn't half bad.

Sonya's teaching me how to knit, and I started making her playlists again.

After every one of my excursions, I ring Henry's doorbell. I usually find him in sweats, unshaven, going through edits from photo shoots. He pulls me in, kissing me like he missed me. Really missed me. He asks me if I've found my passion yet, and I shake my head no. Not yet.

This morning, we're at my place.

"Can you grab me a spoon?" Henry pours himself a cup of coffee from my French press.

"Mm-hm." I yawn. I have to be at the library in an hour and Henry has a closing shift at the restaurant, which means we'll have to spend the night away from each other.

My finger grazes a piece of paper in the silverware drawer. I pull the heavy card stock out and pinch it between my index finger and my thumb, holding it delicately, as if it's a bomb that might explode at any moment. The invitation to Andy's wedding. I'd completely forgotten. Actually, I hadn't forgotten. I'd been ignoring it.

The Chases. How can I face them? The doting family I let fall out of my life? A pit sinks in the bottom of my stomach.

I've been prancing around New York, the home I was supposed to share with their son, with someone else. And I've been happy. It feels like such a slap in their faces.

Henry comes up behind me, kissing my neck, and my brain is quiet. "Sonya's not here, is she?" he whispers.

"Nope." I pull his arms around my shoulders, letting him hold me close.

He slides his hands down my body, pressing his palms into my stomach. "I'm going to miss you tonight," he whispers as he nibbles my ear.

"Down, boy, I have to get ready for work," I say, but I don't pull away.

"Screw work," he says. One of his hands slides up my body and lands on my chest, fingers lazily tracing my nipple through my shirt. "What's that?" he asks, noticing the invitation.

This is the moment. I can't keep pushing it off. "The wedding invite."

I turn around to face him, holding the card stock between us.

"I kill it at weddings," he says, grinning. His bright eyes burn a hole in my heart. "And I crush it with parents."

"Do you think . . . maybe . . . it's a little weird for me to bring my new . . . um . . . *something* to the wedding of my dead ex-boyfriend's sister?" I know I already asked him to go with me, but now that our relationship has changed, it feels strange.

He pulls back slightly, rubbing at his jaw. "You don't want me to come?"

"No, it's not that." I take a breath. "Is it inappropriate?"

"Depends." He shrugs. "On what you mean by *something*."

I fold my arms across my stomach. "I don't know."

"I don't usually get caught up in semantics, but if by *something* you mean *guy who's just a friend I sleep with*, I'd say I shouldn't go. But if by *something* you mean *boyfriend* . . ." He smiles sheepishly. "I'd really want that, actually." He pauses, noticing my hesitation. "Unless you don't want to . . . you know. Make it official."

"I don't know," I say, because it's the truth. "I'm scared."

"That's okay." His face lightens. "Anything worth doing is at least a little bit scary."

"What if we break up?"

"What if everything is fine and we're happy?" he says, cupping my face with his hands.

I close my eyes, imagining what it would be like—it wouldn't be much different than how we are now. How everything we've done this summer has scared me a bit, but it's also been worth it. How I tackled plenty of fears, including dangling off the side of a skyscraper, and I came out on top.

I open my eyes to him looking hopefully down at me, feeling that same adrenaline buzz as I did on that skyscraper.

"Okay," I say, with a little catch in my voice.

"Okay?" His eyes brighten and a slow grin spreads across his mouth.

I take his face in my hands and kiss him. His arms hook around my waist and he holds me against him. How can he taste this good in the morning? It's tingles, it's warmth, it's hot buttered bread. "Yes," I say.

"You're my girlfriend," he whispers between kisses.

Girlfriend was only ever a thing I was in relation to Sam. I feel dizzy hearing it again. Being it again.

He hoists me into the living room, laying me down on the couch. I peel his shirt over his head. *Girlfriend.*

His hands move down my back and land lightly on my hips. I reach between his legs, pleased that he's already ready and I won't have to wait long for him to be inside me.

I grab a condom from my purse on the floor and help him get it on.

He tugs my pajamas down and tosses them to the side. I pull his hips back to mine, squeezing my legs around him. The couch creaks under our weight. Let it crumple. I don't care.

"My girlfriend," he breathes as he dips inside me. I cling to his shoulders, wishing that being Henry's girlfriend made the fear go away.

At the library, I open the wedding website, my chin resting in my hand. I take a quick look through their engagement photos, beautifully bright and popping off the screen. Andy and Theo look so happy I could cry.

When I read about the wedding party, I'm embarrassed that I don't know anyone in it. How could Andy's life have changed so much in just a couple of years? Theo's brother, Alonzo, is the best man, and a woman named Vanessa is the maid of honor. Once, Andy wanted me to be her maid of honor and Sam her best man. Neither of us are either of those things.

I keep scrolling until I hit the bottom of the page and I see it. A small picture of Sam under a caption. Honorable best man: Samuel Chase. I clench my jaw. I haven't seen his picture in years. I haven't let myself look. He's wearing a suit and tie, smiling in front of a hydrangea bush. It's from graduation. I tied his tie that day.

I remember watching him walk across the stage, my throat tight with the fear of the post-graduation unknown. I remember being proud, but selfishly sad because I knew everything would change. Andy and I sat together in the crowd with Mr. and Mrs. Chase, the four of us each hiding our tears from each other, swallowing the emotions that come along with growing up and moving on. After the ceremony, the Chases took me to dinner, and it felt like a moment suspended in time. I wished I could be at that table, squished in a restaurant booth between Sam and Andy forever, sipping on iced teas and nibbling on french fries.

I scroll down to read the text.

Brother of the Bride. Samuel Chase passed away in a tragic accident, but the family feels his presence every day. The bride will wear a small patch of one of his baseball jerseys stitched into the bodice of her gown to honor him and to keep him with her every step of the way.

My breathing shortens to shallow pants. A lump rises in my throat. I click off the page and pretend I didn't see it. My fingers shake as I scroll to the RSVP section and find my name in the computer system. I click yes to the rehearsal dinner, and I pick the chicken and the steak so Henry and I can share.

Oh god, what will they think of me?

The Chases accepted me the minute Sam introduced me to them. They showered me with gifts at birthdays and holidays, they invited me to family vacations, they loved me because Sam loved me. They used to call me their third child.

How could it be okay that I'm bringing someone new to this wedding? That I haven't spoken to them in so long and now I'll be showing up with a new boyfriend who's not their son?

Inviting Henry was a spur-of-the-moment thing. I thought he would be the perfect person to bring, since pretty much everyone who meets him loves him. When I asked him, I pictured introducing the new friend I met in New York City, not my boyfriend. Those are two hugely different things. The former tells them that I'm doing well, trying to get my life together. The latter tells them I've moved on from their son. That I'm happy when I should be grieving.

I pull my phone out of my pocket and open my messages with Andy.

> Are you still at the same address?
> Sending our invites soon.

I never responded. God, I can be such a jerk. I debate with myself for far too long over whether I should acknowledge the fact that I never responded, or if I should act like it never happened and tell her I'm coming to the wedding. I debate for so long that Andy beats me to it, and my phone pings.

> I just got the RSVP notification.
> You're coming? With a plus one?

My lungs tighten, and so does my grip around my phone. Andy texts again.

> Who are you bringing?

How the hell am I going to explain this? I did not think this through. Not at all. I type out a response.

> I'm bringing my new boyfriend which feels like a massive betrayal to you and your family seeing as I used to date your brother and now he's dead because of it.

Delete.

> Can't wait to rub my new boyfriend in your face when I've completely abandoned our relationship.

Delete, delete, delete.

I clasp my phone between my hands and squeeze my eyes closed. Panic rises up my chest, until it feels like it's choking me, stopping the blood from flowing to my head.

Plus one is just a friend.

Send.

Immediately my stomach churns. I'm pretty sure the worst option for me was to lie, and that's exactly what I did. Henry is very much *not* my friend, and one look at the way we interact with each other will make that extremely obvious. I open my messages to see if by some miracle it didn't send, but Andy is already typing her response.

If you want a room for your friend, one of my cousins dropped out last minute so we have an extra one on the block. Yours, free.

You don't share hotel rooms with people who are just friends, right? Not if there's also a free one hand-delivered to you by the bride herself. This lie is already ahead of me and I told it two seconds ago.

I'll take care of it, but thank you.

Andy types back.

I know how you are about your personal space. Just send me your friend's name.

I can't argue with her. She's the bride. The bride always wins.

Henry Adams.

The blue dots appear at the bottom of the screen and Andy's message pops up.

I'll send you the confirmation.

My heart is beating like a damn jackhammer. She texts again.

Weekend is going to be pretty
busy but I want to catch up.
Sunday morning?

I bite my lip and hope I don't bleed.

I'd love that.

Within seconds I get confirmation from the hotel in L.A. with a room under my name and a room under Henry's. I flop my head down on the desk in front of me and wallow for a couple seconds, and then I bury my phone out of sight. I can't even look at it right now.

How will I explain the two hotel rooms to Henry? If I tell him I lied to Andy and told her we're just friends, it will hurt him. If I tell Andy I lied to her and Henry is really my boyfriend, it will hurt her. I'm trying to salvage this relationship, not set it on fire.

Get it together, Bennet.

Maybe it'll all be fine and Henry won't be mad that I

booked two separate hotel rooms, and Andy won't ever find out Henry's my boyfriend, and rainbow pigs will fly out of my ass and start dancing the Macarena.

I hunch over my desk, pressing my palms to my face. I don't know why I can't stop screwing things up.

Chapter Twenty-Nine

I booked us on the cheapest flight I could find. Henry is staring out the window, hand drumming on the armrest between us.

"You good?" I ask, noticing his jitteriness in the sky. He insisted that despite his fear of heights, he preferred the window over the aisle so I wouldn't have to crawl over him to use the bathroom if I had to.

"Yeah," he says, nodding. "Heights don't bother me so much when I'm *inside* something. Instead of, you know, standing on top of a skyscraper with no safety net."

I laugh. "We both survived, didn't we?"

"We did." He reaches across the seat and squeezes my knee. I rest my head on his shoulder, feeling that instant serenity that comes with Henry's contact. There's a screaming baby two rows behind us and a man eating a rancid sandwich across the aisle, but with my head on Henry's shoulder, the world calms down a little bit. Maybe this weekend won't be such a disaster. I catch a glimpse of the earth below us through the window on Henry's side, then check the in-flight tracker on the screen in front of me. I poke him in the ribs.

"That's Colorado," I say, pointing out the window.

He smiles, glancing out the corner of his eye. "So it is."

"Do you miss it?"

"Yeah." He keeps his eyes locked on the window, gazing at the ground below us. "One of these days I'll take you to Denver and we can go hiking."

"You're going to dump me when you see how out of shape I am."

"It'll be worth it, I promise." A thought flickers across his eyes. "Like Jane Austen said, *What are men to rocks and mountains?*"

"Wait." My heart tingles. "No way."

He nods, satisfied. "Mm-hm."

"*Pride and Prejudice.* You watched it?"

"I read it and I watched it. I had to know where your name came from. You realize you're not Lizzy, though, don't you? You're hard to read, dark, brooding, kind of cold but in a sexy way . . . extremely kind and soft when you get to know you. You're Mr. Darcy."

"So, what, that makes *you* Lizzy?"

He shakes his head. "I give off Bingley energy."

"So in our version, Bingley and Darcy get together?"

He shrugs. "I think that would make a lot of fan-fiction writers very happy," he says.

I gape at him, my mouth hanging wide.

"What?" he says. "I may have skimmed a couple in my research."

"Wow. I can't believe you read it."

"Anything for my girl." He kisses me, a tender, comfortable kiss that makes even the tiny cabin of this airplane feel like Pemberley. With Henry, I'm warm and soft and melty and . . . fuck. It will be impossible for us to keep this under wraps.

I settle my cheek onto his shoulder, feeling the rise and fall of his breathing under my head.

"Can I ask you something I've been wondering for a while?" he asks.

I nod.

"Why does Alexandra go by Andy? It doesn't seem like a natural nickname."

I feel a smile pull at my cheek as a flood of a memory overtakes me. "Because when Sam and Andy were kids, they watched *Toy Story* together and Andy was obsessed with it. She wrote *Andy* under all of Sam's shoes and . . . it just stuck."

It goes silent between us as my eyes start to sting. Henry pulls me closer to him, kissing me on the forehead.

We only have a couple of hours until my worlds crash into each other. I picture Henry congratulating Andy, shaking hands with Mr. Chase. I imagine him goofing off with Theo and refreshing Mrs. Chase's glass of champagne. Everything he does will highlight his not-Samness in their eyes. His Henryness. The way he talks, the way he laughs, the way he dresses, will all be compared to Sam. Isn't it wrong? Isn't it an invasion? Shouldn't I be more miserable?

I suddenly feel hot, my body sweating and screaming for space. I unzip my hoodie and wrestle it off as fast as I can. It's little relief, but I feel less restricted.

Henry rests his palms on his knees. "I know it'll be hard, but I think this weekend is a big step for us."

Tell him about the hotel rooms now, my brain screams. But my heart just wants this moment to pass.

"Me too," I say, dread building in my stomach.

"It means a lot that you want me there. It always did, but especially now that we're together." His breath rises and falls. "Thank you for letting me in, Bennet. I do not take meeting them lightly."

I close my eyes, leaning against his shoulder again, pretending to fall asleep as he strokes my hair.

All I can think about is how earnest Henry is, how he's not asking for much from me, yet I can't seem to give it to him. How badly I *want* to give it to him, yet I'm making the worst possible choices.

The baby two rows back lets out a bloodcurdling screech.

Me too, girl. Me too.

The Hotel Amaya is a social media dream location. Every surface is Instagrammable. The walls are painted a creamy white, with glossy floor tiles to match. There are succulents on every table, potted palms in every corner, long confetti-like ferns hanging from the ceiling. Colorful flowers dot the walls and give off the perfect sun-soaked Los Angeles vibe. It's beautiful, if slightly insincere.

I try not to seem panicked as I scan the lobby for one of the Chases. The ceremony will be on the beach tomorrow at sunset, but tonight's rehearsal dinner is at the Amaya's outdoor restaurant overlooking the ocean.

"Hello, welcome to the Amaya," the front desk lady says as we approach. "How may I help you today?"

I clear my throat and speak low. "We're checking in. Bennet Taylor."

"We're in the Chase wedding block of rooms," Henry says.

She types away at her computer, looking for our reservation. "Ah yes, here it is."

"Hey." He turns to me, beaming. "Think we'll have a view of the ocean?"

Oh god. I have to tell him. I have to tell him now. "Listen. About the room—"

"Two rooms with queen beds. Room 307 for Miss Taylor and Room 407 for Mr. Adams. Looks like they're right on top of each other."

"Oh no, there must be a mistake," Henry says. "We only need one room."

She frowns at the computer screen. "It says here that the reservation was originally one room, but it was changed to two rooms a couple days ago."

Henry looks at her, his brows knitted together. "I think it meant two people, one room."

"Henry." I turn to face him. "She's right. It's two rooms."

"What?" He looks at me, shocked. "Why?"

"I'll explain later," I mumble under my breath.

"Rooftop pool access is on the fifteenth floor with your room key. Towels are available for your use at the pool or by the ocean." She gestures to sliding glass doors at the back. "The beach is right through those doors. I hope you enjoy your stay."

Henry's jaw clenches as he takes his key. He rolls his suitcase toward the elevator. I shuffle after him.

"Why did you book two rooms?" he asks. "When were you going to tell me?" He stops to press the elevator button.

"I don't know. Now?"

"I'm confused," he says as the elevator doors ping open and guests flood past us, like we're boulders in the middle of a rushing stream.

We roll our bags into the elevator. I hit floor three. Henry grits his teeth as he hits floor four. "Andy had an extra room, and I just . . . I felt like I couldn't say no."

He runs his hand through his hair as an indecipherable expression flashes across his face. "I guess I was just looking forward to spending time with my girlfriend."

I have to tell him the other thing. That they don't know we're dating either. Just rip it all off like a Band-Aid.

"There's one more thing." I hesitate as the elevator begins to move. "They don't know you're my boyfriend, and . . ." I breathe through my teeth, heartbeat pulsing in my neck. "And I kind of want to keep it that way."

He looks over at me, eyebrows furrowed. "Oh," he says. He opens his mouth as if to say something more, but decides against it.

We pass floor two. Only thirty seconds to make this right. "I feel like it's disrespectful to be, like, touching and kissing in front of them," I say. "Because of Sam."

He scrubs his hand down his face. "I get that," he says. "But I thought you at least wanted me to meet them."

"I do," I say. "And you still will!" The doors fling open on my floor. I step out and turn back to face him. "Maybe in a couple months I can reintroduce you as my boyfriend. Think of this as a warm-up round."

He breaks eye contact with me. "A . . . test?"

"Not a test." I wince. "I just don't want to dump it all on them at once when they haven't seen me in years."

"No, I get it," he says, frowning. "It makes sense."

"None of this has to change anything. You'll still meet them, you'll still be your charming self—it'll just be slightly different. We can still have fun, right?"

"My charming self," he mutters. He swallows, his body tense. "Why didn't you tell me sooner instead of springing it on me at the last second?"

I bite the inside of my cheek, wondering how I can possibly explain all this. "Because I didn't want you looking at me the way you're looking at me right now," I say. "And also because I'm so nervous to see them. I really need this to go well."

"You know what . . ." He twists his mouth and looks at the floor. "You're right. I don't want to be mad about this," he says. "This weekend is important to you and I trust your judgment. If this is what you want, I'm okay with it."

Thank god, I think. "You have no idea what a relief it is to hear that," I say. "I was so afraid you'd think I didn't want you here. I do want you here. I need you here."

He shakes his head, holding the elevator doors open so we

can finish talking. "I'm just going to miss sleeping next to you. That's all."

"Me too," I say. "Can we continue this talk later? Let's unpack and then maybe pick me up for drinks before the rehearsal dinner?"

"Sounds like a plan." He smiles, a genuine smile, and my heart is reminded all over again why his being here is a good idea. Why *he's* a good idea. His endless empathy and understanding, his kindness and sincerity even when I make mistakes . . . it's almost too good to be true. Too good to be true for me, at least. Too good for me to deserve.

The elevator doors close and I wheel my bag across the outdoor hallway. I stop at Room 307 and unlock the door with my key. The carpet in my room is squishy under my feet. The decor on the walls is made up of generic pictures of palm trees and cacti against cotton-candy skies. Hanging above the bed is a gigantic black-and-white print of the HOLLYWOOD sign.

Across from the entrance there's a glass door that opens onto a balcony. I curl my fingers around the handle and slide it open, revealing a breathtaking view of the crystal-blue ocean. Warm, salty air fills my lungs, and the sun heats my skin. From here the waves look no bigger than ripples. Kids splash and bodysurf while parents lie out and pretend to read books under large sun hats. Boats swirl by, carrying people on blow-up rafts and tugging them in parasails.

I sit on one of the chairs on the balcony and fold my legs to my chest, resting my chin on my knees. I try to make up little stories for the people in the water, like Henry and I did that afternoon in the park, but it's not the same. It feels silly doing it alone. Contrived.

Why did I do this to myself? And to him? I don't want to be away from him, even if it's just for a couple of nights.

I do miss Sam. I do. But maybe I feel a bit guilty about how missing him doesn't feel the same anymore. Maybe I feel guilty that at this present moment, I miss Henry more. And he's just a floor away.

What kind of a person does that make me?

I tilt my head back and look at the balcony above me, the same size and shape as mine, and I wonder if Henry is out there, looking at the sea just like me.

Chapter Thirty

I slide a thrift-store-bought orange dress over my head and adjust the ties on the shoulders so they lie like perfect little bows. I slip on a pair of beige strappy sandals and brush my hair into place. I smear some pink blush over my cheeks and roll Sonya's perfume across my wrists.

I may not actually be put-together, but I certainly can look it. At least enough to face the Chases.

You can do this.

I flop down on the bed, careful not to get any makeup on the white pillows, and text Henry.

Ready for that drink?

Blue dots appear on my screen as he texts back.

Just got back from the beach. Let
me shower quick. Five minutes.

I close my eyes, head against the pillow, and try to center myself, but my stomach is twisted in knots so tight I can hardly breathe. I haven't been able to eat any food all day in anticipation of this night, and I feel lightheaded and woozy.

A knock at the door tugs me from my mind, and I roll out of bed to answer. Henry's hair is damp and disheveled and his cheeks are pink from the sun. He's wearing a light green button-down with the sleeves rolled up to his elbows and a pair of dark blue fitted pants. He smells divine, like coconuts and salt.

"Hi," I say, suddenly shy around him.

"Hi," he says, stilled by the door, not moving toward me.

"You're, like, super-hot. Did you know that?"

"Look who's talking." He smiles at me and my heart jumps.

He takes my face in his hands and kisses me slow. I go limp in his arms, wanting to pull him closer, but my head is full of buzzing bees. I wrap my arms around his waist, feeling the warmth of his body recharge me.

He tucks my head under his chin. "It's going to be hard not to act like I'm crazy about you tonight," he whispers as he tightens his grip around my shoulders.

Me too, I think.

And then Sam's eyes flash through my mind. His big, soulful eyes. Suddenly it feels like I'm choking. Suffocating. Like the walls of this hotel are collapsing in on me, and I'm powerless to move.

I pull away from Henry quickly, brushing my hands down the front of my dress, hoping it didn't wrinkle while we were pressed together.

"Shall we?" I say as I grab my key card and purse.

Henry guides me by the small of my back into the elevator. I look around to make sure the hall is empty. Satisfied that we're alone, I grab his hand and hold it the whole way down.

The elevator doors open into the lobby and we make our way to the hotel bar. I take a seat on a high-top stool, swinging my legs above the floor. He gets a beer for himself and a rosé for me, which we sip silently as gentle music wafts over the veranda.

"So . . ." My stomach boils with nerves. I take a breath. "What's our story?"

"What do you mean?" he asks as he inspects a cactus bloom on a succulent on the bar. This place is full of them.

"I mean, like . . . how did we meet? How do we know each other? For the Chases."

He folds his hands in his lap and purses his mouth. "What's wrong with the truth?"

"We can't exactly tell them how we really met," I say, my cheeks getting hot remembering that awful night. How Henry was asked to go out with me. How I puked my guts out and spilled wine everywhere. "How about we met at work. You temp at the same place I do and we became fast friends after a couple of shifts."

He frowns. "I can't even be honest about who I am now? What I do?"

"Don't think about it like that," I say. "You're still you, just slightly different. We don't have to tell them about the Passion Project or anything, because that's kind of embarrassing."

"Since when is it embarrassing?" He crinkles his brow, looking distraught. "That's kind of important to this entire summer," he says. "Don't you think?"

I tap a fingernail on the stem of my glass. "I just want to be on the same page, that's all."

"If you wanted us to be on the same page, you'd have told me you wanted to hide our relationship from the beginning," he says, tearing at the edge of a bar napkin.

"I thought you weren't mad," I say, turning toward him.

"I'm not," he insists. "I'm just feeling a bit jerked around."

I open my mouth to say something, but I come up short. The pit in my stomach grows, threatening to drag me under. I turn back to my glass of wine, tapping at the stem again.

"I'm sorry," he says, scratching his chin. "I'm sorry. I know this weekend is hard on you and I don't want to make it harder. I'll play along, okay? We met at work. No Passion Project talk. I'm fine with that."

I close my eyes, trying to banish every dark thought creeping into my brain. Thoughts about how Henry deserves someone better. Someone who wouldn't put him through this.

He taps my ankle under the bar, a subtle touch that no one besides Henry or I would notice. "It's going to be okay," he says. "I promise."

Henry's optimism never wavers, and it feels a bit naive.

"Yeah," I say, trying to seem convinced. "It's going to be okay."

"Good," he says, nudging me on the shoulder. "That's what I like to hear."

"Bennet!" a voice booms from behind me. I hop out of my seat as quickly as I can as a big barrel of a man heads toward us.

"Theo!"

"Where have you been hiding?" Theo's muscular arms

wrap me in a big bear hug before turning his attention to Henry. "And you must be Henry."

"Yeah, I'm Bennet's—"

"Friend," I spit.

"Thank you for letting me crash your wedding." Henry eyes me as he shakes hands with Theo, but it's only for a moment. Then his attention is fully back with Theo. "This place is gorgeous."

"Alexandra picked it out. The woman's got great taste. She's going to flip out when she sees you, Bennet."

Is *flip out* a good thing or a bad thing?

"I'm excited for her!" I try to sound as peppy as I possibly can, hiding my panic. "And you. I'm excited for both of you! To get married! Yay!"

Henry chuckles a bit beside me, no doubt an endearing poke at my lack of social skills, but it doesn't put me at ease like his teasing normally does. I take a step away from him.

"How did you meet?" Henry says, noticing my retreat. "You and . . . um . . . Alexandra?"

Theo beams, hearts practically flying out of his eyeballs. "Alexandra was buying art for one of my clients. I deal with musicians mostly, and this one woman couldn't find the perfect piece for her living room. Alexandra was just an intern at the time, but she swooped in with this portrait of a butterfly stamped in this purple fabric, completely on a whim. My client fell in love with it. So much that she made it the cover of her new album, actually."

I know the album cover immediately. A black butterfly stamped over purple waves of velvet with Pollock-esque splatters of red paint on top. I knew Theo's clients were big, but this particular pop princess is huge. That album cover is everywhere. A bit of pride wells up in my chest for Andy.

"Anyway, my client invited us both to her housewarming party out in Calabasas. As soon as I saw her . . . I knew." Theo laughs, the sound like tambourines. "You know the effect Alexandra has on people, right, Bennet?"

I smile. "She sparkles."

"I can't wait to meet her," Henry says, beaming.

"The party should be starting soon." Theo checks his watch. "Oh, and the open bar starts in five minutes. We'll see you over there, right?"

"Yeah." I swallow down a huge gulp of wine and also the feeling of dread pooling in my stomach. "Congratulations again!" I call after him as he speed-walks toward the patio.

My heart is beating so hard I can feel it in my fingertips as I adjust the straps on my dress.

"Breathe," Henry assures me. "We've got this."

The bartender returns his card and a hotel employee ushers us to the patio for the reception.

Time to face the music.

The patio is on the backside of the hotel overlooking the ocean. The dim crashing of waves on sand fills the air with a salty mist. Lights hang like weeping willows from the wooden beams overhead. The breeze is sweet and warm and gently blows Henry's hair off his forehead. We stand at a table by the edge of the patio so that we can look out over the ocean.

A cocktail waiter offers us a tray of coconut shrimp and I grab two. The irony that I'm usually the one passing out shrimp is not lost on me.

With not one, but *two* shrimp tails hanging out of my mouth, I finally see her. She's wearing a clean white strapless jumpsuit with delicate feathers floating along the neckline. Her crimson hair bounces as she glides across the patio to greet her guests.

I spit the shrimp tails into a cocktail napkin.

Henry leans back on his heels. "Is that her?"

"Yeah." I swallow. At one point, that woman was one of the most important people in my life. Now . . . practically a stranger.

I check my pulse with my fingers against my neck. It's racing. "Should we go say hi? Or should we wait for her to come here? Or should we hide in the bathroom?"

"Let's wait for her," Henry says, squeezing my wrist. "She's the bride, everyone will be shoving through the crowd to talk to her."

I jerk my hand away, trying to be discreet. Henry seems to have already forgotten we're *not dating*.

I follow her with my eyes, heart thumping, throat constricting. When she reaches Theo, he breaks off a conversation with his brother to kiss her. They kiss like the longest they've ever been apart was the amount of time Theo spent talking to Henry and me earlier. He whispers something in her ear and then points to me, smiling.

When she looks at me, her expression is stony. She waves from across the room, a tiny delicate wave.

"She's waving," Henry says.

"I can't move."

"Go say hi to her," he whispers.

In a flash, Andy turns toward Theo and laughs, presumably at something he just said. Her attention on me was fleeting, like I'm a fly to bat away. Butterflies don't bother with gnats, do they? Not when the gnat flew away after the butterfly's brother died. She doesn't want me here, otherwise wouldn't she have come say hi? Wouldn't she do more than wave?

"I have to go," I mumble. I can't be here.

I crumple my cocktail napkin into a ball and nudge my way through the crowd back into the hotel lobby. I don't look back to see if Henry is following me.

In the bathroom, I splash cold water on my wrists. I take a deep breath, making eye contact with my reflection. I wasn't in this position too long ago at L'italiano, yet so much has changed. I've changed. But, being here at this wedding . . . I feel exactly like that girl on the bathroom floor of a restaurant, puking her guts out.

"Bennet?" A twinkly voice says my name as the bathroom door cracks open.

Andy steps inside, her white heels clacking on the tile.

I whip around to face her, my cheeks and chest hot from the stress. "Andy." Looking at her feels like looking at a memory. At once, I'm transported to her dorm, a pencil eraser pressed to her lip as she studied for an art history final. I was reading a book I don't remember while sipping chamomile tea from a dining hall mug.

You know what? she said, turning toward me. *You should meet my brother, Sam.*

I blink, staring at her as the faucet runs. She's slightly older yet entirely different. All that's been broken between us, all that's been lost, hangs in the air like laundry clipped to a line.

"Why did you run out?" she says, playing with her engagement ring.

I turn the faucet off. "Sorry." I gesture to the stalls. "I had to pee."

"Oh," Andy replies.

"I'll be out soon." I grab some paper towels from the dispenser. "You should be outside with your guests."

"You're my guest too," she says. Her eyes are glassy and blue as the ocean.

"I, um . . ." I toss the paper towels into the trash and turn to face her. "I don't know what to say."

She frowns, still twisting her ring around her finger. "This is weird."

"So weird." I pinch the fabric of my dress, feeling the cool cotton against my skin.

"You didn't really have to pee, did you?"

I shake my head, my nose stinging. "No."

To this, she laughs, despite the awkwardness. "How have you been?"

"Shitty. You?"

She wipes her nose. "Shitty. And good."

I nod, swallowing the knot in my throat. "That's good."

She looks down at her perfectly clean shoes. "I know you said your date is just a friend . . . but when I saw you standing there with him . . . for a second, I swore it was Sam." I'm surprised to see a tear rolling down her cheek as she looks up at me again. "I'm so used to seeing you with him. I know that doesn't make sense."

My throat stings, and I try to breathe through it. "I shouldn't have brought a guy. Even just a friend."

She shakes her head, glancing at the floor. "It's just hard. Not having him here. I keep looking for him."

"I hope me being here . . . I hope it doesn't make things harder for you," I say.

"Of course not," she says, wiping the corner of her eye. "I'm glad you came. You'll always remind my family of Sam."

I'm not here out of pity. I'm here because I remind them of Sam. Because I'm their closest connection to him. If there was any question as to whether or not I should hide my relationship with Henry, it's crystal-clear now. They don't need me to be Bennet with a new boyfriend. They need me to be Sam's Bennet. At least for this weekend.

I can do that.

"I always thought I'd be at your wedding with him," I say.

"Me too." She steps forward, grabbing my hand. "Me too."

I swallow my tears, gathering myself. "Sorry for crying before anything even happened," I say. "You haven't even put your wedding dress on yet."

"Weddings make people cry," she says. "It's okay. We can talk about it after."

I dab my cheek with a paper towel and take a deep breath. "Should we go back to the party?"

She nods, and I watch her transform back into sparkly Andy before my eyes. Her cheeks are dry and perfect, and her mascara didn't even run. She grabs my hand. "Let's go before they do the toast without us."

We enter the patio hand in hand, like the sisters we might've been. I spot Henry at our table, still standing there, abandoned.

"That's your friend, right?" Andy says, leading us toward him. "I want to meet him."

I gulp as we approach him.

"Alexandra Chase, this is my friend Henry," I say when we get to the table. "Henry, Andy."

His forehead creases as he reaches out to Andy. "Nice to meet you, Andy. You look beautiful." He shakes her hand. "This place is amazing. I can tell you put a lot of thought into it."

Andy laughs. "I like him already."

Henry leans against the railing, being as friendly and charming as ever. "It's a pleasure to be here. Thank you for having me."

"If you've got Bennet's stamp of approval, you've got mine." Andy pats him on the arm. "It's hard to crack her."

"What?" I let go of her hand and cross my arms.

"You made the Chases work hard," she jokes.

"I loved you all from, like, the moment I met you," I say.

Andy raises an eyebrow. "I thought you hated me at first. Sam too."

"Me too," Henry agrees. "She's not the best with first impressions . . . but in a good way, I think."

"I object to that," I say, shooting daggers at him with my eyes. "I wasn't trying to impress you."

"Yeah," he snorts. "Believe me, I know." He turns to Andy. "When we met, Bennet got way too drunk and puked in the bathroom instead of going on a date with me." He laughs to himself at the memory. "Definitely thought she hated me after that."

"Henry." I snap my head toward him, my heart thumping.

"What?" he says, squinting at me, then turns back to Andy. "Took all summer to win her over."

"Oh," Andy says. "You two *are* dating?"

Henry's eyes widen, realizing his mistake. Not only did he let it slip that we went on a date, he also told my ex–best friend I'm trying to act normal in front of about one of the most embarrassing nights of my life when I explicitly asked him not to.

He turns to me, his mouth agape, but nothing comes out.

"No," I cut in. "No. We're not dating. I mean, I guess we went on one date, but I . . . That's how we met, but . . ." I turn to Henry, whose face is turning red. "But we're just friends," I stammer.

Henry shakes his head, pressing his eyes closed. The skin behind his ears starts to turn red. "We're not together . . ." he says, swallowing back his embarrassment. "That night was a mistake. It didn't mean anything to her. It's not like that between us."

"Long story short," I bluster, "we went on a date, but I realized I wasn't ready to move on from Sam." It's the truth. That is what happened.

"You can be honest with me," Andy says. "You know that, right?" Her expression is hard to read, but I know she's thinking about Sam.

I nod. "Of course. Yes."

She grabs my wrist. "I just want you to be happy," she says, her eyes watering again.

"I know," I say. I can't make this woman cry at her wedding. Not when I've already caused her so many tears. "If I was with someone, I'd tell you," I say. "But I'm not. And that's the truth."

Henry stills beside me. I can't look at him.

"Okay." Andy squeezes my wrist and smiles before letting go. "Have you seen my parents yet?" she asks.

A cement brick drops in my stomach. I shake my head no.

"Mom! Dad!" She beckons across the crowd to Mr. and Mrs. Chase. "Bennet's here!"

Mrs. Chase makes a beeline for our table, squealing. Her hair is trimmed to a white bob, and she's wearing huge green seashell earrings that swing as she walks. She's wrapped in a paisley shawl with long black tassels over her simple black dress. Mr. Chase isn't far behind wearing a camel-colored suit he's probably had since the seventies.

"Our third baby," Mrs. Chase sings into my ear as she hugs me. "How are you doing, sugar?"

"I'm good. I'm okay." The air leaves my body.

She releases me, but keeps her hands on my shoulders. "Oh, my love." She pulls me into another hug, soft and warm. "We're so happy you're here."

"Me too," I say into her cheek.

She lets me go, brushing a strand of hair behind my ear as she spots Henry. "Is this your boyfriend?"

Static fills my ears and my pulse starts to throb. "No, Henry's just a friend."

Be Sam's Bennet.

"Nice to meet you, Mrs. Chase." Henry shakes her hand, his face still pink from the embarrassment earlier.

"Please, call me Laura." Her voice booms louder than the din of the crowd. "And the silent one back there is Jon. My husband."

"Pleasure." Henry takes a deep breath after greeting the parents. "I'm, uh . . ." He clenches his jaw. "I'm going to go grab a drink."

"Good idea," I snip. Henry gives me a tired and disappointed look. He's tense as he walks toward the bar.

Mrs. Chase looks me up and down. Her lips tremble into a smile. "We've missed you so much."

"I've missed you too." My hands are sweaty—I ball them into fists. "More than you know."

Her eyes go misty. Sam's eyes. She tilts her head, studying me, placing a hand on my cheek. "I feel him when I look at you."

Be Sam's Bennet.

Mrs. Chase. Sam's mom, here in front of me. How can I express what she means to me? How can I express the guilt I feel? "I feel him too. Everywhere."

She buries my body into an embrace that's just like home, covered in her familiar scent. The scent Sam would bring back with him from Christmas break.

My muscles shake as I squeeze her. This is the person I need to be for them. And it's who I should still be. Who I would still be if Henry never came around.

She lets me go and wipes a tear from my eye. "I know," she says. "It'll take a long time to heal."

Part of me knows I've been healing this whole time. But part of me wants to take a knife to the stitches and pop them open. Mrs. Chase looks up at me with Sam's eyes, pulling me in like a gravitational weight. Her heartstrings pulling on mine.

"I hope you know how much Sam still means to me," I say. "He's the love of my life, and I don't think I'll ever stop loving him. With him I was the best version of myself. He's the only person who has ever really seen me. Sometimes I feel like . . . like I'll never know love like that again. Even if I'm with someone else, I'll never feel that way again. Never."

Right as the words leave my mouth, I spot Henry in the corner of my eye, holding a fresh glass of wine for me. He freezes; his face looks pale.

My stomach sinks and all the blood in my body goes cold. I feel my face flush as a tear spills down Mrs. Chase's cheek. "Sugar," she says, brushing a hair from my forehead. "We all love you, I hope you know that. Always will."

I breathe a shallow breath as she shakes herself out of it. "But this is a party." She sniffles and grabs a napkin from a cocktail waiter. "We don't need to get emotional yet, right?"

"You're right." I clear my throat, noticing Henry retreat to another corner of the party. "Tell me about your trip to Alaska."

I keep the conversation going for as long as I can. Luckily, it's easy with Mrs. Chase. She's such a dynamic woman, telling stories and jokes from her travels. She's always been like this, adventurous. She and Mr. Chase started traveling when Sam and Andy were in college, and they're well on their way to spending time on every continent. While she recounts an ice-fishing excursion, I scan the room for Henry.

After a few minutes, I excuse myself from the conversation and search for him at the bar. The sun has completely set by now, making the patio glitter with the lanterns burning against the night sky. Every party guest is speckled with tiny spots of firefly-like freckles. It's beautiful, but makes finding Henry difficult.

I check inside the hotel lobby. I peek my head into the men's bathroom. I go back to the patio and nudge my way through the crowd hoping to run into him. I scan the beach. The cool shores are empty except for one lonely person with his toes in the water. A lonely person I know.

I kick off my shoes and carry them by the straps as I walk through the sand. He doesn't turn to face me when I reach the shore, he just stares off into the water. We stand shoulder to shoulder, gazing at the black horizon.

He takes a deep breath, blowing it out his lips. "Hey."

I feel the cool water rush between my toes and up to my ankles. "Hey."

"Did you mean that?" he asks, his tone even and low. "What you said to Sam's mom?"

"You weren't supposed to hear that," I say, my heels digging farther into the wet sand.

He shakes his head and looks down at his feet. "That doesn't answer my question."

The salt spray of the ocean mists my shins and I shiver. "Yes. And no. It's confusing. I mean, I'll always love him, but with you . . ." I let my voice trail off.

He tucks his hands in his pockets, shifting his weight from foot to foot. "I'm starting to think I was right, in the bathroom at that party."

"What does that mean?" My voice cracks slightly at the end.

"That you're not ready. I'm not sure you will be for a while. I mean, I thought you were, but then we came here. You hid me from the people you care about, and you only invited me here to be charming. You said so yourself. And then to hear that you'll never love anyone again . . ."

"What was I supposed to do?" I turn to him. "You outed us in the first three seconds. I had to do damage control."

He almost laughs at this, and then shakes his head. "I'm really sorry I messed that up, okay? I didn't mean to. But you didn't exactly give me enough time to prepare for lying about our entire relationship."

"It's not that hard," I say, gritting my teeth. "You did lie to me for months, remember?"

His expression gets very stern. Serious. "I don't believe you're still mad about that, Bennet," he says, turning toward the ocean again. "I just think you want to be mad about something. I think you want to be miserable because you're afraid to be happy."

"That's unfair," I say, my throat tightening. "I don't *want* to be miserable."

He takes a frustrated breath. "Think about this weekend," he says. "You built up this entire lie about our relationship for no reason. They are lovely people. They want you to be happy. But you'd rather complicate things."

"You don't know them," I say. "You don't know the history."

"All I know is what I see. And what I see is a group of people who love you and want the best for you. You are the one who wants to be restricted by the past. Not them."

My heart starts to race and my fingertips buzz. "I've had such a shitty few years, Henry," I say, heat rising up my chest. "If I want to be miserable, that's my problem."

"Well, it's also my problem because you're in a relationship with me," he says.

"I wasn't ready to be in a relationship!" I throw at him, my ears ringing.

"Why did you agree to be with me, then?" he says. "Why do any of this?"

"Because you pushed me," I say, anger clouding my decision making.

"What? I didn't push you," he says, confusion in his eyes.

"Did I not tell you multiple times that I needed patience?"

He folds his arms around him. "Yeah, but—"

"But nothing," I say.

He presses his fingers to his forehead. "If I pushed you, Bennet, I'm sorry. I didn't mean to. And I definitely don't want to continue to push you into being with me if you don't want to be. I want to make you happy, and I think that I do. But sometimes it feels like you won't let me in all the way."

He pauses. All I hear is the sound of the ocean, crashing up against us over and over again. He looks away for a moment, back to the glow of the party on the patio. Then he bows his head, almost in defeat.

"You know . . ." He frowns. "It took me being here to realize it. It took me seeing all this to really understand you. And I really think you meant it," he says, his voice shaky. "I think you meant what you said to Sam's mom. That you don't want to move on." The breeze from the water sends a chill through my bones as he steps away from me. "And if that's the case, I don't know where that leaves us."

I want to scream. I want to run into the ocean and dunk my head under and wash up on a shore where no one knows me. I want to cry. I want to hit something with a baseball bat. I want Sam. I want Henry. I want all of this to stop.

Instead of any of that, I take a deep breath and try to shove all my feelings into an airtight box. "This is who I am," I say. "This is what I deal with. And I've been pretty clear about it from the beginning. Maybe you weren't listening."

He looks at me in a way I've never seen from him. And I realize it's because he's crying. His eyes are shimmering in the night air and his lip is shaking.

"I'll keep up the act through the end of the wedding," he says, his voice wavering. "Just so they don't ask questions. But after that . . ." He swallows, his eyes flicking from me to the rest of the party. When his attention is back on me, he looks more resolute. More sure. "When we get home, I think . . ."

The waves fizzle in front of us, white foam slowly disappearing back into the earth. Henry and I stand like statues, letting the water spray us and dampen our clothes. He is silent, the kind of silence so loud it pierces your eardrums.

"I don't want to be with someone who will never let herself love me back fully. We've had fun this summer, and I've loved every second of it. But you're not always there with me. I've sensed it, and I think deep down you know it's true too. You deserve to be happy, Bennet, but so do I," he says.

I can't even look at him, at the hurt in his eyes. I feel grief in my body, spreading out into my vision. Grief that has lived with me since the day Sam died. Grief that will always be here, suffocating me, making me make the people around me miserable. Maybe he's right. Maybe I'm not ever going to be happy. Maybe this is who I'm supposed to be.

"I know," I say, folding my arms around my stomach.

"Do you? Love me?" he asks, not looking at me.

I stand, silent, unsure of everything. Beyond how I feel, I know that Henry deserves full love, unabridged. Someone who won't be haunted by ghosts, by her own mind. Someone who is ready to jump in feet-first at a moment's notice. I want that for him. I want him to find that girl.

When I finally look at him, I'm shocked that he doesn't seem mad or even sad. He looks at me with one thing he never has: *pity*.

"I think that's my answer," he whispers.

My skirt ripples around my hips as a gust of wind blows by. "You should go back to the party," I say, dabbing my eyes. "They'll be wondering where we are. I need a minute, but I'll be back there soon."

He nods. "Okay."

"Okay," I say. "See you out there."

He scratches behind his neck. "See you out there."

I squeeze my eyes shut as he walks away. Music swirls in the air and the scent of hors d'oeuvres mixes with the salt of the ocean. I catch the lilt of Mrs. Chase's laugh, the cadence of Andy's speech, over the crowd. I hear the sound of Henry's voice and then the chime of Theo's laugh.

I take a deep breath, swallowing back the feeling that I'm losing the best thing in my life, and I head back to the party.

Chapter Thirty-One

The whole ceremony and reception will take place on the beach. I sit on the bride's side alone, saving the seat next to me for Henry. I'm not sure he'll even show after last night.

The rest of the rehearsal dinner was as smooth as it could be. Henry was charming, I didn't make a fool of myself, no one got angry and threw mashed potatoes at each other. There were no more tears.

But memories of Henry's face, the pity in his eyes when we parted ways, invaded my dreams all night.

He thinks I *want* to be this miserable? Why would anyone want this? Why would anyone want to feel like everything you do, everything you say, causes pain? Why would anyone want to be the cause of so much suffering?

If I could forgive myself, I really would have by now. But Sam will never be around to forgive me.

Of course I don't want this.

My pineapple-yellow dress sticks out in a sea of pinks and blues. I wish I had brought something a little less loud, but when I packed my suitcase I was hopped up on Henry hormones and must've wanted to stand out. Now I want to disappear.

I'm bouncing my knee up and down so violently that I'm tunneling a hole in the sand at my feet. It's five minutes until the ceremony and Henry's still not here. Maybe it's best if he doesn't show. We've already made such a mess, him blowing our cover, me blowing my lid.

I use the wedding program as a fan, because it's hot and also because I need to get these jitters out of my body.

A wave of spearmint and sugar wafts in on the breeze when he finally takes a seat next to me.

"Sorry I'm late," he says as he settles in, wearing khaki pants and a pale blue button-up.

"It's fine," I say, handing him a program.

For the first time since maybe the night we met, I'm at a loss for what to say. It feels like we're on different sides of the subway platform, only catching glimpses of each other through breaks in the rushing trains.

"Henry . . ." I say.

"Yeah?" He looks at me like I'm a stranger, not someone he loves. Loved.

"I—"

The sound of ukulele music and Israel Kamakawiwoʻole's voice singing "Somewhere Over the Rainbow" cuts me off. I honestly don't know what I was going to say anyway.

Theo takes his place at the altar, the ocean as his backdrop.

His parents are next, meeting him up front and kissing him on both cheeks before taking their seats in the front row. Everyone in the bridal party is wearing warm taupe with pops of bright orange in the floral bouquets.

We all stand when Andy arrives. She links arms with both her parents.

Breezy fabric drips off her body and flows in the wind like a jellyfish. Her hair is swept off her shoulders and pinned in place with a bright orange tiger lily. A tiny patch of blue is stitched into the back of her dress. Sam's jersey.

When it's time to exchange vows, Theo goes first. He says he loved Andy from the minute he saw her. He promises to support her dreams and make her life as full of adventure as possible. He wishes to stay by her side in sickness and health and, while he is not a perfect man, he wishes to be perfect for her.

Andy clears her throat. Her turn.

"Theodore, my love, my favorite person on the planet." Her hands shake. He takes them into his. "When I met you, I was grieving the loss of my brother, Sam."

My breathing gets more ragged. My throat tightens. Henry puts his hand on my knee. This is the hardest part, and despite our distance, he knows I need him.

"My entire world shattered. I didn't know how to pick up the pieces." Andy takes a moment to get through the tears. Theo waits for her patiently. "And then . . . I met you. You didn't pressure me to heal, you didn't tell me to get over it, you didn't try to fix me. You just sat with me in my pain and allowed room for me to put myself back together."

My eyes sting. Henry squeezes my knee.

"I remember there was this day back when we first met when I was having a tough time. I drank, what was it, half a bottle of Bordeaux while you were at work?"

Theo laughs. "More than half."

The crowd murmurs in laughter. "You came home and you said, 'Baby, if you're drinking, I'm drinking.' And you put the bottle right to your lips and took a swig. The wine exploded all over your face and I started laughing so hard. And then you started laughing. We laughed until our stomachs hurt, me covered in tears, you covered in wine. I have loved you every day, more and more, ever since. You are my true north, my compass, my light in the dark, and I'm so happy I get to marry you today. I know Sam is looking down on us, and even though it breaks my heart that you'll never meet, I know he approves."

I tense every muscle in my body to keep from crying. A sniffle from Mrs. Chase prompts me to shift in my seat. Henry's hand falls from my knee.

Andy and Theo look at each other with googly eyes as they each slide a gold band around the other's finger. They giddily say, "I do," when it's time.

Everyone stands and claps for the bride and groom, who float back down the aisle to a string version of "Another One Bites the Dust." Mr. and Mrs. Chase, and Theo's parents, walk arm in arm with each other like a united front.

Henry and I trail the other wedding guests toward the beach reception. We are handed bright orange Aperol spritzes when we check our table number. Leave it to Andy to pick a wedding cocktail that perfectly matches her color scheme.

The sun setting over the ocean creates a juicy orange sunset that ripples out over the horizon. That's one thing Andy couldn't have arranged for. It had to be Sam.

We take our seats at a table with some of Andy's high school friends, still not talking.

"Testing, testing, one two three—" Alonzo taps the mic by the head table. "Introducing the couple of the century, Theodore Brightwood and Alexandra Chase!"

The bride and groom come rushing onto the dance floor, and the bridal party showers them in orange flower petals. When the applause from the crowd dies down, they fall into a gentle sway as they dance their first dance to "The Way You Look Tonight." It's hard not to look at Henry, to remember the way he whistled this very song on the way home from seeing Fred get adopted.

The waiter puts a plate of chicken down in front of me and steak in front of Henry. I push the potatoes around on the plate and pretend to have an appetite as Alonzo makes a speech. Henry won't look at me.

By the time the DJ picks up the pace with "September" by Earth, Wind & Fire, Henry and I are the only two not dancing.

The sky is inky now and the dance floor is lit with paper lanterns and candles. The breeze kicks in, sending prickles down my arms.

The DJ plays the first slow song of the evening: "First Day of My Life" by Bright Eyes.

Henry stands up and offers me his hand.

"Dance with me."

"You want to dance?"

He nods. "Yes."

"With me?"

"Yes." He stretches his hand out. "They won't think anything of it. Friends dance."

He leads me to the dance floor, my bare feet cold against the tile. We snake our way through swaying couples who seem to be in rhythm with each other, back and forth, back and forth. Henry stops in the middle, glancing over his shoulder at Mr. and Mrs. Chase, who are cradled in an embrace, paying us no attention. When he looks back, he takes my hand, pressing it to his chest, and wraps his other arm around my shoulders.

"So . . ." he says as we rock back and forth.

"So." I glance over his shoulder to see Andy wrapped in Theo's arms, her head resting on his shoulder as they dance.

"I . . . uh . . ." He swallows. He still won't look at me. "I'm leaving tonight."

I tighten my grip on his hand, pausing our dance. "I thought you might," I say.

"Yeah." He twists his mouth. "I wanted to get through the wedding, but . . ."

"It's pretty much over now," I say.

He sucks in a breath and blows it out his lips. "I know there's always going to be a piece of you that's Sam's," he says. "And that's okay. He's a part of you . . . but all I wanted to know was that there was a possibility of a future for us too. That you could at least try."

"I was trying," I say, my nose stinging.

He nods, closing his eyes. "I know," he says. "I know you think that."

This is so unfair. I wish I could do this. I wish I wasn't broken. I wish I was the kind of person who never knew grief. Who only knew love. But I'm not. I'm just not.

It's not fair to Henry to trap him here with me in a messed-up relationship with a messed-up person. Even if I do like him as much as a human possibly could.

I swallow the lump in my throat. "When do you have to go?" I ask.

"The plane leaves at eleven thirty, so . . ." He pulls me in, tucking my head under his chin. "After this song."

I'm wrapped up in Henry for the last time, I know it.

When I pull away to look at him, his expression is sunken, his sadness cloaked by the night sky. "So this is it?"

He brushes a strand of hair out of my face and doesn't say a word.

I nod, swaying back and forth to the song. "Okay," I whisper. And it feels so definite.

He pulls me tightly to his chest and we stay there for the next minute and a half, until the guitar stops, until the song changes tune.

He kisses me on my temple and whispers a short goodbye before heading to our table to grab his things. I watch him walk along the shore back to the hotel. I follow his path until he shrinks to the size of an ant.

I stand alone, barefoot on the dance floor, surrounded by people singing to Whitney Houston, watching my favorite person walk away.

The rest of the night moves in slow motion around me. The lights look dimmer, the cocktails taste bitter, the ocean seems less beautiful. The sounds of the wedding are muffled as I go through the motions of small talk. I walk barefoot into my hotel room. As soon as the door slams behind me I collapse into the bed, burying my face in my pillow, trying to bite back my emotions.

It's for the best, I think. *It's for the best. It's for the best. It's for the best.*

As if saying it over and over again will make it true.

Chapter Thirty-Two

I wake up with my face pressed to my pillow. My dress is crumpled on my body. I never changed into pajamas or brushed my teeth. My head is pounding and I feel drunk even though I'm dead-sober.

There's a knock at my door. Henry.

I spring to my feet and head to the bathroom to wash up. My mascara ran down my face and my eyes are crusty and swollen. My cheeks are raw from crying.

"One second," I shout as I throw some water on my face.

"Bennet? You up?" It's a female voice. Not Henry.

I forgot I was meeting Andy for coffee.

I squirt toothpaste on my toothbrush and vigorously scrub my teeth. "I'm changing," I shout. "One minute."

I spit into the sink and rinse my mouth, and then I dig through my suitcase to find my denim shorts and a tank top.

When I look presentable, I crank the door handle open to

Andy. She's fresh-faced, wearing a white sundress, and holding two coffees and a greasy brown paper bag.

"Breakfast on the porch?" She smiles as she holds up her gifts.

"Sounds perfect." I let her into my room, which looks like a tornado has recently passed through it.

"Classic Bennet. You could never keep your room clean."

I kick a pile of clothes out of our path to the balcony. "I've actually been doing a pretty good job keeping my room clean lately," I say. But clearly that hasn't lasted.

"I got you a cappuccino," she says, handing me the cup. I take a sip of the foamy coffee as we both settle into the hotel chairs on the balcony. It tastes heavenly.

"Thank you." I wipe the foam from my upper lip. "I can't believe you're married."

"It's crazy, right?" She holds her ring out in front of her to inspect it. "Did you have fun last night?" She reaches into the paper bag and fishes out a croissant.

"I think the more important question is, did *you* have fun?"

She tears off half the croissant and hands it to me on a napkin. "I got to marry Theo. Nothing else mattered."

I pick at the croissant in my hand, tiny flakes of pastry blowing off into the wind. "Andy, I owe you an apology."

"What for?" She sinks her teeth into her half.

"That I wasn't there. Through everything."

She wipes a crumb off her chin, shaking her head. "I'm not upset with you, Bennet."

"You could be. I ditched you and your family after everything happened. I feel so guilty."

"That's the last thing I would ever want you to feel."

"I was so embarrassed that my life was a wreck and it seemed like yours was going so well. I felt like my presence would make everyone miserable."

She laughs, her groomed eyebrows crinkling. "Bennet, what you never realized is that I'm just a hell of a lot better at hiding my mess than you are. Always have been."

"What do you mean?"

"I mean," she says, crossing her legs, "I got so mad at you the day you left L.A. because I was mad at myself for not opening up to you, for not sharing my pain with you. You thought I was fine, but, god, I was not. And I wanted you to see through my act."

I shake my head. "I didn't."

"That's the thing," she says. "I got so good at putting on this facade, being what the world expected of me, that when Sam died . . . I couldn't drop it. If I could keep up the act, maybe it wouldn't feel so awful. But of course it felt worse the more I pretended it didn't hurt."

My mind goes to Henry, how he said almost the same thing about being what the world expects him to be—outgoing, happy-go-lucky. And I still pressured him to be *his charming self* this weekend when I know he doesn't feel like that person inside. I stare into the foam of my cappuccino, feeling more and more shame for how I handled this weekend.

"Thankfully I've been in therapy for a couple of years now," she says, shifting in her seat. "Working on that. Among many other things."

"You're in therapy?"

She nods. "Every week," she says. "But, yeah. I never got to tell you how sorry I was for acting like everything was fine when you visited me. Nothing was fine."

"I should never have said the things I said to you that day, regardless. And I shouldn't have disappeared."

"Babe," she says as she puts her croissant down on the table between us, "we all lost Sam. We all dealt with it in different ways. I knew you needed space. I could never be mad at you for taking it."

I frown. "I had this whole story built up in my head that I was going to get here and you all were going to hate me. But the only one who hates me is me."

"Would I have appreciated a call once or twice? Of course. But losing Sam . . . that's bigger than either of us. You don't need to hate yourself for dealing with loss the way you had to."

"Andy," I say, my hands gripping the paper coffee cup so tight it creases on one side. "If Sam never met me . . . he never would've been driving that night."

Her mouth tightens into a thin line. "Bennet, don't go there."

"He was driving to see me because we were breaking up. It's all my fault. Everything." The truth. Finally. My hand trembles. She reaches across, takes the cup from me, sets it on the table, and replaces it with her hand.

"Every one of us has felt like we were to blame. My dad encouraged him to go talk to you in person that night. It took him years to feel like it wasn't his fault."

My stomach drops. "You all knew we were breaking up?"

"Sam couldn't hide his feelings. Not when it came to you. It didn't change how much he loved you, and I'm guessing it didn't change how much you loved him."

I shake my head. "No. I never stopped. I don't think I ever will."

She reaches to my face, cupping my cheek. "That's what life is about. Never stop loving. No matter what." A flicker of a smile flashes across her face. "We love you. We always will. And it is not your fault."

I let out a huge breath. "Thank you, Andy." I hook my arms around her neck over the table. "I didn't know how badly I needed to hear that." She settles back into my shoulder. Andy Chase, holding me. I could fall apart right now and she'd keep me together.

When we come apart, I wipe a tear from her cheek. She takes a deep breath. "So tell me about Henry. He's not just your friend, is he?"

I *knew* she knew.

"No." I lean back in my chair. "Well. I don't know." I puff out a breath of air. "Not anymore."

"Why?"

I take a bite of croissant. "He overheard me tell your mom that I'll never love anyone like Sam again," I say.

"Holy shit," she says, her eyes wide.

"And when he was upset about it . . . I couldn't lie to him. I couldn't tell him that wasn't true. Not when I haven't moved on. Not really."

She takes a deep breath. Her red hair blows gently in the

breeze. "Moving on doesn't mean we don't love Sam or miss him every day, because, trust me, I do. It's that we open ourselves to love and to all of the things life has to offer to us. Sam would want you to live. I want you to live."

"It's easier said than done."

"I know," she says. "But you're not doing yourself any favors by self-sabotaging like this. You have to try. And I don't mean half-assed, Bennet. I want a full-assed try."

"What if I can't?"

"You can," she says. "You are not defined by any of the choices you made with Sam, or even the mistakes you make with anyone else. If you're really not ready to be with someone new, that's perfectly okay. But if you are ready, Bennet, that's okay too. You don't need my permission, but if you thought you did, there you go. Permission granted."

I let out a shaky laugh, grabbing my coffee and taking a sip. "Okay," I say.

"Okay," she says.

I look out over the water, at the crowds laid out on beach towels, kids hunting for seashells. In this moment, I feel it. I miss Henry so much. I miss his hair, his eyes, his voice. I miss his laugh, I miss his glass-half-full attitude, I miss the way he talks to people and really listens. I miss the way I am when I'm around him. I miss it all.

I look down at my lap, at my grip around my coffee cup. "I love him," I say, mainly to myself. After a moment, I glance up at Andy, who's got a huge grin plastered across her face.

"I knew it," she says.

"How?"

She shrugs, looking at me under glittering eyelids. "I know what you look like when you're in love."

I sink into my chair, hugging my arms to my body. "I don't think he wants anything to do with me."

"I think you'd be surprised. You didn't think I wanted anything to do with you, and I love you a fuck-ton, Bennet Taylor."

"I love you a fuck-ton, Alexandra Brightwood."

She bats me away. "Chase. I'm staying a Chase."

"Thank god." I smile. I make a silent promise here and now never to let her get away ever again.

The seat on the plane next to me is empty, where Henry should've been. I flop my bag on it so it doesn't remind me that I'm flying back to a city that doesn't even feel like home without him.

Some of the contents of my purse spill out, my headphones and sunglasses and a pack of gum slide onto the seat. I shove them back inside. Something in my bag catches my eye, something new I don't recognize immediately. But when I do, the air is sucked out of my lungs.

I curl my fingers around it, feeling the familiar weight of the ball—the soft leather, the bumpy stitches running down its round surface.

Andy must've slipped it into my bag before she left my room this morning.

I pull the baseball out, turning it over in my hands. Through blurry vision, I see her handwriting. *I'm sorry. I love you*, in faded red Sharpie.

My lips quiver as I hold the ball to my heart, breathing through the emotion building in my body.

She kept it. After all this time, she kept it.

I'm holding something in my palms that not only Andy and I held, but Sam also held—it's the most cherished gift she could've given me. A relic from the past, a totem of forgiveness.

All those nights in the batting cage together, all those mornings in Sam's bed, all those breakfasts and dinners and tears and smiles, they all come swooping in, each memory like a bird fluttering under my skin.

The tears dry up and my throat loosens as I smile thinking about him. I smile remembering the first time he kissed me, in the arboretum. I smile remembering the sound of his laugh. I smile remembering how jealous Andy got when we would leave her out of our plans.

The realization that I've been avoiding Sam just as much as I've been avoiding everyone else in my life punctures my heart. He feels like a part of me, yet when was the last time I really welcomed his memory?

This is all about forgiveness. I've been asking it of so many people this summer—Andy, Sonya, the Chases, Henry . . . but I haven't asked it of myself. I haven't asked it of Sam.

And I want it so badly. I want to heal. I want to grow and flourish and see my future as something that could be happy. I want to go back to school. I want to go to therapy. I want to learn more about people, about grief.

And I want Henry by my side as I do it. I want my love for

him to be just about him. Just about us. I want it more than anything I've wanted in a very, very long time. It's simple. It's so simple. Because he is a love of my life. One of two.

I clutch the ball in my hands through the entire plane ride home. I hold it as I walk through the airport and take the AirTrain back to Manhattan. I'm barely thinking, just moving, the baseball almost guiding me toward my destination. I clutch it the entire subway ride to Yankee Stadium.

Chapter Thirty-Three

The late afternoon sun burns my eyes as I emerge from the subway station. It's an off day for the Yankees, so it's not too busy here, just a few people snapping pictures or going about their days.

I stand by the stadium and take three deep breaths, my suitcase handle in one hand and the baseball in the other. I close my eyes and prepare to do what I came here to do.

A shadow falls across my face and I open my eyes to a man standing next to me.

"Sorry." He winces. "I didn't mean to interrupt."

His face is young but aged by the sun. He's wearing a Yankees cap and a sweaty blue shirt.

"It's okay. I'm Bennet."

"Mike." He wipes sweat off his brow and squints up at the stadium. "It never gets old, does it? I mean, I work here and I'm still not used to it."

Normally a random interaction like this would send me running the other way, but I channel Henry, and I welcome the conversation.

"You work here?"

He turns to show me the back of his shirt, which is drenched with sweat. The word MAINTENANCE is written across his shoulder blades.

"Very cool," I say. I remember standing here not too long ago, wishing I could see Sam somewhere in the stadium's infrastructure. Wishing I could feel him. "The Yankees were my boyfriend's team," I say.

"Were? Don't tell me he's a Mets guy now."

"He passed away while I was in college." Mike looks caught off guard, mouth slightly open, as if trying to conjure something to say. "Sorry, I know it's an overshare. But I'm working on being open."

"I'm really sorry."

"It's okay. Really." I look at him, daring myself to be bold. To be brave. "Mike, you ever take people inside the stadium to see the field?"

He looks at his watch and bites his lip. "I'm not supposed to. . . ."

"I'll be super quick," I say. "I won't touch *anything*."

He glances over his shoulder as if he's looking for his boss or supervisor. I feel bad for the position I've put him in, but I have to see it from the inside. I just have to.

"I just want to see it," I say. "I never got to go to a game with him."

Mike blows a breath out through his lips and puts his hands

on his belt buckle. "In honor of your boyfriend, I'll make an exception."

"You won't get in trouble?"

He shrugs. "I caught the head of maintenance having an affair in one of the locker rooms. He owes me one." He starts walking briskly toward the stadium and gestures for me to follow him.

I trail Mike through a small side door, rolling my suitcase behind me. He leads me through a series of hallways and stairwells and I worry that following a strange man into a dark alley was a terrible mistake. But as light streams into my eyes, and we pour out into the open air, I know I'm supposed to be here.

The field is gigantic and filled with turf as green as apple Jolly Ranchers. It smells of freshly cut grass and dirt. I lose my breath at the scale. I feel like I'm standing in the middle of a thumbprint made by a giant.

"Pretty wild, huh?" Mike takes his baseball cap off and fans himself.

"I feel so small," I say.

"Puts things into perspective."

"Thank you for this, Mike. You'll never know how much it means to me."

He brushes it off. "Sure." He points to a small door across the field. "I'll bring your bag through those doors over there for when you're done. Take your time." I watch as he wheels my suitcase off the field.

I turn to face the pitcher's mound and walk carefully toward it. I line my toes up with the plate and stare at first base. My heart is beating fast.

I place the ball on the center of the plate and sit down criss-cross applesauce facing it. I stay there for a moment, letting my body soak in the atmosphere of the stadium, the massiveness of it all. I will myself not to feel self-conscious about what comes next.

"Hey, Sam." A breeze blows across my face. "Hey, my love."

I drag my fingers through the silky dirt near the plate. "So . . . I went to Andy's wedding. I'm sure you already know that. Or, I don't know what you know . . . I don't know what I believe you know. But if you are around somewhere, I'm sure you were there on the beach with us. She looked beautiful. You'd like Theo, I think."

I take a shaky breath and skate my fingers across the top of the ball, turning it so the words *I'm sorry* are facing me.

"I saw your parents. They're doing great. They miss you so much. We all do." I glance at the sky to choke back the stinging feeling in my throat.

"Listen, Sam, I never said I was sorry. I'm so sorry. I've wished every single day that I could say that to you, but it never felt like enough. Such a trivial word against such a colossal thing. I've gone over in my head what I want to say to you a million times and nothing seems right. It doesn't feel like any words could fill the magnitude of your loss."

A cloud casts a shadow over my eyes, relieving the intense heat.

"And I love you. I will probably love you until the day I die. I can't see a world where I stop loving you. I need you to know that. I never stopped and I never will."

The wind picks up, whipping my hair in my face. "I want

you to know that even if I love other people, it is only possible because I also love you. I am forever better because you were in my life."

I drag my thumb over the words *I love you* on the ball.

"I thought living in New York would be the best way to honor you, but I know now that the best way is to never stop loving. So I won't. Ever."

All of a sudden, the sky opens up and rain pours down over my head. The bright kind of summer shower that is warm and gentle. It soaks through my clothes. I stand up in the middle of the field and stretch my arms out to the sky. The rain streams down my face and into my hair. It floods my eyes. It fills my ears. I run to first base, my lungs tight and wheezing. And then I keep running. I round second base, my breath labored and heavy. I round third, my legs screaming for me to stop. But I don't. When I reach home, I press my lips to my fingers and then to the plate, and I mouth the words, *I love you*.

I leave the ball on home plate and run toward the stadium exit. The rain splashes down my face and pools in my shoes and washes away the cobwebs that have settled in my life for far too long. Suddenly thunder claps against the late summer sky. Sam.

As I leave Yankee Stadium, I turn back one more time and smile through the rain. I whisper, "Thank you," to everything around me, and then I leave it all behind.

As soon as I get home, I tear off my drenched clothes, change into something dry, and pace the living room, sweating in the sweltering September heat. I think about what I learned about myself the past few months, about Sam, and Henry, and Andy, and Sonya, and Jamie. About happiness. About passion. About grief. I think about the Passion Project and all it represented, the hope it gave me for the future, and I realize I have one final thing to do for myself to finish the project once and for all. It involves three phone calls:

One, to a therapist. Two, to my undergraduate guidance counselor. And three, to Sarah.

Chapter Thirty-Four

I stand behind the bar, wringing a kitchen rag between my hands, twisting it over itself until it's as taut as a rope. Sarah peeks her head out from the kitchen.

"He's on his way," she says. "Everything okay?"

She was skeptical at first. I guess she was always skeptical of me, the same way I was skeptical of her, but after some apologies on both sides, she agreed to help me. Plus, Jamie pleaded my case pretty hard over text. She agreed to unlock the restaurant an hour early so I could surprise Henry here.

"Thanks, Sarah," I say, releasing the twist in the rag. "For all of this."

She bites her bottom lip and sighs. "What I said to you a few weeks ago about you making him miserable wasn't fair," she says. "It wasn't nice and it also wasn't true. Before he met you, he used to hang out with the rest of the staff after work. Now he rushes out of every shift as fast as he can to see you. He comes in late, he's distracted when he's here, and he's always smiling at his phone like a goofy idiot. He's going to be happy to see you."

I swallow, my heart beating faster. "I hope you're right."

Her phone dings, and she pulls it out to check the text. "He's almost here," she says. "You have the envelope?"

I nod, pulling a white envelope from my back pocket.

"Great," she says. "I'll go to the back."

The kitchen doors swing closed, and Sarah disappears behind them. Now it's just me alone in L'italiano behind the bar. The lights are dimmed, the rich lilt of Ella Fitzgerald's voice dances in the air, and a pepperoni pizza sits in front of me. Just like the night we met. Henry will come pick up his paycheck, like I came to pick up my wallet, except he'll find me here waiting for him, just like I found him waiting for me.

My heart squeezes in my chest and my stomach churns. I keep my eyes trained on the door. Any second and he'll be here.

It's been two weeks since I've seen him. Two weeks of wishing I'd handled everything better. Two weeks of knowing I love him, of not being afraid anymore, of formulating the plan that I am now executing. I let the image of Henry walking away along the beach flicker into my mind, but this time I don't wonder if I could handle the heartbreak again. I've handled so much in my life that I never thought I could. I'm ready for heartbreak just as much as I'm ready for love.

But, god, do I hope this doesn't end in heartbreak.

I grab two empty wineglasses and set them on the bar, and I put a bottle of Chianti next to them. I bend down to the cooler below the bar to grab a bottle of the grapefruit wine I drank that first night, so everything's the same. As I do, the little bell above the restaurant door chimes.

I freeze, crouched below the bar so he can't see me.

"Sarah?" he says.

Just his voice alone makes my heart jump. He's right there, two feet away.

Henry.

It aches.

I stand up to reveal myself, clutching the cold bottle of wine between my hands. He looks at me, eyes wide, and takes a step back.

"Bennet?" There's a hitch in his voice, a shakiness I've never heard from him.

I uncap the wine. "Red or white?"

"What—" he starts to say, scratching his chin. "What's going on?"

I take a deep breath, trying to recall everything I've planned to say to him. Everything I feel, that I hope he feels in return.

I pour the white wine into my glass and the red into his. He watches me carefully but doesn't budge. "A few months ago, I stumbled into this restaurant after a really horrible day," I say, watching the red liquid pool into his glass. "There was a guy behind the bar who, against all odds, made me believe that maybe life was worth living." I set the bottle down and slide the red wine toward him. "All it took was one glass of wine for him to convince me to go on this crazy quest for my passion. He was really convincing and, honestly, a little pushy."

Henry snorts out a laugh. It's enough to keep me going.

"Anyway," I say. "I was a wreck that night. I was embarrassed, grieving, pushing every single person in my life away in favor of being alone. But something deep down told me that I should say yes to him. That he is important. He's going to be important to me. And he was."

Henry looks away, into the light.

"He helped me look for my passion all summer," I say. "It was a wild goose chase, really. We did a bunch of odd things trying to find it. But now I've figured it out. Do you want to know what it is?"

He turns back to me, his eyes glassy, and nods.

"It's not a job, it's not a hobby, it's not even a person. It's just . . . loving. It's loving, and it's trying. It's giving people a chance. It's standing on the ledge of a skyscraper to appreciate the view. It's sharing stories while sharing a pizza. It's making new friends and putting in the effort to visit them in New Jersey. It's taking a business class because someone you care about wants to. It's whacking a vase with a baseball bat when you haven't let your emotions out in a long, long time. It's holding someone's hand. It's doing something that scares you with someone who scares you. It's realizing that you might be broken, but that doesn't mean you can't heal. That doesn't mean you can't be loved. It's going to therapy and finishing my undergrad degree. It's restarting my life. It's waking up every day and deciding that it's worth it. It's so simple, and I feel stupid that it took such a journey to figure out, but that's all it is, and I think the rest falls into place."

He closes his eyes and takes a deep breath. I think he might say something, but he shakes his head, swallowing it back. He feels so far away. I ache to touch him.

"I spent so much energy worrying that I was behind, or that the world was moving on without me, or that having a passion would fix me, but I realized that *I'm* the only one who can fix me. No one else. Not a fancy job, not a passion, not you, and not even a therapist. Me. So I'm not waiting for some magical key to unlock my life anymore. I'm doing it myself. Starting over. Committing to waking up every morning and trying with my whole heart. I may never find a passion or a career or anything like that, but screw that, Henry. I don't think it even matters.

"The Passion Project is the best thing I ever took a chance on, but not because I found a passion. Because it made me happy. You made me happy. You showed me love doesn't care about whether or not you have your shit together, or if you're a grieving mess. Love doesn't care if you're anxious or depressed or drowning in everyday life. Love just loves. I feel grateful, every day, that I puked my guts out in the bathroom here, and that's insane because that was one of the worst nights of my life, but it led me to one of the best things in my life. You."

It's all spilling out, everything I feel about him in one fell swoop. I press forward, hoping it's not too much.

"I want to do this with you, for real. I want to kiss you, and sleep with you, and laugh with you, and tell stories, and watch movies, and cry with you. I want to watch you take pictures and I want to meet your dad, and I want to hike mountains and hold you when you're falling apart. I want to fight with you and make up with you and roll my eyes when you stop and talk to the millionth person in the park. I want to rescue a mean old dog with you and name it Falkor the Third. I want to drink wine with you and make fun of people and admire people and talk to people with you. I want to take care of each other and take turns leaning on each other." A tear slides down my cheek. I wipe it away. "I'm ready. I'm so ready. I'm done being sad. I'm done being angry at the world, and with myself. I'm done latching myself to the past because I'm afraid of the future."

Henry's eyes betray nothing. If he hates me, if he loves me, I don't know, because he's quiet.

I hold the envelope up. "The night we met, you made a bet with Sarah that you'd see me again, and you won that bet." I open the envelope and pull out a twenty-dollar bill, setting it on the counter. "I want to make another bet now."

He comes closer to the bar and traces the bill with his hand, feeling it beneath his fingers. "Okay," he says. "What do you bet?"

Here it is, the final confession. "I bet you don't know that I'm in love with you. I'm madly, deeply, insanely in love with you. What I said to Sam's mom was wrong. I thought it was what she needed to hear, but I was so wrong. I love you so much it hurts. I love you so much I thought I didn't deserve it. I love you so much that I found a therapist so I could love you right. So I could love the world right. I bet you don't know that I have felt more passion in my life in the last summer than I have in years. I bet you don't know that you're my favorite person. I bet you don't know all of this, because I was too afraid to tell you. But I'm telling you right now, everything out in the open: I love you. And it has nothing to do with how much I loved Sam, because you're different people, and it's a different love." I feel my hands start to shake as I press on. "And I really, really hope I'm right about this final bet, otherwise I'm going to look incredibly dumb, but . . ." I take a deep breath, allowing myself to say the scariest part. "I bet you love me too."

What follows is silence. A long silence, an eternity that seems to pass as Henry and I stare at each other, unmoving. He takes the twenty-dollar bill in his hands, turning it over once, but he doesn't say anything.

"What do you think, Henry?" I whisper. "Do I win the bet?"

Please say yes. Please, for the love of god, say yes.

His green eyes are trained on mine, swimming under a layer of tears. "You win the bet," he says. "Of course you win the bet."

A rush of air leaves my lungs and I almost let out a sob of relief. I run around to the other side of the bar and he opens his arms for me as I engulf him in a hug. I inhale his spearmint-and-sugar scent, clutch my fingers to his shirt, and feel his rib cage shudder with a laugh or a cry, I'm not sure. He lifts me off the floor, holding me tighter than he ever has.

"I'm so sorry," he says into my neck. "I'm so sorry I left you there."

He sets me on my feet and I pull away so I can look at him. I brush his hair off his forehead as he holds my waist close to him. "I pushed you away," I say. "What were you supposed to do?"

He twists his mouth. "I said some terrible things."

"I needed to hear them," I say. "I really did. And I told Andy we're together. Well . . . were together. You were a hundred percent right. She was happy for me."

"Still. I feel awful. It was so important to you."

"Of course it was important to me, but so are you, and I didn't treat you like it," I say. "I should've introduced you to the Chases proudly as my partner, not hiding how much you mean to me. Neither of you deserved that. We both could've handled it better, but all that matters is how we handle it now. No more pushing each other away, okay?"

"Okay," he says. "No more pushing each other away," he repeats.

He hugs me close to his chest and we rock back and forth. "You looked good behind the bar," he says. "I like how the tables have turned."

"You didn't puke in the bathroom," I say. "So the tables haven't completely turned."

"Yeah." He laughs. "I won't be doing that."

I pull away to look up at him. "God, I've missed you so much," I say.

"I've missed you too," he says, a soft smile spreading across his lips. He lifts the twenty-dollar bill up to show me. "And I kind of feel like I deserve half the prize money."

I smirk, knowing he would say this. I pull a ten out of my pocket and hold it up for him to see. "All yours," I say.

He cups my face with his hands and kisses me, letting the money flutter to the floor. Warmth fizzles through my body as I let my hands brush against his waist. I grip the fabric of his shirt, making sure it's real. Making sure he's real.

"I want this so badly," I say. "Can we be together again? Please?"

"I'd like that," he says, smiling down at me. "For as long as humanly possible."

Our lips come together, his mouth as soft and loving as ever. I wrap my arms around his ribs and pull myself flush against him.

"I love you," I whisper.

He kisses my temple. "I love you too. I have for a while now."

I press my cheek to his chest, listening to his heart beating under his shirt. He tangles his fingers in my hair, holding me as if I'm something precious, something cherished.

"Henry?" I say, my voice muffled against his chest.

"Yes?"

"Where do you want to go on our next Passion Project date?" I ask.

He strokes the back of my head, tipping my chin up to look at him. "Right now? I just want to go home with you," he says. "Can we do that?"

"Of course," I say. "Always."

He slings his arm across my shoulder, holding me close. I hug his waist with one arm, not wanting to let him go, and I push the restaurant door open with the other.

Outside, I look up at his face, his kind, open, gentle, charming face. His eyes, his hair blowing in the wind . . . I couldn't imagine it better if I tried. I don't know where we go from here or what happens next. I don't know if I'll ever find a passion or if it was always an arbitrary goal that never really mattered. All I know is that this matters. He matters. I matter. I let the feeling rush through me like a ripple in the water as I kiss the beautiful boy who makes every match in my body light on fire. The first breeze of fall brushes past us as the oppressive summer heat melts away.

I am going to be just fine.

October,
One Year Later

"P*ush!*" Henry's voice echoes as I thrust my body.

"What does it look like I'm doing?" My back seizes up. "Oh shit."

"Should we take a break?" He wipes a bead of sweat from his forehead.

"Yes, please." I set my side of the wooden dresser down on the steps. We made it halfway up the single flight of stairs to our new apartment in Brooklyn.

"Why is this thing so damn heavy?" Henry pants.

"I don't want to hear it. You actually have a rock collection we're going to have to move up these stairs."

"Little tiny rocks, not boulders."

"Let's rest here for a minute." I lean my body on the dresser sitting crooked in the middle of the flight of stairs. Henry holds it steady a few steps above me. This is the first piece of furniture we've moved out of the truck, and I cringe at the amount of heavy lifting we're going to have to do today.

If you asked me a year and a half ago if I'd consider moving to Brooklyn, I'd have laughed. I barely wanted to live in Manhattan, let alone put roots down in another borough. But here I am, pushing an incredibly heavy dresser into a place in Bushwick that has my and Henry's names on the lease. Our one-bedroom apartment has rooftop access and enough space for Henry to have a real photography studio. He took engagement photos for Terrance, our friend from the animal adoption center, and got three more couples to hire him from that alone. Martin helped him set up an LLC, and ever since, he's been busy every day. He hasn't quit L'italiano yet, but I know it's because he's nervous about doing photography full time. I tell him every day how much I believe in him and his business. I know he'll make the transition when he's ready. The studio in our apartment is step one.

I finished my undergrad degree last winter, and I've developed quite a fascination with psychology brought on by a book I picked up at McNally Jackson. I grabbed it because I thought I recognized the face on the cover, and bought it when I realized it was written by the psychologist who gave a talk at the library at the beginning of last summer. Dr. Barrera. I've now read everything he's written, every psychology book I can find. I'm planning on applying to clinical psychology programs once everything is settled, and I want to become a grief counselor someday. Baby steps, but it turns out I do have a passion after all.

Henry's back and forth from Denver fairly regularly, and I

accompany him when I can. His dad is the sweetest man I've ever met, and I can tell it tears Henry apart that he never remembers who I am despite having met me several times. Sometimes I catch Henry looking at old photos of the two of them together, and I let him cry into my shoulder. But we never push each other away anymore. We always let the other in. We take care of each other.

My own parents have fallen deeply in love with Henry as well. I took him home for Christmas, and he absolutely crushed it. He was right. He is *great* with parents.

Sal and Mary moved permanently to Maplewood to be near their grandchild. He sends us photos of one-and-a-half-year-old Michael constantly. We try to visit them every couple of months if we can.

Sonya and Jamie decided to live together when our lease ended, and Sonya started her own business designing and selling jewelry. Her designs are sold in several New York City boutiques, including Harper & Jane, and she's working on a website to sell her pieces all over the country. Jamie is having her design a ring for her mom and dad's vow renewal, but that's just a cover story. Sonya doesn't know it yet, but she's designing her own engagement ring.

After living in Henry's tiny studio for two months, we decided enough was enough. We needed more space.

"Is it bothering your arm? Lifting the dresser?"

Henry rolls his long-sleeved shirt up to his elbow, inspecting the fresh tattoo on his forearm under a clear plastic bandage. "Nah. It seems fine."

I take a moment to admire it, a ten-dollar bill. Our ten-dollar bill. A reminder to always bet on each other. Bet on ourselves. God, I love him.

"It looks good," I say, a flush rising in my cheeks at the fact that he wanted something, some piece of us, permanent on his body.

"So this was just your excuse to look at it, huh?" He stretches his arm out so I can admire the whole thing in its beautiful glory.

"You know how much I like it."

"I'm going to be covered in tattoos for you in no time, babe." He smirks. These are his horny eyes. I've unleashed the horny eyes.

My phone buzzes against my leg. "Andy's calling."

"Damn." Henry sighs.

"We don't even have a bed yet," I say. I dig the phone out from my back pocket. "I'm picking it up."

"Tell her I booked the place for December."

I slide my thumb across the screen to answer.

"Andy Chase!"

"Bennet!" Her voice is cheery on the other end.

"Henry got the Airbnb."

"Bless him. Theo sent our flight info to your email."

After our trip to L.A. and my vow that I would never let Andy slip away, I made efforts to stay in contact. We're all going to New Orleans for an early Christmas celebration with Mr. and Mrs. Chase, who moved down there not too long ago.

"How's the move going? Do you want to kill each other yet?"

"This woman picked the heaviest furniture on the planet," Henry shouts from the other side of the dresser, a few steps above me.

My cheeks get hot. "It's only one flight of stairs, he'll live."

"I will not live." He fans himself with his hand.

"Andy, we've got to finish moving this dresser. I'll call you tomorrow?"

"Sounds good. Love you."

I beam at the phone as I click the screen off. "You ready to move this sucker?"

"Let's do this."

"Three, two, one, lift!" I exert my muscles as much as I possibly can to lift the dresser slowly up each step. Henry grunts as he arrives on the landing in front of our door, and we set the dresser down with a thump.

"Welcome home," he says as he dangles the key in front of me. "You want to do the honors?"

My pulse quickens with adrenaline as I take it from him. I slide the cold metal key into the lock and turn it.

I let my fingers trace the walls as I take my first steps inside. We've seen the place before, but never alone, just the two of us. It feels sacred, magical, to be two people standing in an empty room full of possibility. I put my hands on the cool countertops by the kitchen sink to remind myself that they're real.

There's a small window seat that I imagine drinking coffee at while looking out over our new neighborhood. I'll fill it with plants and books, for Sam.

This city that I wanted to leave last year has become my safest place. I know it's not exactly the life he envisioned for us, but Sam led me here. Without him, I never would've found my home.

Our bedroom is full of sparkling light; shadows from the

trees outside move over our eyes. I can't believe so much has changed in a year. I spend my time laughing until my stomach hurts, kissing until my eyelids droop and I drift off to sleep in the arms of a man who loves me, trying to cook dinner before burning it and ordering takeout. I am strong. I am resilient. I am kind. I always have been. I am proud that I'm able to say it, and even more proud that I believe it.

I'd like to say that finding something I'm passionate about is what made me finally feel happier, but my therapist reminds me every session that it's because I opened myself up to love from Henry, Sonya, Jamie, Sal, Marjorie, Andy, Mr. and Mrs. Chase, my parents, and even my own little heart beating in my chest.

This life is one that I didn't feel worthy of, but I now know I am. It's *not* too good to be true. It's just true.

"Henry?"

He drapes his arm across my shoulders and squeezes. "Yeah?"

"I love you."

He brushes his lips against mine, so softly it's almost imagined. "I love you more."

In his arms I'm reminded that happiness doesn't need to be shrouded in guilt. Love doesn't need to be shrouded in disbelief. Sometimes it just *is*.

And that's enough.

I take his hand in mine and we walk toward the door for the dresser, our first piece of furniture in our new apartment. Even though this place is brand-new to me, I know that I'm home.

I can't wait to fill it with the heaviest furniture I can find.

Acknowledgments

This book was born on the front porch of my parents' house in upstate New York over a few frenzied months of summer, and has been lucky enough to be looked after by the most adept caretakers every step of the way since. It takes a village to raise a book baby—a clichéd statement perhaps, but I've always liked clichés.

Passion Project would truly be nowhere if it were not for my dream agent, Lily Dolin. Thank you for taking a chance on me and for being this book's fiercest advocate. Your sharp eye, tenacity, and brilliance are in constant competition for what I admire most about you. Thank you for constantly reading my mind, for answering every neurotic text, and for always approaching everything with confidence and wisdom. Thank you, as well, to everyone at UTA Publishing—it is an absolute dream come true to be a UTA author.

Thank you to my incomparable editor, Marie Michels, who made this book soar. It's such a gift to work with someone who *gets it*, whose vision is so aligned with mine, and who sees the true heart and soul of the book and understands how to make it stronger through developmental edits and line edits alike.

Thank you for making this book better on every single page. Thank you, also, to everyone at Pamela Dorman Books and Penguin—Brian Tart, Andrea Schulz, Patrick Nolan, Kate Stark, Pamela Dorman, Nick Michal, Norina Frabotta, Nicole Celli, Sabrina Bowers, Mary Stone, Rebecca Marsh, and Andy Dudley. Thank you to Jason Ramirez, Nayon Cho, and Katie Smith for the most beautiful cover ever.

Thank you to my family, who didn't think it was *totally* crazy when I announced I was writing a book. You have encouraged me through the loftiest and least practical dreams and have never made me feel like I was choosing wrong, or like I should screw my head back on my shoulders. You've always let me be me, and your love and support are the greatest gifts I'm sure I don't always deserve.

Thank you to Amber and Danielle Brown, who are two of the most talented writers I've had the privilege of crossing paths with—you helped shape this book and my career in immeasurable ways and I am forever thankful for your guidance, editorial eye, and encouragement.

Thank you to my early readers, critique partners, and tour guides in the publishing world, without whom I'd be fumbling around in the dark. Meredith Schorr, CL Montblanc, Bridey Morris, Shoshana Grauer, Samantha Bansil, and Famke Kim-Thy Halma—thank you for your advice, patience, and most importantly, friendship.

Thank you to my besties, drinking buddies, unpaid therapists, and soulmates—Richard Spitaletta, Rachel Fairbanks Adaran, Isabelle Germano, my Lion Pride and more. I wouldn't have been able to do this without you. Thank you to Eric Price and Will Reynolds, who weren't the first people to tell me I was a writer but were the first I believed. Thank you to Kyrie Ellison-Keller, who gave me the lowdown on what the bathrooms at the Frying Pan look like.

And thank you lastly, but most fervently, to readers. I am forever grateful for book people, especially those who are as enthusiastic about happy endings as I am.